Praise for *Planetside*

"Mammay capably writes Butler's gritty, old-school soldier's voice, and the story delivers enough intrigue and action for fans of military SF."

—*Publishers Weekly*

"*Planetside*, the debut novel by Michael Mammay, is an easy book to love. [. . .] a page-turner and an extremely satisfying read."

—*Washington Independent Review of Books*

Praise for *Spaceside*

"Highly recommended for military sf lovers, who will savor his perspective and probably want to buy the man a drink."

—*Library Journal* (starred review)

"Wow, just wow. This was another exceptional book from Mammay, who has once again produced a fantastic science fiction thriller hybrid with some amazing moments in it. [. . .] *Spaceside* is an incredible second outing from Michael Mammay, who has a truly bright future in the science fiction genre."

—Unseen Library

Praise for *Colonyside*

"Highly recommended for readers who like their heroes cynical, their mystery twisted, and their sf thought-provoking."

—*Library Journal* (starred review)

"I'm certainly on board for this author's next book. And the one after that, and the one after that, and all the ones after that."

—Reading Reality

THE
MISFIT
SOLDIER

Also by Michael Mammay

PLANETSIDE
SPACESIDE
COLONYSIDE

THE
MISFIT
SOLDIER

MICHAEL MAMMAY

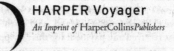
HARPER Voyager
An Imprint of HarperCollins Publishers

First Harper Voyager mass market printing: February 2022

Print Edition ISBN: 978-0-06-298100-4
Digital Edition ISBN: 978-0-06-298101-1

Cover design by Guido Caroti
Cover illustration by Jeff Brown Graphics (jeffbrowngraphics
.com)
Space station art © tsuneomp / Shutterstock, Inc.

FIRST EDITION

Printed in Lithuania

22 23 24 25 26   SB   10 9 8 7 6 5 4 3 2 1

To all the people in the world like Gas.
People who look at something wrong
in the system and say, *That's messed
up. I think I'll burn it to the ground.*

THE
MISFIT
SOLDIER

WHEN YOU JOIN THE MILITARY, NONE OF THE recruiting material shows you trying to stow away on a bot freighter headed to a war zone on a hellhole of a planet.

But there I was.

Add to my list of crimes that I'd sort of stolen my power armor. I say *sort of* because technically, I signed it out of the armory to do perfectly legal cleaning and maintenance. But somehow, I don't think a military judge would see it that way at my court-martial.

Hopefully it wouldn't come to that.

I walked down the station's wide docking corridor, trying not to draw attention. Not that I could remain inconspicuous while wearing a sixty-kilogram armored bioenhancement suit—that was the official name for what we grunts called power armor. Each fall of my polymer boots thudded on the deck, screaming for everyone passing in the busy walkway to look at me. I kept my eyes forward, my pace steady, trying to project the image of someone who belonged. Everyone on station had seen augmented infantrymen before. Nothing new here. If I acted like I belonged there, the maintenance workers and cargo specialists would have no reason to question me.

Technically (there's that word again), I hadn't broken any rules.

Yet.

I rationalize once more because while I didn't belong in the loading area, nothing prohibited it. Given my rank of sergeant, nobody would say anything about me taking my suit for a stroll. Nope. At this point, I could talk my way out of everything right up until the point where I stepped onto United Federation of Planets supply ship S4044, berthed at bay lima 9. The moment I crossed that threshold, I ceased being a sergeant in the augmented infantry and became a common stowaway. Or, rather, an uncommon one, considering I was going *toward* the war zone, rather than away from it like a sane person. But I had my reasons.

I passed the wide bay doors of lima 8, the curve of the station keeping lima 9 out of sight. I had a hundred meters of corridor left to change my mind.

Not likely.

I kept my pace steady, not hurrying. I couldn't appear nervous. That would just make me more obvious. This was the only supply ship headed to the surface of Gallia in the next twelve hours, and I had a ticking clock. Every hour made it less likely that I'd find Kendrick, the soldier we left behind when we pulled out of combat under duress. We don't leave people behind in my squad. Except we did, and I had to fix it. Now, almost a day later . . . he might be alive, he might be dead. But my suit's display said he was alive when we left, and I'd trained my squad well. I'd trained this soldier especially well. I fully expected to find him alive and holed up, waiting for us to come get him. But even if the worst had happened, I could recover his body. At least then we'd know.

It wasn't going to come to that, though.

I tried to do it the right way first. But the captain—my company commander—told me they couldn't support a mission for a single soldier stuck behind enemy lines. I'd expected that. He might have been right, though I'm not sure he asked. My captain didn't like to rock the boat with his higher command. And if he *did* ask, he didn't ask hard enough. At least that was my considered opinion.

I'd expected that too.

Well, fuck him. You know, with all due respect . . . which was none. I took care of my people, and they took care of me. I needed to find Kendrick, and if the captain wouldn't help, I'd do it myself.

Despite what it sounds like, I'm not stupid. I did recognize the inherent flaws of my plan. *Plan.* I probably should put that word in air quotes. It was more like a series of ideas at this point—an initial concept, and then some branches, depending on what happened. There were too many unknowns to get much beyond that. Truth be told, I hadn't thought much past the point of getting to the planet. That alone seemed daunting enough. I'd figure out the rest once I got there, find a way to get to Kendrick's last known location, and then play it by ear. Things would work out for me. They always did.

Mostly.

I want to stop right here and make something clear, because I think it's important. Going back into a combat zone after a missing soldier looks like something a good soldier would do, but I'm not a good soldier. Never have been, never will be. I didn't even want to *be* a soldier, but three years ago I was running from some stuff, and the military seemed like a pretty good place to hide. I probably should have thought that one through a little better, because now I had served three years of a six-year contract, and I couldn't get out. And I had a guy who counted on me stuck down behind enemy lines in a war zone.

I wasn't a good soldier, but I was a good friend. A good person to know. If you're in trouble, I'm a guy you want on your side, because I'm going to help. I'm going to lie, cheat, steal, or whatever else it takes to protect my friends. Period. That includes stowing away on a supply ship to a combat zone. Was it the right thing to do? Who knows—right and wrong are personal judgments that people use to make sense of things. To pretend their actions have some sort of justification. Usually, what they really mean when they say *right* is that it aligns with their personal moral compass. Unless we're talking about some sort of super-evolved person who can see with true objectivity. Maybe you think that's you. You're probably wrong.

My personal moral compass? It has a *lot* of wiggle to it.

But I digress.

I needed to focus. The foot traffic slowed after I

passed dock 8—just three people in the wide corridor, two walking the same direction as me and one coming toward me. According to my source, they'd have the ship loaded already, everything completed for launch except for the final inspection by the loadmaster. I had a ten-minute window to get myself on board and hidden well enough that the loadmaster wouldn't find me. Staff Sergeant Ella Jandus had a reputation as a hard-ass. With most people, I'd have tried to make a deal. After all, that's what I do best. But not Jandus. She wasn't the type to turn a blind eye for a favor. That's okay. We need honest soldiers like her to make up for ones like me. It just didn't happen to fit my needs at the moment, and unlike Jandus, I always put the needs of my friends above the needs of the military.

I adjusted my pace so I'd hit the bay door at a moment where nobody else would be close. The ship didn't have dedicated security. It didn't need it. Nobody *wanted* to go to Gallia. People tended to avoid areas that might kill them unless they didn't have a choice. Soldiers might try to get on ships *leaving* the planet, up to the relative safety of the well-defended space station. On the off chance that someone *did* want to head planetside, they'd take one of a dozen daily shuttles. I'd considered forging orders to get me on one of those, but that would have taken time that I didn't have, and then I'd still have had to explain my armor . . . and where I was going once we landed.

This was easier.

Kind of.

There might have been a lack of security, but there

was no shortage of cameras—they covered everything on the station. After the fact, once someone realized I'd gone, perhaps they'd look back through the footage and see me, but I trusted that nobody would notice one random video in real time. The station had thousands of cameras, and I had to believe the AIs had other priorities. Hopefully. As I mentioned, it wasn't a great plan.

But you go with what you've got. I stepped through the bay door onto the ship, crossing the line of no return.

The sensors in the face shield of my helmet automatically adjusted to the lower light inside the freighter's cargo bay, allowing me to see. I hurried past the first stack of crates to obscure myself from anyone outside, then triggered the camouflage feature in my suit. My dull gray armor would change to blend with its surroundings. I didn't have the near invisibility of a scout's suit—they can't build every feature into every suit because of the power drain—but I'd take any advantage I could get.

I moved quickly through the chained-down pallets and webs of cargo-strapped material, searching for a hiding spot. I looked up to the ceiling, some four meters above me, and found what I needed. I opened a storage alcove marked *Tie-Downs* and grabbed two short straps. Gotta love the military for conveniently labeling everything. I could have clamped onto the ceiling using the magnetic grip of my suit, but the less power I burned now, the better.

I climbed up a stack of crates, balanced myself on top, then leaped for the ceiling using the mechanical assist in my suit's legs to propel me the extra meter I needed. I grabbed both sides of a support beam, then held myself there with one mech-assisted hand while I snapped the hook at one end of a strap to a D-ring in the roof. The rings were probably meant to help tie down cargo, if needed, but now I used them to form a make-shift hammock that would keep me up on the ceiling and hopefully out of sight. My suit's camouflage would hide me, but the straps would stand out clearly if anyone looked. I had to trust the shadows and the hope that the loadmaster wouldn't look up.

The good thing was that she had no reason to look up, with all the cargo below me, but even so, I put my odds at around seventy percent for success. I'd bet more on worse, and as always, I had a backup plan in case I got caught. I liked plans on top of plans, in case the first one went wrong. Because the first one always went wrong.

At least in my experience. Which is part of how I ended up in the military in the first place.

The loadmaster entered through the bay door what felt like an hour later but according to my HUD was only a few minutes. She bent to check the straps on the first pallet, unaware of me hanging above her like some sort of camouflaged space spider. She stood so close I could hear her breathing, and after that, all I could think about was my own breathing. I had my helmet on, but still I concentrated on every breath, holding my mouth open wide and controlling the air flow to make no noise.

She worked her way through the cargo compartment slowly, checking every connector. Staring down from above, I had time to memorize everything about her. She wore a dark blue jumpsuit, and had close-cropped hair except hadn't had it cut recently, so a layer of fuzz grew on the back of her neck. She hummed a song to herself that I didn't recognize.

After she checked the last pallet, she stood, stretched, and leaned her head back as if to pop her neck. She couldn't miss seeing me. I waited for her to call out, tried to come up with a pithy line that I could use to defuse the situation. Maybe I could get her to keep it between us. Maybe I could get her to throw me off the ship, but not report it. No harm, no crime.

She didn't see me.

I don't know why. Regardless, she gathered herself and made her way back down the dual rows of pallets and out through the bay door. A moment later the back hatch of the ship whirred to life and closed with the sound of hydraulics and success. The lights went out, quickly replaced by the low light amplification of the sensors in my helmet, which cast everything in shades of gray. I considered letting myself down from my ridiculous hiding spot, but decided I'd wait for the ship to start moving to be safe. Then I'd have to bullshit whoever I ran into at the other end, but that was my strong suit. I had *plenty* of ability to bullshit.

The deep thrum of the ship's engines kicked in, and the hull shimmied a little, shaking me in my roost. The pitch grew higher, rising from an almost imperceptible bass note up through the register to what would soon be a high-pitched whine. I'd heard that sound dozens of times.

The engines died, the wail fading away like the desperate gasp of an electric horn with a dying battery.

My brain whirred, running through a dozen possible scenarios. There could be a legit reason for—

My thought cut out as the lights blazed on in the compartment, blinding me for a split second before my sensors adapted. The ship's door lowered slowly, like the maw of impending doom.

"Come on out." The person spoke with authority, like they were used to being obeyed. A lot of people in the military had that. I think maybe they teach it in a class somewhere.

I didn't answer. I mean . . . what could I say? I hadn't thought through the part of the plan where I got confronted after the loadmaster left.

"We know you're in there. Stand down."

My mind finally clicked into gear, riffling through potential responses, possible actions, any way out. After a few seconds of thought, I dismissed them all as useless.

"I'm here. I'm coming out."

I unstrapped myself and fell to the top of a pallet of packing crates with a thud that reverberated through the too-quiet compartment. My armor absorbed the minor shock, and I quickly hopped down to the deck and headed for the bay door.

"Halt there." I got my first look at them. A station police sergeant, wearing a black armored vest over a tan utility suit. Three companions flanked them. The team didn't quite have their weapons raised at me, but they certainly had them ready.

I showed them my empty hands, leaving my rifle clipped to the side of my armor. I still presented a threat, wearing power armor—in fact, I could have taken them all out. But attacking UFP soldiers doing their duty was too far. Even though I didn't like it, *I* was a UFP soldier, and most days we were on the same side.

No, I was caught, and it served my best interests to appear as friendly as possible. Always good business to be friendly when staring down four people with weapons. Besides, now that they'd caught me, I was on to plan B, and for that to work, I had to be alive.

"No trouble from me. Promise."

The four SPs didn't move. "Remove your armor."

"Understood."

Friendliness aside, for a second I considered making a break for it. It didn't fit my new designs, but habits are hard to break. Fight or flight and all that. I moved my hand slowly—no need to make anyone jumpy—and pressed the two buttons on my clavicle while simultaneously flicking my eyes across my heads-up to enter the code that triggered my suit's exit function. I stood perfectly still for the twelve seconds it took for the suit to unhinge itself and release me, and then pulled my helmet off and—still moving slowly—set it on top of a crate to my left. That left me unarmed, standing in my undersuit, my weapons staying attached to my armor. But I kept my hands visible anyway.

"Gas?" The lead SP stepped forward into the light. Sergeant Ken Burrows. I hadn't planned for them to be there, but I knew them well.

"What's up, Ken?" I asked.

"Gas . . . what the fuck? Why are you stowing away on board a supply ship going to a combat zone?"

"You know me, my friend. I've always got an angle working."

Ken looked at me, trying to find the story. "This about Kendrick?"

"You heard about that?"

"Of course. Everybody has. We all love Kendrick."

"Yeah," I said. "I had to try."

Ken hesitated, as if they were afraid to say the next bit. "I'm sorry, Gas, but I've got to run you in on this."

"No problem. We've all got jobs to do."

"If it was just me, you know I'd let you slide."

"I know you would." I believed them. They weren't a bad person, and I did them favors from time to time. I did a lot of people favors as part of my side hustles. I got them things, provided services—whatever I could do to make a buck or favors in return I could cash in later. The military could keep me under contract for six years, but they couldn't quash my entrepreneurial spirit.

"It's just that this one came from higher. You know how it is." Higher, meaning this wasn't random. Someone sent them after me, and that meant somebody higher would be following up to see the result.

"I get it. You had no choice." I gestured to the other soldiers. "You don't need your squad, though. I'm not going to give you any trouble. I know the way to D Cell." D Cell was short for detention cell, short-term holding for people who broke the rules but hadn't been convicted of a crime. Not a great way to spend a day, but better than the brig, where they kept the convicted criminals. If all went well, I wouldn't end up there.

They thought about it. "I better keep one with me. Just for appearances."

"Sure. You know best. Could you make sure my suit gets back to the armory?"

"Will do."

We headed out toward D Cell—I really did know the way. I'd been there often enough, though never for long. Funny thing, somehow nothing ever seemed to stick. At least they didn't cuff me. We'd be traversing public corridors, and it was already embarrassing enough walking with SPs. Ken did their best to make it cool, keeping pace beside me while their partner trailed behind.

"How'd you know I was in there?" I'd told Putty I'd be away, and for him to cover for me, but he hadn't told anyone. He wouldn't. Not Putty. He was part of my team, and I trusted my team as much as I trusted myself. It had to be something else. Someone else.

"Someone from higher called dispatch. Dispatch called me. That's all I know."

"That seems unusual," I said.

"A little," said Ken. "But it happens."

It happens. But that didn't explain why it happened to me. I smelled a rat. "If you find anything else out, you'll let me know?"

"Absolutely." They walked in silence for a few seconds, as if afraid to bring up the next subject. "Hey . . . with Kendrick gone . . ."

I knew what they wanted to know, so I made it easy on them. It pays to keep customers happy like that. I spoke in a lower voice. "You want to know about the card game."

"Right. Sorry."

"No worries." Ken loved their cards. They weren't any good, so other players liked having them in the game too. "Putty will run it now that Kendrick's out. You know what they say—the show must go on."

"Thanks, man." Ken cocked their head, the way people do when they're getting a message in their ear. "That's weird."

"What's up?" I asked.

"Change of plan. We're not going to D Cell. We're going to the command group."

We continued on for a bit. If I had to guess, Ken was wondering what the fuck was going on.

Me? I had at least some idea. I intended to try to get to Kendrick on my own if I made it down to the planet, but that was always a long shot. What I *wanted* was attention, and our detour to the command group said I had it. I could work with that.

We turned right at the next corridor and walked through a narrower hall to a lift that most soldiers avoided if possible. The words *Command Group* were stenciled on the closed door, as if everyone didn't know where it went. Command group implied the station commander. The general. No soldier wanted her to know their name, and most would go out of their way to avoid her.

As I said, I'm not your regular soldier.

I didn't let Ken in on the fact that I didn't mind the new destination, but I didn't pretend that it bothered me, either. I had a rule I lived by: wherever I found myself, that was exactly where I wanted to be. It's an attitude that people gravitate toward, for whatever reason. So that was my play. We were at the command group, and I tried to act as if it was normal and expected. As far as anybody would see from me, I owned the place.

Ken held their wrist device up to the scan pad, and the door opened.

We went up four decks, and the door whooshed open into an elegant room just outside the command suite. I'd been there once before, supervising a cleaning detail as they vacuumed the deep blue carpet. But I didn't pay attention to the well-appointed surroundings this time. My eyes went to the person waiting to enter the lift after we disembarked.

Sergeant Kara Miller.

We called her Killer, because, well . . . it rhymed with Miller, and her first name started with a *K*.

Cut us some slack. We're soldiers, not poets.

Killer led third squad. In theory they were sister squad to my fourth, but if we were siblings, we were the kind who didn't get along.

I stared at her, and she met my eyes for a split second before turning her head and pretending she hadn't. Despite being my age—twenty-two—she looked older. Apparently being an evil minion of the lord of the underworld aged a person. I stared at the back of her head, her textbook blond bun. By-the-book Killer Miller leaving the command group. That explained how I'd been caught.

CHAPTER 2

I STOOD AT ATTENTION, MY EYES LOCKED ON THE tasteful framed picture on the far wall without really seeing it. It allowed me to avoid eye contact with the crisply uniformed staff of the commander's office who sat at polished desks or walked around pretending they had something to do so they could sneak peeks at the convict headed for the gallows. I wore the gray utility clothes that we wore under our armor, form-fitting and glistening with the moisture that it wicked away from my body. Not the best look to meet the general— I really didn't think she wanted to check out the bulge in my pants—but I didn't think I should ask to go change. Non-coms who worked in the command group had a notorious deficiency in the sense of humor department. Not to say they weren't good at their jobs. Everyone in the office had been chosen from a group of excellent candidates, all of whom were better soldiers than I'd ever be.

At least on the surface. From my alternate line of work, I knew a lot of their vices. But I don't judge, and I don't tell. Those are two things you can count on when you do business with Gas Gastovsky.

"Sergeant Gastovsky, the colonel will see you now," said a sharp-looking staff sergeant, poking his head out of the office of the deputy commander. *Colonel.* I was seeing the deputy commander, Colonel Gwan, instead of the general. That was very good news.

I did a crisp facing movement and marched to the door, my head level. We weren't big on drill and ceremony in the augmented infantry, but when you're in trouble, it never hurts to show the brass what they want to see. I was where I wanted to be, but I didn't want to explain that, so it was best if they thought me suitably intimidated.

The staff sergeant with the perfectly trimmed buzz cut held the door for me, then let it slide shut after I entered. The large office—large for a space station, anyway—reeked of furniture polish as I stood at attention again, just inside. An officer with the regulation salt-and-pepper hair of a colonel focused on a screen that rose from his immaculate desk.

"Sergeant Gastovsky?" He looked up.

"Yes, sir," I said, a little louder than I needed to, maintaining my show.

"You can relax."

I snapped from attention to parade rest, spreading my legs to shoulder-width apart and placing my hands in the small of my back.

"Really," he said. "Relax."

I didn't move. I heard him, but the concept of "relax" did not mix with the concept of "in a colonel's office and in trouble." It was one thing to work to get myself into this position. It was another thing altogether to actually be there, and I have to admit that it had me a little on edge. He sighed, then stood up and came out from behind his desk, his feet silent on the thick carpet. He gestured to the round table in the corner. "Have a seat." When I didn't move, he added, "That's an order."

I walked to the table and sat stiffly in one of the fake leather chairs, not letting my back touch the backrest, my feet flat on the floor, eyes forward. He'd expect me to be nervous, so I leaned into that part to make sure he saw it. Any good soldier would be nervous, and he'd be suspicious if I wasn't. The colonel made some noise that might have been suppressing a chuckle and took the seat across from me.

"I'm Colonel Gwan, the deputy commander." He held out his hand, and I stood back up to shake it.

I knew who he was—probably more than he thought. Sergeants weren't really supposed to know much about colonels, but I make it my point to keep abreast of things. You could never tell what might give you an advantage. Gwan had been an up-and-coming star as a brigade commander, but he didn't follow orders on an important mission, so his career had stalled, and they'd buried him in the number two position—a desk job—at a nowhere station. They would have fired him outright, except they couldn't. You see, the orders he disobeyed were *stupid*, and they would have gotten soldiers killed needlessly. He was *right* to disobey them, and he won the battle. But for whatever reason, it pissed off the wrong people. I had theories, and if they were correct,

I might be sitting across from the man who could help me—directly or indirectly. But I needed confirmation before considering Gwan an asset, let alone an ally. Officer politics were confusing.

"Good to meet you, sir."

"Good to meet you too. I deal with things the general doesn't have time for." He smiled, as if that was a joke, then continued when I didn't react. "Look, Gastovsky, I just want to talk to you."

"Yes, sir." From what I was reading from him, he didn't want the scared soldier, so I visibly relaxed my shoulders and let my body sag a little in the chair. I transformed into a picture of a soldier ready to talk. "What can I do for you, sir?"

He nodded once. "Good. First off, you're not in trouble."

I met his eyes for the first time. They were dark brown, bordering on black, lines crinkling away from them. They struck me as eyes that had seen too much. I pretended to stumble over my words. "I'm not?"

"I don't see the point in it. Nothing really happened, right? You were in an unauthorized area, but that's not exactly a major crime."

I hesitated. Was he baiting me? I mean . . . his explanation . . . that was how *I* would try to sell it, sure, but as convincing as I can be, I wouldn't expect anyone to actually buy it. "I stowed away on a ship, sir." He had surprised me enough that now I was championing my own guilt. But he had to have known what happened, and I didn't understand what game he was playing yet.

Maybe he wanted to offer me the chance to rationalize my own crime so he could shoot me down.

"Eh. Maybe you did, maybe you didn't. The ship didn't leave, so I guess we'll never know for sure." He smiled, but again, I couldn't tell if the joke was *with* me or *on* me. The deputy commander was acting like a private trying to get out of work detail, and I didn't know what that meant.

I almost explained that the doors had closed on the ship, but my brain finally caught up, and I let it go. "Thanks, sir."

He gave me a flat smile. "If it makes you feel better, I can assign you to a week of extra duty."

"I'm good, sir."

"Oh, you're not good. But it's not as bad as you think, either." He laughed, which put me at least a little at ease considering what he'd just said. "Look. I get it. I was line infantry before I got promoted up to this post. Twenty-four years of it. I'd have done the same thing you did."

That I didn't believe. It sounded too much like an officer trying to show himself as *one of the grunts, just a regular soldier.* I didn't begrudge him the lie. People have secrets. I lie a lot too. But either way, he had my attention, and either way, I needed to see how he fit into my constantly changing plan. "Really, sir?"

He paused. "No. I'd have been smarter. You had no chance of getting away with it. What the hell were you thinking?"

I smiled. I couldn't help it. We were back in territory

I understood. "I wasn't thinking, sir. I just know I need to find my soldier."

He nodded. "Private First Class Kendrick."

"Yes, sir." I have to admit, it surprised me that he knew Kendrick's name. Then I glanced at the screen on his desk—someone had probably fed it to him while they escorted me up.

"Tell me this," continued Gwan. "What were you planning to do to find him? They'd have discovered you when you landed, and even if they didn't, you wouldn't have been anywhere near Kendrick's last location."

"I was going to wing it, sir."

He chuckled. "Yeah, I definitely would have come up with a better course of action."

"I had to try, sir." It sounded a little more belligerent than I intended.

Gwan pretended he didn't notice. "Yeah . . . yeah, I guess you did. So what do we do now?"

I looked at him, only half pretending to be confused. I didn't know. That's what I needed *him* to tell me. "What do you mean, sir?"

"What I mean is, when you walk out of my office, looking suitably chastised, are you going to forget about going planetside?"

I thought about it for a moment, as we were getting to the important part. The good soldier would say, *Yes, sir. I'm going to forget about it. You'll never hear from me again.* I could pretend to be that guy—normally I would—but something told me Colonel Gwan didn't want to hear that, and I'd get more out of him by letting him know I *didn't* intend to follow the rules. He wouldn't believe me if I lied anyway. Whatever game he was playing, they don't make you deputy commander if you're an idiot. That's an important thing to remember when you're working an angle: the other guy might be smart too. "No, sir. I'm not going to forget about it."

He measured me for several seconds with his eyes. I felt like he was reading my soul. "No, I didn't figure you would. I wouldn't." He stared at me for what felt like a solid minute. Finally, "Okay."

A silence drew out, getting awkward, so I broke it. "Okay? I can go to the planet, sir?"

He smiled, almost laughed. "Hell, no. I just finished telling you how pointless that was. You don't know where Kendrick is. You don't even know if he's alive."

I *did* know he was alive, but I didn't think the colonel would have taken kindly to *how* I knew. So I kept that to myself. "I don't understand, sir." I really didn't. He had his own motives, and while they seemed to align with mine at the moment, there were a lot of potential outcomes, and we definitely had different end goals.

"Look, you told me that you're going after Kendrick again, right?"

"Yes, sir."

"And you're a resourceful soldier. I figure the only way I'm going to stop you is to lock you up or give you a better way, and I told you I wasn't going to lock you up." He paused, and this time I didn't interrupt, as I got the impression he was thinking. "But first, I want you to do something for me."

"What's that, sir?"

"I want you to give me some fucking credit."

My heart almost stopped. Had he seen through my bullshit? More important, *which* bit of bullshit had he seen through? "Excuse me, sir?"

"Do you think you're the only person who wants Kendrick back?"

"No, s—"

"He's my soldier too." Gwan slapped his hand down on the table to emphasize his point. "Yeah, you want him back—probably more than anybody. But I want him back too. It's just not that easy."

I cut my eyes down to the shiny polymer tabletop, then back up to meet the colonel's. "Why isn't it, sir? We've got the assets, and we know his last location. Give me a team, and I'll go get him right now." He wasn't going to do that, but I wanted to push back on him, see how he reacted.

He shook his head, but not in an angry way. More sad. "That's not how it works."

"It should, sir."

"It should. You're right. But *should* is a fucking fairy tale. Let me tell you how the real world works. It's a numbers game. I had Medical Ops run the monitoring data from Kendrick's augmented suit. Twenty-two hours ago, four hours after you pulled out, Kendrick's vital signs went blank all at once. What does that tell you?"

The man had done his homework. I had to give him that. "Sir, that's consistent with a catastrophic kill, a total system malfunction, or a manual deactivation of his armor."

"Right. His heart rate didn't spike before the system cut out, so if he died, he didn't see it coming. Based on historical data, Medical Ops estimates that there was a seventy-nine-percent chance he was alive at that time."

"Seventy-nine percent is pretty good odds, sir."

"I'm not done yet. That was twenty-two hours ago. I'm going to save you the details of how we got all this and just give you the results of our analysis. There's a sixty-eight percent chance that Kendrick is still alive," he continued. "In about half those chances, he's wounded, and in three quarters of them, he's under enemy control. A prisoner. Overall there's a fourteen-percent chance that he's well enough to move and still on his own recognizance."

I sat there, stunned into silence. The numbers he stated might not have been correct, but he spoke them with such confidence that I believed him. Or, more accurate, I believed he had figured out the best possible answer based on his limited information. On the surface, I hadn't expected him to be so sure at this point. Of course, he had a huge staff at his beck and call, and all I had was a bunch of contacts and a whole pile of motivation. But I knew things he didn't know—things beyond the pure numbers. I knew where Kendrick would be. I had contingencies for everything, and that included a plan in case a soldier got left behind. Everyone in my squad knew that if we got separated, they were to make their way to the town of Kiergard and hole up there until we came to get them.

And I knew Kendrick. The colonel said fourteen percent. My number was in the nineties. But despite the colonel being so forthcoming, I wasn't sharing that with him. Not yet. Because I didn't know if I could trust him enough to explain the difference, and regardless, I couldn't prove it. We both wanted Kendrick back, and Gwan had directed his staff to put energy into trying to find him. I believed that. I just didn't know why. And call me cynical—or someone who tends to live his life this way himself—but I don't believe that anybody does something for nothing.

"Fourteen percent is still a chance, sir. Even if he's injured or captured, we can find him and get him back." It was a weak argument. I think I only made it because he expected me to, and it would help him make his next point. As I mentioned, I go out of my way to make other people comfortable. It's part of the game.

"Again, that's not how it works. The important numbers aren't just the odds of finding him. It's the cost of going after him in material, personnel, and risk."

"What's the worth of a human life, sir?" I didn't expect him to answer, but he didn't hesitate.

"Not nearly as much as you'd hope."

I sat there with that for a good while, and to his credit, Gwan gave me the time. I think if he'd said it ironically, it would have pissed me off, but the sadness in his voice struck me. That meant it was time to get to the point. He wanted something, and he wanted me to ask what it was. Who was I to disappoint the boss man? "So, sir . . . you didn't call me to your office to tell me why we couldn't do something. Why am I here?"

A smirk touched his face for just a second. "I thought I had the right guy, and now I'm sure of it."

"Right guy for what, sir?"

"I'm a big believer in motivation. Motivated soldiers are the most effective soldiers. And I've got a feeling that when it comes to Kendrick, there's nobody as motivated as you are."

He certainly has that right. "I think that's a good assessment, sir."

"I've also done some checking. You're not only motivated, you're resourceful."

My heart rate spiked a bit, but I kept my face as flat as I could. How much did he know about exactly how resourceful I was? He couldn't know everything. I was in his office, not in prison. But I didn't appreciate him knowing *anything* about me. He did, though. "I've been known to make some things happen from time to time, sir."

He half grunted, half laughed. "Well, it's time to see if you can make something happen for Kendrick. I'm not lying to you when I say I want to go after him, but I'm also not lying when I tell you I can't."

"Yes, sir. I understand. The numbers."

"Right. The numbers." He paused. "I want you to find me better numbers."

I took my time thinking about what he said, because we had reached the critical moment. He was correct, of course, about better numbers. With the right motivation, you can change *any* situation. You just have to want it enough to take the risk. To pay the price. And I was more than willing. We probably weren't going to agree on *how* to change them, but that didn't matter at the moment. He had presented me with the opportunity

I needed, and I was going to take it. I wasn't asking for clarification, though, because I didn't want it. I wanted the broadest possible authority I could get.

That wasn't why I took time to think. Every agreement has two sides. He was giving me what I wanted, but he wanted something too, and I had to make sure to get it right, to give him—or at least let him think I was giving him—what he expected from me. If not, he could pull back what he offered with a snap of his fingers. I figured it out after a minute. He wanted plausible deniability. He was a colonel, and I was a sergeant. His risk was significantly higher than mine. He had more to lose. Still, I hesitated, this time for effect. I didn't want to come across as too eager.

He fixed me with his officer eyes, that look that makes you want to agree. A look that makes you want to do anything you can to gain the man's approval. If circumstances in his life had gone differently, he'd have made a good con man.

"Okay, sir. I'm in."

"Just like that?"

"Just like that, sir. I go with my gut."

He pounded his fist on the table. "Good. Here's what I've got for you. There's a lieutenant colonel who works in Operations. She's one of mine. Her name is Barnes. She's expecting you, and she's going to help you with intel assets. Your job is to get me enough evidence to justify a mission."

I twisted my mouth slightly. He said it like it was simple, but he had just given me a task that his entire staff couldn't accomplish, and I didn't have an immediate idea about how I could improve on their result. He smiled, having read my mind. "What, you thought it was going to be easy? If it was easy, it would be done already."

"No, sir. I didn't think it would be easy." I *did* think it would be possible. "I'll speak to Lieutenant Colonel Barnes." I paused before the next bit, as if I was thinking about it, though that was an act. I knew what I wanted to ask. "Sir, I assume that I'm allowed to use my own means as well as those of Lieutenant Colonel Barnes to change the numbers. Is that correct?"

"Did I say 'change'?" he asked, his eyes crinkling with an almost-smile. "I most certainly did not say *change*."

"Of course you didn't, sir." We understood each other. He was protecting himself with precise language.

"As for outside help? Oh yes. I'm counting on it." He stood, and I followed suit. "Don't waste time. Every hour he's missing, the odds of finding him go down. Any questions?"

I hesitated, considering one more thing before he threw me out, and then decided, why not? He had an angle behind the deal he gave me, and one slightly insubordinate question wouldn't change that. "One more question, sir, if you don't mind."

"What's that?" He moved back toward his desk.

"How did you know I was on that ship, sir? What tipped you off? Did routine camera stuff spot me, or did someone rat me out?"

Colonel Gwan turned back toward me and paused. For the first time since I'd entered, he didn't have an immediate answer. "I think I'm going to keep that one to myself," he said finally.

"Roger, sir." I didn't know why he wouldn't say. I already knew it had been Miller. She had no other reason to be up there in the command group. Soldiers like her and me didn't *just happen* to stroll on through this level. I guess I wanted to hear him confirm it. But I couldn't blame him for holding it back. He didn't owe it to me. He'd done enough by giving me the chance I needed. Of all the outcomes I could have hoped for when I started out on my ridiculous attempt today, I got the best possible one.

But Miller was going to be a problem.

CHAPTER 3

PART OF ME WANTED TO CHASE DOWN MILLER AND let her have a piece of my mind, but I couldn't. I'd *just* left Gwan's office, and I didn't want to be back there anytime soon. Not until I'd found the proof I needed to convince him to okay the mission to go get Kendrick.

I'd settle up with Miller after that.

So I did exactly what the colonel told me to do. There's a first time for everything, I guess. I made my way to Ops to meet with Lieutenant Colonel Barnes and see what I could learn about the area around Kiergard. I already knew quite a bit, which was why my squad had orders to hole up there in an emergency. To start, neither side ever bombed it. Not once in twenty-two years of war. But Ops might have something useful, like a disposition of enemy forces, and for sure they'd be able to show me the closest friendly units. Maybe they'd have a surveillance feed or some other intel asset I could use to find my wayward soldier.

In my head, I thought of him as alive. Given what I knew, Gwan's numbers didn't apply. Of course there was risk. It was a war zone, and anything could happen. But I trusted Kendrick to follow his training, and that upped his odds significantly.

I reached the door to the operations center and put my palm against the hand sensor. Something somewhere decided I had the right clearance, so the door zipped upward. I stepped inside and stopped, staring at the huge room. They called it the Ops floor, but *floor* failed to describe it. In front of me rose a multi-tiered stadium of computer terminals, flashing lights, and technicians. Twelve screens, each the size of a barracks room, stretched across the top of the front wall—the wall I had entered through—showing all sorts of video feeds, maps, and other information I couldn't quickly decipher. What struck me most, though, was the sound. Or rather the lack of sound. There had to be three hundred people at work, and the loudest sound in the room came from the ventilation system that kept the air cool enough to make me shiver.

"You lost, Sergeant?" A corporal heading toward the door I'd entered through stopped to speak to me.

"No. Just taking it in. I'm supposed to find Lieutenant Colonel Barnes. She's the deputy chief of Operations?"

He chuckled. "Yeah, I know who she is. She runs this place during the day shift. Good luck."

"Good luck finding her, or good luck talking with her?"

"More the latter than the former, but I don't know exactly where she is right now." He pointed. "She usually hangs out at the big command suite at the center, though. The one with all the fancy stuff."

"Thanks," I said, but he didn't wait around. I made my way across the floor level to the metal stairs that ran up the center of the stadium, going slowly to avoid the constant stream of soldiers moving from one place to the next. They all wore wireless headsets and tiny throat microphones. That explained the silence.

"Hey!" bellowed a stern male voice that carried the weight of command behind it.

I turned instinctively, even though he probably wasn't talking to me. A short, stocky colonel with a shaved head stared directly at me. "Come here."

His tone didn't leave room to question it, but I still didn't know if he meant me. I couldn't form any words, so I looked back at him blankly.

"Are you dense?" he asked. Definitely talking to me.

"No, sir. Sorry, sir, I didn't know you meant me."

"Who the hell else would I mean? Everyone else here has a headset on."

I walked over to his station on the opposite side of the stairs from my original destination and assumed a loose position of attention. "Sir, I'm here to see—"

"I know why you're here, and I don't care. This is my operations center, and you don't belong."

I hesitated. His narrowed eyes and flaring nostrils almost screamed, *I dare you to question me. Go ahead. See what happens.*

"Sir, Colonel Gwan told me to contact Lieutenant Colonel—"

"I told you *I don't care*," he interrupted, spitting each word. "I don't work for Colonel Gwan, and he doesn't run Operations."

I glanced down to the colonel's name tag, trying to be subtle about it.

"Dentonn," he said, obviously catching my eyes. "Two *n*'s at the end. Make sure you spell it right in your complaint. I'm chief of Operations. You run back and tell Gwan I'm not playing his games here."

A dozen questions flashed through my mind, but the Colonel's tone told me that asking the foremost one on my mind—*what the fuck is happening right now?*—was a bad idea. One more word from me and I thought he might explode. I was smart enough to know when to retreat. "Yes, sir."

He turned away from me and back to his station as means of dismissal, and I immediately headed back down the stairs and out the way I came.

Confused as I was, I almost ran into someone in the corridor on the other side of the door.

"What are you up to?" she asked.

Miller. Because of course it was. "None of your business," I said. "Are you fucking following me?" On the other hand, she made a good target. I'd just had my ass handed to me by a colonel for something I didn't understand, and while I couldn't say anything back to him, Miller was a different story. "Or are you here to gloat?"

"About what?"

I stared her down. Rationally, she couldn't know what happened a moment ago, but *rational* wasn't at the top of my list right then. I tried to move past her, but she shifted to block me. "Get out of my way."

"Is this about Kendrick? You've been acting funny since we lifted off the surface."

"Maybe you should focus less on following me and more on your squad," I said, ignoring her question.

"Kendrick used to be in my squad, in case you forgot."

"*Used* to be." And just barely. He'd been with her for about two weeks before I'd had a soldier get injured, and I worked the system to get him transferred over to my squad. "But I'm sure the people who *are* in your squad need you."

"My squad is fine. Unlike yours, who left someone behind and have no idea what training they're doing tomorrow."

"Fuck you. And my squad knows their schedule."

"Not according to Erickson." She smirked, which made me want to punch her in the face. Erickson was *my* squad's medic, but she and Miller lived together in the room across the hall from the rest of us.

I got past her and walked as quickly as I could to leave her behind. Her footsteps sped up, ringing on the grated floor of the space station. So much for her going away. I wanted to lash out, to bitch at her for turning me in. At the same time, if she hadn't, I wouldn't have talked to Colonel Gwan, and I wouldn't have his assistance getting to Kendrick. She'd actually helped me, but no way was I telling *her* that. I settled on neutral. "I'm not in the mood to talk about it, Killer."

She fell in beside me, matching my quick pace. "I just want to help find Kendrick. Don't be pissed at me because you fucked up."

I clenched my fists at my sides. I *hadn't* fucked up, but her saying it still stung for whatever reason. No peer would blame me if I punched her. But we were certainly on camera, and I didn't need that kind of trouble. Shit, maybe she wanted me to hit her, to get myself locked up. I couldn't be sure. What I *did* know was that if Miller was offering to help, she had an angle. She'd earned her sergeant's stripes faster than anyone in recent memory, and she didn't get them by helping people out. Especially not peers who led rival squads. On top of that, I couldn't rule out the idea that she was working for someone else. She'd been in the command group and now around Ops. I should have kept my mouth shut, but I couldn't hold back. "If you wanted to help, you wouldn't have turned me in when I tried to go after him."

She stared at me for a second, meeting my eyes without blinking. She started to say something, then changed her mind. A few seconds later she began again. "That's what this is? You think I turned you in?"

"Who else would have?"

She shook her head. "Pretty much anyone? You're not exactly subtle, Gas. You probably got picked up on standard surveillance. But go ahead, blame me. Blame anyone, as long as you don't have to take responsibility yourself."

"What's *that* supposed to mean?" I consciously relaxed my hands, unclenching them. As rational as I was with most people, something about Miller just messed with my head.

"You don't think things through, Gas. You wing everything and then try to get by on your bullshit, and then when it inevitably falls apart, you wonder why. Why else do you think it took you a year longer than me to make sergeant?"

"Because I don't brownnose command like a good little soldier." What I didn't tell her was that she only *knew* about the ones that fell apart. Many more worked just fine, which meant they never came to her attention.

She blew out a breath in disgust. "Whatever. You do your thing. Let me know if I can help." She turned to walk away.

"I'm good," I said to her back. "You don't even like Kendrick."

She didn't turn around. "Kendrick is an asshole."

I did snort this time. "He might be. But he's my asshole. My squad, and we don't leave people behind."

"But you did," she said over her shoulder.

It was a good thing she was already walking away, because if she was still standing in front of me, I *would* have hit her, cameras and consequences be damned.

I RAN ON a treadmill, my feet pounding on the spring-loaded platform as I tried to work away the anger and embarrassment from my visit to Operations and my confrontation with Miller. Every minute I wasted made it less likely that I'd find Kendrick alive, but I needed to clear my head, and running helped with that. I'd dragged Putty, one of the soldiers in my squad and my top confidante now that Kendrick was missing, with me. He ran on an identical machine next to me, though at a slower speed. One of the difficult things about being a grunt on a space station was staying in the sort of shape required for combat. It was especially difficult for Putty, who would only willingly run if there were doughnuts involved or if some girl's father was chasing him.

"How come whenever *you're* pissed off with the galaxy, *I* get punished for it?" he asked, huffing a little.

"That's how the military works, Putty. The officer shits on the sergeant, and the sergeant takes it out on the people below him. It's in the manual."

"I don't read much," he said.

"I saw you reading on your tablet this morning."

"That had pictures. *Naked* pictures."

"Sure," I said.

"Your sister's fine, by the way."

I tried to hold in a laugh but ended up snorting. "Fuck you."

"Is that any way to talk to your future brother-in-law?"

"My sister has better taste than that. Colonel Gwan brought me into his office to talk about Kendrick," I said.

"I don't know how you talk and run at the same time." Putty wiped sweat from his round face, his short brown hair already matted to his head.

"And I don't know how you made it into the infantry without liking to run. Or at least being better at it."

"Just lucky, I guess. What did Gwan say about our man?"

"That he wants to help, but his hands are tied. Yet not so tied that he doesn't want me to do something that changes that."

"That sounds vague and useless."

"He's a colonel. What do you expect?"

"What does *he* expect? It was a shitstorm down there," he said. "When that air strike came in and the world exploded, anything could have happened."

"The thing is, the colonel gave me what I wanted. He gave me an opportunity to go after Kendrick. I just can't figure out how to make it work."

"Well," said Putty. "Start with what we know."

"Med Ops reported he was still alive for at least a few hours after that."

Putty didn't answer for a minute, huffing to catch his breath. "So we left him there. We're assholes."

"Sure we are, but not because of that. We'll get him back," I said.

"Still, that's a shitty thing to have to live with."

I punched the speed button up a notch. "Yeah. It is. What if we didn't have to live with it?"

"I don't know. It's not like we can go back in time and change what happened."

"But we can go back for him," I said.

"I assumed that's what you were doing when you thought you were being sneaky and headed out in your power armor."

"You knew about that?"

"Come on, Gas. Who are you talking to?"

I'd been mad at Miller when she'd said basically the same thing, but with Putty, I was proud. It was good that he noticed things. If he was going to fill in for Kendrick, I needed him to think. "You're right. You know with Kendrick gone, I need you to step up, right?"

"I kind of figured."

"I need you to pick up the new soldier. Name is Stimpson."

"You don't take just anyone into the squad. What's his deal?"

"I knew his sister. She called in a favor and wants me to take care of him. Says he's a good kid."

Putty waggled his eyebrows, implying something about why I might owe his sister a favor. It wasn't true, but I didn't disabuse him of the notion. In truth, she was dead, and the favor only existed in my head. But if I told him that, he might take me for sentimental or something. "Roger that. I'll get him."

"I also want you to run the card game. And handle the distribution of the Viper." We didn't deal in hard drugs, but I did supply people with mood enhancers—Viper. They were legal everywhere and harmless, but the military never met something that it didn't want to regulate. We kind of disagreed on that. People wanted things, I got them for them. For a price.

"Sure. I can do that."

"Just until we get Kendrick back," I said. "After that we'll work it out."

Putty stepped off his treadmill onto the rails, turned, and looked at me. "You really think he's coming back? Even if he was alive then, he's probably not anymore. Sorry. Just being real."

"But what if he was? You know what we do if we get separated."

"Head to Kiergard. I never understood why, but yeah, Kendrick would definitely go there if he could. It wasn't too far, I don't think." He shrugged. "Still not much we can do."

"Not by ourselves." I looked around the gym, which was mostly empty, only one behemoth doing power jerks on the opposite side of the room. "You've got to keep this quiet. Especially around anyone in Miller's squad. But the deputy commander said if I can find evidence that Kendrick's down there, he'd launch a mission."

He stepped back onto his treadmill and stumbled for a moment until his feet caught up. "That's a little less useless. You believe him?"

"Yeah. I think he's got a secondary motive, but I believe that he'll come through on that part of things. Problem is, not everybody is on board. I tried to go to Operations, and the colonel there shut me down before I could even talk to my supposed contact. There are definitely competing agendas, and I don't know all of them."

Putty grunted. "Sounds like officer politics. One colonel pissing in another colonel's breakfast cereal. And you know who gets the brunt of it?"

"Don't say the little guy," I said.

"The *little* guy."

I smiled, despite myself. Putty was obsessed with the oppression of the little guy. "Lucky for you that you're not even close to little."

"It's a metaphor," said Putty. "Try to keep up."

"Your conspiracy theories are a bit out there."

"Doesn't mean they're wrong."

I thought about it. I didn't buy into many of Putty's thoughts on how things worked in the galaxy, but I had also just experienced a strange situation with the two very different colonels. There were clearly issues there. I didn't care if Gwan and Dentonn had it out for each other. The only thing that mattered was how I could exploit it. Every seam created a weak point—I just had to figure out where to tear. "So, what do I do?"

He punched the off button on his treadmill, and it ground to a halt. I didn't say anything about him quitting early. "It's easy," he said.

"Sure. Easy."

"It is. Right now, you're trying to do things the officer way. You need to stop that and do it *our* way."

"So I do it the enlisted way," I said. "Yeah."

"Sure," said Putty. "I was going to say 'the dirty way,' but 'enlisted way' works."

CHAPTER 4

AFTER I SHOWERED, I SET OUT WITH PUTTY'S MIND-set. I had Colonel Gwan's authority, but clearly not everybody cared. As chief of Ops, Dentonn controlled a lot of the assets I needed, and I didn't know how deep the feud went, or who might be loyal to whom. Gwan had given me Barnes's name, but not access to her.

He also said he expected me to freelance. That I could do.

The problem was that while I'd built a squad that could make a lot of things happen, there were resources we didn't have. Fortunately, I knew a guy who could get me the info I needed that Ops wouldn't provide . . . and he owed me a favor.

It took me twenty minutes to work my way through the gatekeepers that control access to classified areas—officious little bastards that they are—but finally a sol-dier escorted me to the office of the man I wanted to see: Alex Ortega.

"Gas? How's it going, man? What the hell are you doing here?" Ortega's voice didn't hold any animosity. More like genuine confusion.

"Hey, Ortega. Can't I come by to say hi to an old friend?" As I said it, I cut my eyes at the soldier who had let me in, hoping she'd get my intent. She didn't.

"We're good, Burkett," he told my escort. "I'll walk Sergeant Gastovsky back out once we're done." Ortega waited for her to leave. "Seriously, man, what the fuck? It took me a lot of work to sterilize all my feeds to let you in."

"What's so secret back here?" I said it in a joking tone, but I also meant it. The service entrusted me with a mech-suit that cost approximately forty kajillion credits, but I couldn't see a computer screen? That info was currency, and I liked that currency.

"If I told you that, I'd be out of a job. You trying to ruin my sweet gig or something? So, again: What's up?"

"I need a favor," I said.

He laughed. "I didn't need to be an intel specialist to guess that. I know you didn't just stop in to say hi. When was the last time we saw each other?"

"That would be the time in the K deck bar when I told that good-looking tech specialist how you saved my life back on Kaspar. How's that working out, by the way?" I gave him a pointed look.

"Oh, right. We're still together." He rubbed his hand through his short-cropped dark hair. "So it's *that* kind of favor."

"It is."

He sighed. "Shit. Try not to get me fired, would you?"

"I mean . . . I'll *try*." He glared at me, and I put my hands up defensively. "I'm joking. You're in the clear. I got permission from the deputy commander to query

the staff. They're supposed to give me anything I need."
It wasn't precisely true, but I figured it was close enough.

"You have the entire staff at your disposal, yet you're here, in *my* office. Sure. That's believable." He said it like his office was something special and not basically a closet with a desk and a few computer screens in it.

"Come on, Tega. I wanted someone I could trust."

"Yeah, I'd like that too," he said. "For the record, I think you're full of shit. But what do you want me to do?"

I gestured to his workstation. "Use your magic machines. I need everything you can get on a location." I read him the coordinates. "It's the area around Kiergard, which is where I'm going to find my missing soldier."

Ortega drew his lips to one side of his face. "Interesting. I'm assuming you think he's alive, if you're here."

"Have to believe," I said.

He flicked a map onto the screen on the wall. "Okay, here you go. Behind enemy lines. Twenty-four kilometers. About twenty klicks from the area where we fought recently, but since then, the enemy has moved forward quite a bit."

"Yeah, I was there," I said. "Tell me something I don't know."

He looked up at me. "You were in that? Shit, man. That looked bad."

"It was great, assuming you like getting your ass kicked and trees exploding everywhere."

"Yeah, that had to suck. What do you actually need? I don't have any way to pick up an individual person unless his sensors are hot."

Now we were talking. "Then give me everything. Every feed you've got. Enemy disposition, electronic signatures. Video, if you've got it."

"Come on, Gas. That's a ton of effort." He gestured to three tablets on his desk, which I assumed must be his real work. But I had work to do too.

"That tech specialist at the K deck bar . . . what was her name again? Ashley, right? I wonder what she'd think if I told her how you've never seen combat—"

He stared at me for a few seconds. "Did anyone ever tell you that you're an asshole?"

"All the time," I said. "Didn't bother me when my mom said it, doesn't bother me when you do. Come on, Tega. I wouldn't be here if this wasn't important. It's fucking Kendrick."

He blew air out loudly through his mouth. "Shit. Fine." He punched some more things into his machine.

"No video," he said. "Here's a satellite picture, though. It's dated. From before the battle."

"Can you magnify the built-up area?" I asked.

He zoomed in and enhanced the image. "Older construction. Most of the buildings are two stories. This street here looks like businesses if I had to guess. This large building here looks like a warehouse. Maybe some offices inside of it, given the parking."

I nodded. I already knew that building, and I suspected it was the reason the town never got attacked. "Could you get another pass?"

"Ha! Yeah. I'll just redirect a satellite. Nobody will notice." He did everything but roll his eyes.

"Hey, I need whatever I can get. I don't know what's possible and what's not."

"Sorry," he said. "I didn't mean to be a dick, but there's no chance I can do that. You want a new picture, you've got to go talk to the major. I don't know how far you'll get with whatever authority the deputy commander gave you. I can show you the way if you want. That said, the chances that a random satellite pass is going to help you find a specific person? Almost none."

The thing was, I wasn't really looking for Kendrick. He would be there. I just wanted the most accurate and up-to-date info on the area for planning purposes. But I couldn't tell Tega that. "How about a drone? Could we get one in there?"

"Not even the major could do that," said Ortega. "The Confed Powers would shoot it down. Or, more likely, they'd hack it and steal it."

I huffed out a breath. I had a general understanding that we couldn't fly sensors over the enemy, and even though I didn't know why, it corroborated Tega's assessment. "Okay. What can you tell me about enemy in the area?"

"Hold on." He tinkered with his tools for a couple minutes. "Here we go. Checkpoints templated here and here, based on the signal traffic." He indicated locations on the map that he cast next to the picture of the town. "Movement indicators show a patrol here on the satellite pass fifteen hours ago, but that could be random. Hard to say without a few days' worth of data, which we don't have since the fight happened so recently."

"What do you know about the checkpoints?" He'd lit them up. They were well away from the town but controlled the roads that led there.

"Nothing. But I can guess," he said. "Standard would be fifteen to twenty soldiers at each, along the somewhat acknowledged new line between their side and ours."

I stood and walked closer to the screen. "You'd think they'd have more stuff up on the line, guarding against an attack."

He shook his head. "Nope. They never do. Because we never attack. This line hasn't moved more than fifty or sixty kilometers in either direction in more than five years."

"But they attacked us earlier this week," I said.

He shrugged. "But they know we won't do anything about it. Plus, if we do decide to make a push, they'll see it coming, and they'll bring these forces from back here forward." He highlighted three positions about a hundred kilometers back from the line. "Putting units in static positions on the front line is a good way to get them killed. It's easier to sit back and watch from space, and then react as needed. The closer you get to the enemy line, the more they can bring to bear on you. Especially processing power. The side with more computers wins the hacking battle."

"So if I'm reading this right, the Confed Powers have fewer than a hundred troops within twenty klicks of Kiergard."

He studied it for a moment. "I think that's an accurate assessment. Unless they've got something underground, which is unlikely. I'd have to check the vibration sensors and get a seismic scan to be absolutely sure, but there's no history in this area of subsurface action."

I clasped my hands together. "Okay. Thanks. This was really helpful."

"Anytime," said Ortega. "And when I say anytime, I want to be clear that I mean never again. We're square now."

"I got you. Tell Ashley I said hi."

"Sure. And you tell that girl that you're with hi for me . . . oh, wait. There isn't one. Because you're an asshole."

"I love you too, man."

GWAN HAD GIVEN me one specific directive: I needed to talk to Lieutenant Colonel Barnes. Colonel Dentonn clearly didn't want me to do that, which was interesting on its own, but when taken together hinted at something I could potentially use against one or both of them down the line. But my immediate problem was that Dentonn ruled the Ops floor, and I couldn't risk going back there. So how do you meet someone when you can't go to where they usually are?

I enlisted Putty's aid, and he came through.

I met him in a wide corridor well away from our living area. "She's right where I told you she'd be," he said.

"How did you figure it out?"

His lips turned up in a half smile. "I know a guy."

I could respect that. I wouldn't share all of my sources, either, and as long as he got the job done, that was what mattered. I left him and walked a hundred meters or so, around one turn, and entered the E deck bar. It was an officer hangout, and while there were no rules that said enlisted *couldn't* go there, they usually *didn't*.

Low music played inside, not loud enough to drown out conversation. A group of lieutenants—probably ground pounders from the looks of them—joked loudly at a square table along one wall, deep in their cups, but otherwise the place reminded me of a family waiting room at a critical care facility. Groups of two or three gathered around perhaps a dozen tables, with another dozen or so empty, and none of the conversations drifted beyond the confines of their individual spaces. I scanned the room, pretending to look for someone but not find them. Then I headed to the bar. A couple of sergeants major—the senior-most enlisted soldiers in the force—eyed me from the other end of the bar, which made me self-conscious. Nobody wanted attention from a sergeant major. They kept staring, a little longer than necessary, as if to say, *We're watching you*. Great.

The bartender reached me as I took a seat on a high, round stool. "What'll it be?"

"Beer. Draft," I said. I waited until he served me before I turned back to face the room, leaning against the bar.

I found Lieutenant Colonel Barnes and watched her for a bit over the rim of my plastic beer mug, pretending not to be paying attention to anything in particular. She sat, still in uniform after her duty day, sipping a glass of red wine and talking to one of her subordinates, a female captain whose name I didn't know, who was drinking draft beer. On the surface, I probably looked like a stalker. On the surface, I guess I pretty much was. But Colonel Dentonn wasn't here, and that's what mattered.

When the captain got up to use the facilities about two beers later, I saw my chance. Rationally, the most likely end to my gambit involved rejection and me getting thrown out. But once you decide to make a move, you have to commit, so I squared my shoulders, approached her small table, and sat.

"Can I buy you another glass of wine, ma'am?"

She met my eyes, and her mouth quirked for half a second in what I hoped was an amused grin. Maybe she thought I was hitting on her. "I think I'm okay, Sergeant. I'm here with someone."

"Yes, ma'am. I'll only take a minute of your time. It's a work matter."

She held up her glass of red wine. "I'm trying to forget about work for a few minutes, if that's okay."

I caught one of the sergeants major moving out of the corner of my eye, heading for us. I only had a few seconds.

"It's about a missing soldier, ma'am."

"Ma'am," said the sergeant major, a tall, redheaded man with a hard face, "is this sergeant bothering you?"

Barnes drew her lips into a thin line, then set her glass down deliberately, taking her time. "You're Kendrick's squad leader?"

I started, caught off guard, then took a sip of my beer to cover my surprise. "Yes, ma'am. You know about Kendrick?"

"We're fine, sergeant major," she said.

"Yes, ma'am." He glared at me one more time for good measure.

Glare away, asshole—I was in.

Barnes waited for him to leave before continuing. "I'm the deputy chief of Operations. I know about everything. Plus, I saw Colonel Dentonn toss you out of operations, though I didn't make that connection until just now."

I wanted to press her on that, but I couldn't come right out and ask about senior officer politics. She knew about Kendrick and seemed at least a little sympathetic, so I needed to make it about the mission, first, and then work around to the other stuff. I had a thin margin of error. "So then you know why I'm here."

She picked up her glass and took a sip. "Colonel Gwan sent you."

"Roger that, ma'am."

"Unfortunately, I can't help you."

"I find that hard to believe, ma'am," I said, mustering all the charm I could.

Not even a smile.

I tried again. "But Colonel Gwan said—"

"I know what he said. And at the time I talked to him, I *thought* I could help you. But that was before Colonel Dentonn got involved."

The captain who had escorted Barnes in picked that moment to return from her trip to the latrine. "Excuse me, Sergeant. That's my—"

Barnes moved one finger, slightly, but it was apparently enough to get the captain's attention, as the younger officer stopped midsentence. "The sergeant needs a moment, Cecile. He's lost one of his men. Pull up another chair."

The captain's face didn't register any change, and she pulled a chair over from a nearby table and sat without saying anything. I'll say this for officers. They know how to follow orders.

"Ma'am . . ." I hesitated, not sure how to proceed.

"Go ahead. Ask your question. I owe you that much at least."

"Why would Colonel Dentonn countermand Colonel Gwan on something as basic as this?"

Barnes considered her next words, and I got the impression that she was deciding how much officer business to share with a lowly sergeant. I did my best to project a trustworthy image, which meant, basically, that I just took a sip of my beer and hoped she'd spill some dirt. When she finally spoke, she did it in a measured cadence, and she glanced at the captain more than once, as if looking for approval, which I found weird. "Let's just say Colonel Gwan and Colonel Dentonn have different ideas of how we should prosecute the war."

I tried not to look disappointed. I had figured out that much on my own, which meant I had to press her for more. "That has to be tough on the officers under them, ma'am."

She held up her glass again. "That's why they make wine."

I laughed. I could relate. It was interesting to see that officers had problems with their bosses giving them

crappy orders just like we did. It also gave me an opportunity to keep her talking, and maybe to get something I
could use. "How do you know which orders to follow?"

"You mean besides the wine? There's not as much
conflict as you think. Well, there is, but it doesn't roll
downhill very often. When it does, I put myself between the problem and my subordinates. They never
see it. And on that note, I've already said too much to
you about it. I'm going to trust you not to repeat what
I've said here. You seem like a decent fellow. I'd hate
to see you accidentally end up on the wrong side of an
airlock." She smiled like she was joking. She probably
was. Maybe.

Either way, I decided that I'd enjoy working for a
boss like her. She was taking a risk by even talking to
me, and that told me a lot about her.

"Ma'am . . . if I could . . . just one more question
and I'll leave you to your drinks. I get why two colonels
might disagree, but why on *this*? It's a missing soldier.
It seems pretty simple. The risk doesn't seem that high.
The enemy forces in the area are thin. With a concerted
push, we could be in and out before they can react."

She nodded. "On the surface, yes. But anything we
sent forward would be vulnerable to air attacks or coun-
terattacking ground forces. We could intercept those,
but that would require a much larger investment of force.
Next thing you know, we've got a full-blown battle."

"It's a war. Isn't that what we're here for, ma'am?"

She snorted. "I guess we are at that. But not there.
Colonel Dentonn was pissed that we were fighting in
that area to start. He's weird about it."

Interesting. Now we were getting somewhere. "Any idea why, ma'am?"

"As it turns out, colonels don't have to explain themselves to lieutenant colonels. And . . ." She gave me a pointed look that told me we were done.

"And lieutenant colonels don't have to explain themselves to sergeants." I downed the last third of my beer and stood. "Ma'am, thank you so much for your time. Can I buy your next round?" I offered, gesturing to include the captain.

"We're good, thank you."

"Then, with your permission . . ."

She waved her hand, dismissing me, then signaled the bartender for another drink. She hadn't given me much, but the part about Dentonn had my attention. I knew why *I* cared about Kiergard, but why did *he*? That bore looking into.

As I walked to the hatch leading back to the main corridor that ran the circumference of the circular space station, someone ducked down from a table, as if to pick something up from the floor, and the movement caught my attention. I walked over.

"You often drink alone, Miller?" I asked.

She sat up, her face coloring bright red. I appreciated that she at least had the decency to be embarrassed.

I turned and walked out without looking back. She was obviously there following me. But for whom? That was *two things* that bore some scrutiny.

CHAPTER 5

WHEN I GOT BACK TO OUR SQUAD ROOM, PUTTY and our new soldier, a tall, lanky guy with dark skin and a square jaw, were seated on two of the bottom bunks. The rookie immediately reminded me of his sister, which was a little depressing. The rest of the team was out, except for Patel, my commo specialist, who was hunched over, muttering to himself and digging through his locker, searching for something.

"Everything okay?" I asked him.

He looked at me over his shoulder. "No. My sister Sariah is having problems at her school, and they're threatening to throw her out. Do you know what I went through to get her *in* there?"

Actually, I did. "And you think the solution is there in your locker?"

"What? No. I'm looking for my tablet so I can go down to the comm center and try to get this straightened out."

"It's on your bunk," I said.

He stood and stretched to look up on the top bunk. "Oh. Right. Thanks."

"Don't mention it."

"Sorry, Boss. Gotta run." He grabbed his tablet and headed for the door.

"Just make sure you've got your suit wired to be able to track Kendrick when we get close to him."

"Already done, Boss."

"Thanks. Give my love to your family." Patel was the oldest of eight children and had taken on a paternal role when their father passed away. His mother was still around, but she was disabled and couldn't work. Patel sent pretty much every credit he made back home to take care of them. He wasn't a very good soldier, and he hated the military, but I didn't concern myself much with what the military thought about a soldier, as long as they could do the job *I* needed them to do. Plus, like I said, the guy had a family to take care of, and what kind of monster would let a guy do that on his own? With me, I knew he was safer than he'd be in most squads. That he was a first-class tech head and understood gadgets and communications equipment better than anybody I knew—that was just a bonus. He couldn't find his tablet in front of his face, but he could modify military electronics in ways that the professional techs couldn't. Or wouldn't.

Either way.

"I've got to take Rookie down to tech to get his initial measurements for his mech suit," Putty said.

I nodded. "Good. You seeing the helmet team too?"

"Obviously." Right. I wasn't thinking, still lost in what Barnes had told me and the fact that Miller was definitely following me. Of course they were going to the helmet team too. The helmet of an augmented infantry soldier took a lot of time to fit properly. As the techs explained it, every brain was slightly different, so to get it to pick up eye movement and interpret thoughts, it had to be specifically tailored to each person.

"I'll swing by while they're working on it, pat a few backs." It never hurt to be nice to the techs. Without them we'd just be straight infantry. And as much as I already disliked the military, that would be even worse.

Putty stared at me for a few seconds. "You okay?"

I hesitated. "Yeah. I'm good. It's just that there's more going on here than I originally thought."

"Look, I'm not the touchy-feely kind of person who likes to pry, but if something's bothering you, I'll be happy to get Erickson to talk to you about it." He smiled. Erickson was the best medic on the station, if not in the entire military, but she definitely liked to talk.

Maybe too much, considering that Miller kept showing up everywhere I went.

"I'm good," I said.

"Come on. Who are you talking to? You're not good. Spill it."

So I did. Sometimes saying things out loud helped me make sense of them. "Okay. You know our standing squad rule is that if you get left behind, you make your way to Kiergard. But what I never told you is why."

"That's true," said Putty. "I always kind of wondered about that but figured you know things and you wouldn't tell us to do it without a reason."

"Right. In this case, I know that town has taken no significant damage in twenty-two years of war. It's like a safe zone. But the thing that makes it interesting is why."

"Why?" asked Rookie.

"Hush," said Putty. "Adults are talking."

"I'm glad you asked," I said to Rookie, just to fuck with Putty. "Nobody touches Kiergard because it is the base of operations of Madeleine Ventnor. Better known as Ma Ventnor."

"The gangster?" asked Putty. "I've heard of her, but I always sort of thought she wasn't real. You know . . . a legend."

"Oh, she's real. She's too fucking real." I knew that firsthand, as her anger at me was what had me hiding in the military in the first place. But that wasn't a part of the story I wanted to tell. Not even to Putty.

"Huh," said Putty. "Okay. That seems pretty straight-forward, though. What's it got to do with us?"

"It *didn't* have anything to do with us," I lied. "Not until I talked to Lieutenant Colonel Barnes, and she mentioned that Colonel Dentonn paid special attention to Kiergard. That got me thinking."

Putty paced around the room. "That does seem a little suspicious. Have you got someone who can look into it?"

"I'm going check it out, for sure," I said. "But Dentonn's a colonel. Basically untouchable. I'm not sure I'm going to find anything on him. I caught a break when Barnes gave me what she did."

"You know who can touch a colonel?"

"Don't say Mrs. Colonel."

"I wasn't going to say that," he said. He totally was.

"I was going to say *other colonels*. You said that Gwan told you that he wanted this done."

"Only if I found enough information. I don't have it, and frankly, I don't think it exists."

"Sure. But he doesn't know that. Go back and talk to him and see what he knows about Dentonn."

"I can't walk in there with nothing."

Putty shook his head. "Look. One thing hasn't changed. Kendrick is down there, and you're not okay with that. Dentonn is in the way. So go in there and talk to Gwan and get what we need. Be the Gas that we all know and love."

"You mean like your mom knows and loves me?"

"Hey, my mom has standards."

"Thanks, Putty. You're right. Not about your mom . . . about Gwan. I'll go talk to him."

They headed out the door, and before it closed, I heard Rookie ask Putty if he always talked to the squad leader that way. "Stick with me, kid," said Putty. "You'll learn a lot."

I rolled my eyes and headed out behind them. The last thing I needed was Stimpson learning from Putty. One of him was enough.

IT WAS AROUND dinnertime when I reached the command group, which is a time when things start to slow down on a lot of parts of the base as the duty day ends. You might think of the military as a 24/7 operation—and parts of it were—but the majority of the people on base worked the day cycle and had the evening off. Soldiers need their free time. But apparently not in the command group, which had the same level of activity as when I'd been there earlier in the day. Granted, it was mostly people sitting at desks, but they were *at* those desks for a lot of hours. Definitely not for me, but I did respect them for it.

A lot of them, at least.

I stood for around fifteen minutes in the outer office of the deputy commander. I couldn't measure time directly, because I didn't want to keep looking and seem fidgety. At first, people eyed me surreptitiously, but I didn't let it bother me. Wherever I am, that's where I want to be. After a few minutes, they stopped looking.

"What have you got for me?" Gwan spoke as he walked out of his office. A few heads turned quickly to make sure it wasn't intended for them, but that's the only indication anyone in the office gave that they even noticed.

"I had a problem with something you told me to do." I'd decided to try to exploit the obvious tension between the two colonels. Hopefully I wouldn't get crushed between them.

He looked at me for a moment, then turned back to his office. "Come on in. Shut the door."

I followed him in and triggered the door manually behind me.

He turned to face me. "Tell me I don't have the wrong guy. When I brought you in, I thought you were a soldier who got things done."

He'd caught me off guard with his attack, and I couldn't find words for a moment, suddenly on the defensive. "Sir—"

"If I wanted someone to tell me why it couldn't be done, I have a whole staff full of people."

I took a second to think and centered myself. Gwan was bigger than me, and he could kick my ass. He knew it and used that for intimidation. But he wasn't going to do that. He wasn't going to do anything to me at all. The fact that I was standing in his office—with the door closed—meant he still needed me. Once I figured that out, it got easier to speak. "What you didn't tell me was that when I walked into Ops, an angry colonel was going to jump all over my shit." I paused. "Sir," I added. "Respectfully."

He didn't speak for a moment, and I began to reconsider my thought about him not kicking my ass. Then he started laughing. "Yeah. Sorry about that. If I'd known he was going to go off like that, I would have warned you."

I stood there, confused. I hadn't expected Gwan to apologize any more than I'd expected his initial onslaught. But I was where I wanted to be, and I finally got myself together. "Sir, Colonel Dentonn is holding this thing up deliberately. There's something off about it."

"Yes, there is," he agreed.

By not saying anything more, Gwan put me in a tough spot once again. I wondered if that was intentional. Probably. I didn't want to come right out and tell him my theory about Kiergard and why we never hit it. He either already knew, or he wouldn't believe me, so I'd be showing my cards without even knowing if there was money in the pot. I had to make Gwan respond to me, not the other way around. "Lieutenant Colonel

Barnes couldn't help, sir. Colonel Dentonn is going to block anything we try." I left that hanging.

"You're right. That's the point. I probably should have told you. But it's complicated. And I didn't know he'd go after you directly. I wouldn't have led you into that ambush intentionally."

"Sir . . . I don't get it—why don't you *order* him to do it?" I didn't understand officer politics, but I knew that deputy commander was higher than chief of Ops, even if they were both colonels.

"What would you do if you got an order and you thought it was screwed up to the point of being harmful?" asked Gwan.

I thought about it for several seconds. I didn't have many shots left, so I tried to figure out what he wanted. "I'd run it by some of my peers and see what they thought."

"And if they thought it was messed up?"

"I'd take it higher, sir. Over the head of whoever gave the order. If it was really going to hurt something. I'd just have to be careful about it because I'd be pissing off whoever gave the order."

"Right. Now apply that to Colonel Dentonn."

The light clicked on. "He'd go over your head to the commander."

"Exactly. And he wouldn't care if it pissed me off." Gwan moved to his chair and sat. "And the commander would see exactly what I see, and she'd know in about thirty seconds that Dentonn was right. I wouldn't get the mission, and on top of that, I'd look like an idiot."

"So you're letting *me* look like an idiot."

"Not in so many words," he said with an absolutely straight face. "I'm letting you do something that I can't because, to Dentonn, you don't really matter."

Brutal honesty I could take. "I understand, sir. So . . . what am I missing? I get that the math doesn't currently add up. What would it take?"

He smiled. "Now you're asking the right questions. I told you before that it was fourteen percent likely he was alive and free. To justify a mission, I need that number at somewhere between forty-five and sixty percent. I have no idea how we're going to get that, which is why I need you."

"Sir . . . begging your pardon . . . but if the staff can't get you that information, how can I?"

"Do you think the staff has tried everything possible? Colonel Dentonn controls a lot of the resources."

"Sir, I have to say, this is a pretty fucked up way to run a war."

He met my eyes. "Gastovsky, you don't know the half of it."

I believed him. Though I knew more than he thought, there still remained a lot I *didn't* know, which I needed to fix. The way Gwan said it implied that for his part, there was more behind it than just a difference of opinion with another colonel. I wanted to know more, but he wasn't going to answer, so I held back. Instead, I decided to spell it out and cover my ass. "So we're absolutely clear, sir, I'm going to have to color *way* outside the lines if I want to get that kind of number."

He paused for a moment, as if considering his answer. "Sergeant Gastovsky, I'm still a soldier. If it was me down there, I'd like to hope that *someone* was doing *something* to try to come get me."

That wasn't a yes, but it wasn't a no, either. I met his eyes, trying to find whatever might be lurking there. An agenda, deceit, anything. I got nothing. I had to give him credit. The man was good. One of us was being played, and at the moment, I wasn't sure it was him. That was a weird feeling for me because I'm usually in control. But I'd done all I could do and had to move forward.

"Thanks, sir. I'll get back on it. I won't let you down."

He shook his head. "It's not me. Don't let *Kendrick* down."

CHAPTER 6

WAS PISSED AT MYSELF FOR LETTING GWAN GET ME off my game, and I stormed back into our squad room.

"There's a plate of food on your bunk," said Putty.

I started to snap at him but caught myself. It wasn't his fault. "Thanks."

The rookie lay on the top bunk, looking down at us. Putty nodded once. "No problem. I know you didn't eat."

"Yeah. Not much of an appetite." I picked up a piece of some sort of meat with my fingers and took a bite.

"I take it you didn't get anything useful out of Gwan."

I shook my head, my mouth full of . . . I want to say chicken. "No. The guy is too good to give anything away. Bottom line, the colonel wants more definitive proof of life. I don't have it."

"What are you going to do now?" asked Putty.

"Dunno. Not much to do. I've tried everything I can think of that could prove he's alive." I paused. "Unless . . ."

Putty perked up. "Unless what? I don't like that look on your face."

"Hold on," I said. "Let me think."

"This isn't going to end well," said Putty. I don't know if he was talking to Rookie or himself—I'd stopped paying attention to him.

Because I had an idea.

It wasn't a good idea. It might have even been a stupid one. I'd been counting on Gwan getting me down to the surface, but he'd been pretty clear that I had to make that happen myself. And a stupid idea beats no idea. Mostly. Gwan hadn't put any boundaries on how I should get proof of life—just that I should get it. That left me a lot of freedom to maneuver. As I had told Gwan, it was time to color outside the lines.

Way outside the lines.

"I need to go talk to someone."

"Did you see that, Rookie? Did you see the look that Sergeant Gastovsky got just then?"

"Yes," said Rookie.

"Remember that look. That's the look of us being screwed."

TEN MINUTES LATER I stood outside a barracks door on the opposite side of the base, where station personnel lived. They tried to keep them separated from us temporary inhabitants as much as possible. We were on the same team, in theory, but we were different breeds of soldiers. Still, I don't know why they wasted the time trying to keep us apart. Soldiers would find their way to where they wanted to be as surely as water would find its way downhill. I found Corporal Ariana Kohler's room from a hacked directory I had in my device. She lived with three other techs. Station permanent personnel had four to a room, as opposed to the six to a room for us grunts. I didn't want to talk to her in front of her roommates, so I leaned against the wall on the other side of the narrow corridor. A few techs came by, but nobody entered Kohler's room. She came out twelve minutes later.

She inclined her pointed chin when she saw me. "Stalk much?"

I smiled. "How'd you know I was here?"

She tapped her wrist device. "Got a message that some creeper was hanging outside my door. None of my roommates know you."

"We should fix that sometime."

She chuckled. "Funny, I was going to say how lucky they were."

"Ouch. But I get it, and I swear this is mostly legit."

"Oh? You're just casually staking me out?"

"Sorry about that. I needed to ask you something. I didn't want to talk in front of your roommates."

"Walk with me. I need coffee anyway. We'll go get the good stuff that you have to pay for. You're buying. Because unless I miss my guess, you're about to ask me something that could get me in trouble."

"I said it was mostly legit."

"And all I heard was *mostly*."

I put my hands over my chest. "I'm wounded."

"Yeah, sure. But I notice you didn't deny it." She sighed. "What's her name, and what did you do?"

I laughed. "It's nothing like that. It's work-related."

"Did you ever notice how line infantry look down on us space dwellers, right up to the point where they need something?" She smiled, taking some of the bitterness out of the statement, even though we both knew it for the truth.

I put my hand up in a mock gesture of defense. "I am an equal opportunity soldier."

"Meaning what? That you'll bang either a grunt or a space dweller, as long as she's got a heartbeat?"

I laughed again. "I told you—it's not about a girl. But I do miss you, Kohler. Why don't we hang out more often?"

"Because I refuse to sleep with you," she said.

"Yeah. What's up with that?"

"It's called standards. Now, what do you want that's so important that you had to lurk in doorways and creep out every woman on my corridor?"

Ignoring that, I said, "I have a transportation question." Kohler worked in that department, and she knew everything that happened there. "Hypothetically, if someone needed to get down to the surface, how would he do it?"

She stopped walking and turned to face me, then waited for three soldiers to pass. "Well, first off, you definitely don't try to stow away on a supply ship."

My face heated. "You heard about that?"

"Come on, Gas. I hear about everything. You know that. That's why you're here, right? What the hell is so important on the planet? They'll ship you back down soon enough."

"But they'll ship me where they need me to go and on their own timeline, not where I want to go. Now."

"Is there a resort on Gallia I hadn't heard about?"

"There's a soldier down there. *My* soldier. Ops won't go get him, so I'm looking for other options."

She pursed her lips and drew them to the side of her face, then sucked in a big breath and blew it out. "So . . . hypothetically . . . how many people would need to get to the surface? I can *maybe* forge you a pass for a shuttle. But only one."

I didn't want to share everything with her, as she wasn't going to be part of the team, but I had to give her the parameters if I wanted her help. "Maybe eight or ten, in full kit. You don't want to know any more than that."

She bit her top lip with her bottom teeth, the gears churning in her brain. "If I tell you it's impossible, are you going to believe me?"

"I'd believe that it's impossible for a mortal, but not for a genius goddess such as yourself."

She shook her head but couldn't suppress a smile. "You're so full of shit."

"Come on," I said. "There has to be a way. If you were down there, you'd want someone to come for you."

"Shit."

I couldn't tell if that was anger or acquiescence, so I stayed silent while she thought. I had a reputation for talking a lot, but I knew when to shut up.

"You're a hell of a squad leader, Gas," she finally said. "What you're asking . . . it's maybe the stupidest thing I've ever heard, but also kind of awesome."

"You seem mad about that."

"Well, yeah—this is going to totally blow my opinion of you as just another asshole."

"I'm not *just* another asshole. I'm an exceptional asshole."

She rolled her eyes even as she considered my request for a bit. "I guess there's one way. It's not *impossible*. It's close, though."

"I'll take it."

"Steal a drop ship. The smallest one will do. Ten seats. But then, you knew that."

I nodded. We usually took bigger ships to the surface, but they had ten-person lifts for small missions. Infiltration missions. It was what I had hoped Kohler would say, but I hadn't wanted to put the idea in her head. That she came up with it on her own meant it really *was* possible. And that word she used . . . *steal*. She understood. Gwan wasn't going to authorize it for me, so that's exactly what I had to do. "How?"

She thought about it. "It's been done before. At least, I've heard that it has, but not recently. Legend is that four soldiers took a drop ship out for a joyride. That was before my time, though."

"What happened to them?" I asked.

"Don't know. That's never part of the story."

"Forget the legends. How would I—I mean, someone—do it tomorrow?" I had the idea, but I needed a lead, a thread I could grab onto.

"The problem isn't getting the ship—although that isn't super easy, either. The problem is getting away once you have it. Which means, by the way, you need a pilot so you can manually separate from the base. Even with one, though, flight command would see it immediately."

I figured as much, but I didn't care, as long as I got off station and down to the planet. And an idea was already forming about how to fake the clearance. "They wouldn't shoot me down, would they?"

"They wouldn't have to. They'd override your controls and bring you back."

"So I need a hacker on the mission to keep flight command from getting into my system."

Kohler snorted. "Wouldn't do any good. The hacker would be up against the electronic warfare resources of a fucking space station. Trying to stop that would be like trying to fill a solar system full of air using a blow-dryer. And that's the *good* news. That's if the ship itself didn't turn on you and self-destruct. You have to beat the station, *and* the ship." At first I thought she liked the idea of me blowing up in the ship through my own stupidity. But her expression said that it was more than that.

"Oh. Is that all?" I asked.

"No. You need to promise me: we never had this conversation," she said.

"Why's that?"

"Because I can tell by looking at you that you're going to try to do this, and you're going to get caught."

Maybe she was right. Maybe it was impossible to get a ship away from the base. But she didn't know everything.

She thought that a hacker couldn't beat the space station. But I knew a guy.

"SEE, ROOKIE, I told you we were screwed," said Putty when I walked back into our room.

"What?" I asked with exaggerated innocence.

"Oh, I don't know *what*." Putty got up from his bottom bunk. "But it's bad. You going to tell us, or just smirk about it all night?"

"We're going to get Kendrick."

"So you found him?" asked Putty.

"No."

"But you know he's alive?"

"No."

"So . . . he might be dead, and he's definitely lost."

"I mean, we know where he's supposed to be."

Putty looked at me. "What am I missing?"

"My gut says he's alive, and that he's at Kiergard. And if he's down there, holed up behind enemy lines, waiting for us to come get him out? Then we need to go get him. He's part of the team. He'd come after you if the positions were reversed."

"Again: What am I missing?"

"I've got the beginning of a plan."

"Holy crap on a cracker," he muttered. He stared at me for a second. "It *is* Kendrick, though," he said. "He's so lucky that if he's down there, he probably *is* alive, and he's probably found a whorehouse with a full bar to put him up for a few days."

"So you're in?" I didn't need to ask, but I wanted to hear him say it.

"How are we even going to get down there?" He'd been leaning back in his chair, and now rocked forward to sit on all four legs again.

"I'm in," said Rookie. We both turned to look at him, and his eyes went wider in his dark face. "What?"

"You don't even know what we're talking about," said Putty.

"You're talking about going to get Kendrick," said Rookie.

"Do you know who Kendrick is?" asked Putty.

"He's on our team. That's his bunk, there." Rookie gestured to the middle bunk on the opposite side of the room.

Putty nodded, impressed. "Cool. And that's really stand up of you to want to take this mission on. But nobody would blame you if you didn't."

Rookie's eyes shifted, as if unsure. "Why wouldn't I? He's part of the team."

Putty leaned back again. "Well, for one, there's the space whales."

Rookie chuckled. "Sure. Space whales."

"You laugh. They inhabit this area, and they feed like crazy during mating season. Worse, they've been known to attack our drop ships and—"

"Putty," I said, interrupting him. I didn't have time for this. "Don't listen to him, Rookie. There are no such thing as space whales."

"He says that now," said Putty, "because he wants you on the mission. Then you're out there, cruising through space, minding your own business and wham! Fucking space whale."

"You're an idiot," I said.

"An idiot who's never been eaten by a space whale." Putty stood. "And let's face it. Even without space whales, you still haven't answered my question: How would we even go about it? Kendrick is down on the surface of Gallia, last seen behind enemy lines, and we're up here on a giant orbiting piece of space junk."

I tried not to smile, but probably failed. "Like I said, I have a plan."

"You said you have the *beginning* of a plan."

"Did I?"

"You most definitely did!" He paced the four steps to the door and then back. "I don't suppose you'd care to enlighten me and the brave but stupid newbie here, would you?"

"We're going to steal a drop ship," I said, smirking. I couldn't help it. I knew exactly how it sounded, and exactly how Putty would react.

A laugh escaped Putty, half-choked. "That's a great plan."

"You haven't even heard it yet."

"There's more?"

"Of course." Kind of. I hadn't really worked out the rest of it.

"Rookie, I need you to go get Erickson, our medic. Our fearless leader needs a psych workup." Putty deliberately didn't look at me.

"Come on," I said. "Hear me out."

He blew out a big breath of air. "Oh, Gas, I don't have to hear it to know you're one magazine short of a basic load."

"Still plenty of ammo to get the job done," I said. Putty rolled his eyes, but I didn't buy it. "C'mon—you know you're intrigued."

"Only because I'm an idiot." He rolled his eyes again. "Okay, let's pretend for one minute that you have a plan and it's not ridiculous. And I'm not conceding that, for the record. But if we could steal a drop ship, how would we even fly it? We're not pilots."

"You said *we*," I pointed out.

"Did I?" He looked at me blankly. "I don't think I did."

"You said *we*. So you're in." Like I said, I didn't need to ask, but I think it just helped Putty that we played the game. He liked a show.

"Fine. I'm in. But you're avoiding the question," he said. "What pilot would risk their career to do something so ridiculous?"

"We don't really need a pilot. The AI flies the ship."

"And the AI would immediately realize that you don't have the authorization to do what you want to do and fly you right back. So you *do* need a pilot," said Putty. "You know that. And I can tell by the look on your face that you've got one. Who is it?"

He was right. Even before Kohler brought it up, I already had someone in mind.

"Chang."

"Chang." He stared at me. "*Li* Chang?"

"That's right. I haven't talked to her yet, but I think she'll sign on."

"Oh, Gas, you kill me."

"I aim to please."

"I'm out."

"Putty—"

"What's wrong with Chang?" Rookie asked.

"The problem, Rookie," Putty said, "is that Chang isn't a pilot."

"She's a mechanic. Close enough," I said.

Putty stood there, his lips moving but no sound coming out. "That . . . that is not at all close enough."

"She's flown drop ships before, on maintenance test flights." At least, I hoped she had. I'd sort that out later. She's who I wanted, and that's what mattered.

Putty gestured wildly with his hands, clearly indicating he thought other things mattered more. "Flying laps around an orbiting space station where there's nothing to hit is not the same as dropping into atmosphere."

I shrugged. "You have a better idea?"

"You know I'm not a big thinker. We leave that to you. Or, we did, back before you lost your mind. I can picture it now. I'll be wherever soldiers go when they die, and the spirit of some old veteran will approach me at the bar—you know there has to be a bar. 'How did you die in the war?' they'll ask. They'll tell me about how they died in some heroic action in some important battle. And I'll have to say that I died because a mechanic couldn't land a transport since she *wasn't a fucking pilot.*"

"All I'm hearing you say is, *I'm back in*," I said.

"Yeah. I'm in. Of course I'm in. Fuck it. But you're ridiculous."

"No, *we're* ridiculous."

He paused and locked eyes with me. "Shit. Yeah. *We're* ridiculous."

"They'll never see it coming."

"I think they'll see it coming a mile away, and we won't get to the ship before we're hauled in for court-martial."

"I knew I could count on you," I said.

"Yeah, yeah. What do you need me to do?"

I stood. "Get Rookie his gear, and start greasing the machine to get kit made for Chang as well. Hopefully she won't have to get off the drop ship, but I'd rather be prepared. I need to go put the team together. We've got you, me, Chang if she's willing—"

"And me," Rookie interjected.

I thought about it. I wanted to keep Rookie safe, but there's only so much safety as a soldier, and he'd be in the shit one day. I'd rather that he drop in with me than with someone else. Plus, I could use the extra firepower. "And Rookie. He can be our second heavy." Putty wore the heavy version of the battle armor for the squad, but having another one along would be useful if we got in any kind of real fight.

Putty looked at me. "You're really going to talk to Chang? You know she's insane, right?"

"I'm kind of counting on it."

CHAPTER 7

WE HAD TO HAVE A PILOT, SO I WANTED TO handle that before I got too much further into things. To do that, I entered a large maintenance bay where half a dozen ships of varying classes sat in different states of disassembly. I peeked between them, looking for Chang. I'd checked the schedule, and this was her assignment, but aside from a few maintenance bots, the place appeared deserted.

A hum grew above me, followed by a crazed shriek. "Wheeeee!"

I ducked instinctively and craned my neck upward just in time to see a slight, dark-haired woman whip by on some sort of flying board thing.

That was my pilot.

"Holy shit, Chang, you scared the crap out of me!"

She zipped quickly away, gaining altitude. The bay ceiling had to be maybe fifteen meters up, and she climbed to at least half that height. I didn't know what she was riding, but it didn't look particularly safe, especially since she stood on it with no straps in sight. She banked the contraption into a wide turn, then headed back toward me in a shallow dive.

As she approached, she dropped down to about chest level.

She wasn't stopping.

"Look out!" she yelled, at right about the same moment I'd figured out the danger for myself. I dove to the right and hit the deck.

Chang tumbled from the flying board, hit the deck on her side and rolled several meters, stopping when she *whuffed* into the strut of a one-person spacecraft. I sprang up and sprinted to her.

"Chang! Are you okay?" I knelt beside her slight body and assessed her for injuries, looking first for blood. I didn't find any, but she could have internal injuries. And I didn't want to move her in case she'd damaged her spine.

She groaned and rolled toward me. "What's up, Gas?"

"Holy shit, have you lost your mind?"

She half shrugged from her prone position. "Jury is still out."

"What was that thing?"

"*That* is the Hoverboard 3 Bravo."

I stood and walked over to where the board rested against a large tool chest and picked it up, surprised at how much it weighed and contemplating that 3 Bravo meant she had probably created earlier versions. It had to be almost twenty-five kilos. "How does it fly? Wait—" I looked at the bottom. "Are those anti-grav thrusters?"

Chang looked away in an exaggerated manner. "No.

Of course not. Where would I possibly get anti-grav thrusters? Those things cost more than I make in five years."

"Yes, they do. Got to say, Chang, they really look like anti-grav—"

"So maybe I borrowed them from an in-atmosphere fighter. I'm going to put them back, I swear."

It was none of my business. If anything, this was another reason I wanted Chang on my team.

She struggled to her feet slowly, as if checking herself for damage. She leaned against the single-seater—a ground attack ship, all blocky lines and bomb racks. "What's up?"

I hadn't seen anyone else when I entered, but I couldn't risk it. "We alone?"

"On this station? Probably never. But if you mean is there another person around, no, it's just me and the bots on this shift."

"They let you in here unsupervised?"

"Yeah—how else do you think I get to play around with that?" she said, looking at the illicit board. She turned back to me, a serious expression on her face. "That does seem like an oversight on somebody's part. But my unit's short personnel, so it's one per shift in this bay unless we switch to high op tempo to support a major operation. The bots do most of the work anyway. Why do we need to be alone? Have you worked your way through every other woman on the station and it's only me left?"

I really needed to work on my reputation. "I wanted—"

"Because you're not my type," she added.

For somebody accused twice recently of sleeping with everyone, I sure did seem to be the wrong type for quite a few of them. And considering I didn't sleep with even *close* to as many women as people thought, it seemed unfair how often people pointed it out to me. "Noted. That's not why I'm here."

"What? I'm not good enough for you?"

"You just said—"

"I'm fucking with you, Gas."

"Right." For whatever reason, I was on edge. I'd stood in front of two colonels without flinching, but here, in front of a corporal, I knew that everything rested on the next couple of minutes. I decided not to play coy. "I need your help on a ridiculous mission."

"I'm in," she said.

I stopped short. "What? I didn't even tell you what we're doing yet."

"Okay, tell me. But I'm in."

"I need you to steal a drop ship and fly me to the surface. If we get caught, we'll be in a shitload of trouble." I said it almost as a challenge. She'd asked for it.

She faked a yawn. "Still in."

I paused. "Have you lost your mind?"

She pretended to think about it. "You keep asking that. You're not a very good salesman. When do we leave?"

"We'll be going into hostile territory." It wasn't an answer to her question. I found myself wanting to talk her out of it for some reason. She wasn't asking smart questions herself, and that compelled me to ask them for her.

"You've already got your yes," she said. "You want me to steal a ship and fly it—I'm totally down for that. You can stop selling. Ooh, can I wear one of those fancy bio-mechanical suits you augmented grunts get?"

"Already working on it." Good thing too, because it would need to be a custom job—not too many grunts stood only a meter and a half tall, like Chang.

"That was pretty presumptuous of you," she said. "I guess you're just used to every woman saying yes to you."

"But you just told me I wasn't your type, not two minutes ago."

"Still fucking with you, Gas."

I shook my head, and almost started to regret my decision to recruit her. But I wanted her *because* of her attitude.

I had to keep reminding myself of that.

"Here's the important question: Can you actually *fly* a drop ship?"

She rolled her eyes. "Of course. I do it all the time."

Good. "You ever broken atmo? Flown one to the surface?"

She pursed her lips and glanced down at the metal flooring of the maintenance bay. "Not exactly."

Not good. "How . . . what *exactly* does 'not exactly' mean?"

She shrugged. "I've done it on the simulator. And besides, the ship mostly flies itself unless something goes wrong."

"Okay. So, be honest, here. What chance do we have of you getting us safely to the surface?"

She rocked her head from side to side a couple times. "The truth?"

I stared at her. If I thought she was lying on this one, I'd kill the mission. I had to be able to trust her with my life—with the lives of the entire team—and if I couldn't, no matter how much I needed her, we'd have to find another way. "The absolute truth."

For the first time since I'd arrived, she thought about her answer. "Ninety-nine percent. Maybe a little higher."

I believed her. I've got good instincts about these things most of the time. Her number might be wrong, but I believed that *she* believed what she'd told me. Ninety-nine percent. It seemed like good odds. Until you thought about it the other way. One chance in a hundred that we don't. But then I thought about Kendrick. "What happens the other one percent?"

She grunted. "You don't want to know."

I remembered her spectacular wipeout just moments ago and winced.

"Yeah," she said, clearly thinking the same thing. "Probably best if we tell the others it's a sure thing."

I didn't know if I could live with that. They deserved to know the risks, even if it meant they backed out. That said, I didn't need to make an issue of it with Chang. It wasn't her job to apprise them. It was mine. I'd get them to say yes, but not under duress. The same as her. Which got me wondering . . .

"I thought it would be harder to talk you into this."

Chang shrugged. "What's life for if you don't take some risks?"

I don't know why that made the hairs stick up on my arms. It wasn't like I *wasn't* taking risks. I was in the infantry, for fuck's sake. But the way she said it . . .

I suppressed any kind of outward reaction. "Go see Putty. He's taking Rookie to get his helmet fitted. He's going to work you in. Putty knows everyone."

"Will do. You know we can't land behind enemy lines, right? Too much computing power. They'll be able to do a whole bunch of bad things to us."

"I know," I said. "I'm working on it."

"You seem to be working on a lot of things."

"Story of my life."

WITH CHANG ON board, my next priority was to address the exact problem that she mentioned. She was right. We couldn't land behind enemy lines. The enemy would use their superior ground-based resources to hack our systems and force us to land at a place of their choosing. Probably right outside a detention center.

In theory.

I needed a good hacker. Technically, the military called them *network specialists*—it probably sounded better in a recruiting video. But the good ones got the nickname *hacker*. We grunts like to act like we're the baddest of the bad, but deep down, we know it's all about the nerds when it comes to winning battles. We'd be useless in a hurry if someone took over our suits, which they would if we didn't have our own hackers protecting us. And if someone screwed with our drop ship, that would make for a pretty short trip. And that was if we even *got* to the atmosphere. We wouldn't even get off the space station without someone fooling the network to give us launch access.

Hence hacker.

And not just anyone. We needed a good one. One with a specific outlook on the military. Chang had the right attitude for her role as pilot. For this, I needed something different. Someone less chaotic, but willing to go against the system *and* highly competent.

Luckily, finding one who was a bit of an anarchist wouldn't be hard, as that sort of came with the territory. Finding one who would leave the comfort of the space station and risk their ass in potential combat? Not so easy. I could only think of one guy.

I needed Dex.

Dex had come to my attention for an exceptionally ballsy hack he'd pulled—or I should say, *allegedly* pulled—about nine months previous when he'd had a conflict with a captain who shall remain nameless. No, actually, we'll give him a name.

We'll call him Captain Asshole.

Captain Asshole mistreated soldiers, talked down to them, and generally made himself hated by all. I don't mean in the way that a lot of captains have, where they're too driven, too hard, or expect too much from their soldiers. This guy was beyond that—he was just plain nasty. He made it personal.

Dex figured if the captain wanted a reputation as being nasty, he could have that. So Dex—again, allegedly—filled Captain Asshole's government computer with porn, which was a no-no when it came to the military network. So when a routine scan caught it . . . bye-bye. No more Captain Asshole.

The moral of that story: never mess with a hacker. They should teach that in basic training.

I didn't need anyone to tell me that. Which is why I was going to talk to Dex.

I entered the tech lab through a white-walled airlock. I don't know why they make the walls white. Probably to give the illusion of cleanliness, which in this case probably wasn't an illusion. The lab damn near sparkled. And like a monolith in all that cleanliness sat Dex on a high swivel-stool in front of a workbench, his giant hands working with surprising dexterity, soldering something onto a small circuit board.

"Dex! Big man! I need some help."

"No." His deep bass voice resonated almost like an act of nature, though something in the room dampened the sound.

"Come on, Dex, you don't even know what I'm going to ask."

"I know it will be against the rules, and I can't afford another mark right now."

I clapped my hand on his massive body-builder shoulder. "I'll owe you one."

He swiveled to face me, meeting me eye to eye even though he was sitting down, staring at me with wide-spaced eyes set into the darkest skin I'd ever seen on a man. "You *already* owe me more than you'll ever be able to pay back."

"This is true," I admitted. "So I'll just owe more. But I need the best, and that's you."

"You need a sucker, and that's not me," he said.

"You know, there's this cook I could introduce you to. Good-looking guy, spends a lot of time in the gym . . ."

"I have a boyfriend. I also have a job—one that I like. Go on, Gas. I've got work to do." He turned back to his project, pretending to work his soldering iron, probably building some custom machine that did things I couldn't imagine.

I sighed. "You *are* the best, you know."

"Yeah, yeah. Sell your bullshit somewhere else. I'm not buying."

"It's about Kendrick."

He swiveled back to face me. "I was really sorry to hear about that."

"So help me do something about it. We're going after him."

He stared at me for a moment without blinking. "He's alive?"

"He is. At least, there's a very high probability."

Dex sat, nodding his head slightly, as if thinking something to himself. "I'm sorry, Gas. I can't do it."

I decided to backpedal a little and try a different approach. If I could get him talking about the mission theoretically, maybe it would intrigue him. "Okay. But answer me this. Is it possible to get a drop ship down in enemy territory? Don't give me the book answer— I know that it's not *supposed* to be possible—but can it be done?"

Dex set his project aside and looked at me. "*Anything* can be done."

"Okay, sure. But I'm talking can it be done with the kind of odds that make it worth trying."

Dex's face lit up as he launched into his answer, gesturing with his giant hands.

I guess you could say that he liked to Dexplain.

Sometimes I hate myself.

"There are three main factors in something like this. Computing power, interfaces, and time. Interfaces are generally standard, as both sides buy equipment from the same suppliers, so that leaves the other two. As the drop ship, time is on your side, right? You need to survive for a specific duration—enough time to get to the ground. That's your advantage."

"I'm sensing a *but* coming," I said.

"*But* the enemy has an overwhelming advantage in computing power over their own territory. They're ground-based with what amounts to basically infinite resources versus whatever your ship could muster. That's why we don't try to land on their side of the line."

"Got it," I said.

"So that nullifies your time advantage," he continued. "Because they can present such an overwhelming attack that they'll blow through you in ten to fifteen seconds. Not nearly long enough for you to get down."

"So it's possible, but extremely unlikely," I said.

"*Extremely* unlikely. That's on the surface. But that's just the initial equation. It doesn't take into account game theory, and it doesn't take into account operator skill."

"Those matter?" I could tell the answer to that by

watching Dex's excitement as he explained, but I needed to ask, because my real purpose wasn't to figure out if it was possible (especially since I almost certainly wouldn't understand what he said). What I really wanted was him to decide it *was* possible, and that he wanted to do it.

"Matter?" he asked, taking the bait. "They're everything. Think about it . . . if you see a wave of drop ships, that's a huge threat. You throw everything you can against it as fast as you can. If they get through, you're finished. But one drop ship? How many soldiers does that hold?"

"Ten," I said.

"That's not many. Hardly a major threat. And it's a single ship . . . you don't have to worry about it. You can overwhelm its defenses fast. So maybe you don't react right away."

"Maybe?"

"*Probably.* Because if you use a powerful hack on a single ship, you've shown a piece of your arsenal for something without much worth, and now you've tipped your hand, so there's a good chance you can't use it again, leaving yourself vulnerable to a larger fleet of ships. So you don't use your best stuff. In fact, theoretically, they don't even want to destroy the ship . . . they want to land it in a set location and steal it. It's worth a lot of money. The prisoners could be worth something too, especially if they have power armor, which is also worth a lot. But in this case? They might try that, and if it doesn't work, overwhelm it and smash it into the ground."

"That sounds . . . not great," I said.

"It isn't. Except that's where the exploit lies."

"Getting smashed into the ground doesn't sound like we're exploiting anything."

"Not that. Just that since we can't beat their systems, we go for the weak link. The person operating them. We take advantage of them waiting."

"I'm not quite sure I get it."

I definitely didn't get it.

"There's an opportunity to take advantage of their complacency. But it means a lot of work. Skill alone won't do it, because they'll leave themselves a buffer. What you've got to do is present a target that's significantly tougher than they expect, and by the time they realize it, the window has passed and you're on the ground."

"And I do this . . . how?" Maybe I didn't need him after all.

Dex laughed. "You? *You* don't do this at all. I— I mean, *whoever tries this*—would have to have access to the ship ahead of time. Beef up its systems and throw in some older technology that they haven't seen in a while, to the point where my—*the operator's*—skill would be enough to hold them out."

I didn't understand why he'd want older stuff instead of cutting-edge, but I trusted him. And I liked that he kept slipping up in talking about his own involvement. "So what you're saying is that there's no way I can do this without you."

He paused, probably realizing what I'd done to manipulate him. "I'm not your guy."

"You've done surface missions. You used to be a grunt. How many hackers on this station already have their own suit of power armor?"

"There are enough of them. We send guys to the ground all the time. Most of us hate it. Have Ops task the Tech Shop. They'll give you someone."

I smiled. Here's where I either knew my man or had read him completely wrong. "That's just it. The mission is sort of . . . unofficial."

He narrowed his eyes, and a line creased his forehead. "Like a covert operation?"

"Something like that," I said.

He thought about it. "Who knows about this besides you and me?"

I looked away. "I don't know. A few people."

"But not Ops."

"No."

"And no officers." Dex wasn't stupid. He didn't know exactly what I had planned, but he knew I had an angle.

"That's correct," I said. Gwan didn't know about stealing the drop ship, so I wasn't lying.

Technically.

He stood, and I took a step backward, partially so I didn't have to angle my neck so sharply to see his face, partly because I didn't know what he might do. He was a huge guy, and I half expected him to pick me up and bodily eject me from the room. But he probably wouldn't want to mess up his sterile workshop.

"You're physically going to the planet to get Kendrick?"

"That's right. In and out."

"How are you getting the drop ship?"

"I can't tell you unless you're in," I said.

"Then I'm out."

I considered it. I had to keep the group in the know as small as possible, but if I couldn't convince him, this was probably over before it started. After Dex, I didn't have a backup plan. I'd already started down this path, so I might as well go all the way.

"Okay. We're stealing it."

He half laughed, half grunted. "It will never work. As soon as they know you've done it, they're going to override your systems and bring you back."

"That's why we need you. To make sure they either don't realize we're gone or can't override our systems if they do."

The big man stood silent for a moment, thinking about it. "So you want me to not only pull off the impossible in getting through the enemy defense, but also to hack our own base to get us away."

"Yes." It sounded bad when he put it that way, but I didn't see any point in sugarcoating it.

"Definitely buried the lede there. And that's way harder than you think it would be. You'd have to override some core station systems. We're not talking about a single terminal here."

"I'd need someone on the inside too. Right?"

"For sure you'd need two hackers. One on the station, one on the drop ship. No other way to do it. The station has too many protections from the outside."

"You know anyone?" I asked, hopefully.

"I don't even know if *I'm* someone."

I kept quiet, as he hadn't outright said no yet, and I didn't want to push him too hard into making his refusal official.

"As it happens," he said, "I know a couple people. This kind of thing tends to get most hackers excited for some reason. One woman in particular comes to mind—she would be best for the on-station work. But she's not going to do it for free."

"I'm sure we can take care of her." I'd expected that, and had funds set aside from almost three years of illicit business. Also, if everything went well, I'd be turning a profit on this mission.

I wasn't sharing that part with anybody yet, though.

Dex sucked in a breath through his teeth. "I can talk to her. See what she'd want. But the person on station is a lot less likely to get caught, so that helps. All they have to do is cover their digital signature, whereas the person on the drop ship could get caught physically as well."

"You sound like you're thinking about it," I said. It was a risk to ask outright, but I was running out of time.

"You're not bullshitting me. This is for Kendrick, right?"

"I'm assured by important people that there's almost a seventy percent chance he's still alive. And I have reasons to believe it's significantly higher than that. No bullshit." It was an answer to most of his question.

He remained silent for maybe thirty seconds before saying, "Yeah. I guess I'm in."

Not exactly the resounding vote of confidence I hoped for, but I'd take it. Except, like with Chang, something came over me and made me ask, "You sure?"

"I couldn't live with myself if you got yourself killed and I didn't help. And I know you. You *will* get yourself killed without my help." He wasn't wrong.

"You're doing the right thing," I said.

He rolled his eyes. "Promise me you won't do something stupid and get us in trouble."

I thought about it for a moment, the lie waiting on my lips before I discarded it. "You've heard what I intend to do—you know I can't promise that, Dex." I'd definitely wait and tell him about the other part of the mission I needed him for later, once he got used to the idea of going.

He snorted. "Yeah, I know. I wanted to see if you were going to lie to me. *That* is what you've got to promise me. You can lie to other people if you have to, but if I'm going to do this—if I'm going up against these odds in a hack—you've got to be one hundred percent honest with me. All the time."

"I knew I could count on you." I put my hand out, and he engulfed it in his.

"What did I just say about lying?"

"You're right—I didn't." I smiled. Of course I had already lied to him—or more accurately, withheld part of the truth. But I justified that as a matter of timing. I was going to tell him everything.

Just not yet.

CHAPTER 8

WITH FIVE OF THE TEAM LOCKED IN, I SET OUT TO gather the rest. The three remaining members of my squad were good at their jobs and likely to say yes, though I had to be careful with Erickson due to her propensity to talk and her proximity to Miller. I hadn't seen Miller around for the last hour or so, but that didn't reassure me. I'd rather have known her location.

Regardless of her connection with Miller, I needed Erickson. She was our medic, and while I hoped we wouldn't need those services, I didn't want to tempt fate. Still, I decided to talk to Patel first, because I thought he'd be the toughest to convince.

I grabbed him from our squad room and walked him outside, laying out the basics of the mission as we went. He listened without comment until I finished and thought for some time after that before speaking. "I don't think I can do it, Gas."

"I need you, Patel."

"You can find another commo specialist. We're everywhere."

"Not one who can do what you do. You're the one

who came up with the way to find anyone from our squad who got lost. Nobody else does that."

"It wasn't that hard," he said.

"Maybe not technologically." I didn't know, but I couldn't argue with him. "But just to have the *idea* to do it shows that you think on a different level."

"I appreciate it. I really do. But I've got my family to think of. I've got my—"

"Your brothers and sisters," I finished for him. "I'll keep you safe down there. I always do."

I braced for him to say, "Like Kendrick?" but Patel wasn't an asshole like that. Instead, he said, "It's not that. If I die in combat, my pension goes to my sister, and she can use that to continue to support the family. I'm not worried about dying. But if I get *court-martialed*? If I lose my pay and benefits? I can't risk that, Gas."

I thought about it. Patel wasn't going to budge, and I couldn't blame him. Taking care of his family was the most important thing in his life, and I wasn't ready to promise him a payday from the mission yet. So I had to come up with something better. "I thought you wanted out of the military," I said.

"You know I do. More than anything. But I need the paycheck and the full pension that comes with a complete term of service."

"What if I told you that I have a way to get you out, but you still keep all your pay and benefits?"

"I'd say yes." Just like that, without question. It was almost scary how much he trusted me. For my part, that added some weight to the matter. I lie a lot—that's established—but not to the people I want on my team.

Obfuscate? Omit? Sure, sometimes. But never in a way that would directly harm them. Patel had a lot to lose, and I wasn't going to play around with him.

"I'm thinking, while we're down there, what if you get injured? Right at the end of the mission, after we've got everything we need. After we find Kendrick. I'm not going to sugarcoat this—it's going to suck. We need to injure you badly enough to get you discharged with a medical pension, but where you can still live a full life. At home. With your family."

"Who can guarantee something like that?" he asked.

"Erickson can."

He considered it. "If anyone can, it's her."

He was right. Calling her the best medic on station wasn't hyperbole. I'd grabbed her up when she arrived for exactly that reason. Like me, she shouldn't have even been in the military. She'd been an actual doctor— a wunderkind, graduating from med school before most people her age had even graduated from primary school. Then she lost her license. I didn't have the whole story, but the basics were that she got fed up with the medical system on her home planet and how it favored the rich, and she'd stolen supplies and started her own underground clinic for the needy. Her hospital didn't appreciate that, and she'd run off and enlisted rather than face a trial.

You'd have thought the military would have thrown a party to get her. She'd have been a great doctor in the military, where everyone is treated equally, regardless of their station, when it came to medical care. Mostly.

But never underestimate the power of the bureaucracy to screw something up. Their loss was my squad's gain.

"I'll talk to her," I said, "and I'll make sure she has a plan."

Patel stood, meeting my eyes for several seconds before responding. "Okay. If you and she say we can make that happen, I'm in."

"I'm off to find her right now."

YET I STILL didn't go directly to Erickson, because I didn't want to go to Miller's room. Instead, I pinged her device, asking her to meet me without giving her an explanation why. As her squad leader, it was normal enough that it wouldn't cause suspicion.

Ten minutes later, I stood with Erickson, my back in the corner of an enlisted entertainment room so I could watch everyone else who entered. No Miller, and nobody paying us any attention. Good. Once I briefed her on the plan, Erickson jumped into a series of questions.

"When do we leave? What happens if we get caught before we launch? Should I pack extra medical supplies? I should. Never mind. I'll have to fill out a requisition, but I can cover that."

When she took a breath, I cut her off. "We leave as soon as Rookie and Chang have their equipment. Every minute we delay makes it less likely we find him, but we can't go without their kit. If we get caught before we launch, I'll handle it. Don't worry."

She nodded her head rapidly. "Got it. Anything else?"

With Erickson, I had to play it straight. She was

smarter than me, and if I lied, she'd catch me out. "I need us to fake an injury for Patel while he's down there. Something that gets him out of the military with a full pension."

Erickson whistled. "That's highly illegal."

"Yep. That a problem?"

"This about his family?"

"It is," I said.

She considered it, probably running it through some ridiculously complex ethical flowchart in her genius brain. "Nope. Not a problem. But I'm going to need some money."

I didn't take her for mercenary, so this caught me off guard.

Seeing my look, she said, "It's not for me. If I'm going to injure someone bad enough to get them out of the military, I'm sure as shit going to make sure that it's done right. And what I need for that, I can't requisition, and I can't steal without getting caught. That means I need a bribe."

"Just tell me how much," I said. I didn't need to know the details—I trusted her—and I had the credits. I'd done nothing but store that money away for a rainy day. Today, it was raining on Patel.

She told me the number. I whistled at the figure, but I transferred the credits to her.

Then I put my hand on Erickson's shoulder and made her look at me. "Erickson, this is really important. You can't tell anybody about this. Especially not in your bunk room. *Especially* not Sergeant Miller."

She narrowed her eyes at me. "Why does everybody

always think I can't keep my mouth shut? I talk fast, but I'm not a moron. In fact, I'm a fucking super genius."

"You are. Sorry. Just covering all the bases." I felt bad about saying it, but Miller had gotten into my head.

"Yeah, no problem," she said. "I won't talk."

And again, because I trusted her, I believed her.

I TALKED TO Martinez last, because I knew he'd be the easiest to convince. Everyone in my squad had a skill, and Martinez's was pretty basic. He was really good at killing people. It sounds kind of dark to say it, but as it turns out, sometimes you need that kind of thing when you're in the infantry during a war. It wasn't that the rest of us weren't capable. We were. But Martinez had a gift. He was our best marksman, a master with every instrument of death in the inventory, and had the quickest reaction time in the squad by every testing measure known to the military. He was also as cold and detached as death itself. Martinez was, quite simply, a killer. The kind of guy that makes other people uncomfortable without even knowing why, including me. But he was *my* killer.

I explained the basics of the mission to him and what I wanted him to carry.

Martinez nodded twice. He was in, and he'd be ready.

Martinez also doesn't talk much. I have no idea if that's related to his other skills. It doesn't matter.

I had my team.

WITH THE TEAM set at eight, the next morning I headed over to find Putty, Chang, and Rookie at the armor issue point. Putty could handle it, but I felt restless and wanted to avoid any delays. Dex and his mystery helper were opening a window for us to launch in just over twenty-four hours. I didn't like how long the whole thing was taking, but Gwan wouldn't help me, and I couldn't rush my hackers, so Kendrick would just have to hold on a bit longer. If anyone could do it, he could. His first twenty-four hours would have been the most danger- ous, and those had passed. If he'd made it through the first day—and I had every reason to believe he had—he could make it another one.

I buzzed in through the main entrance and walked between tables and workbenches lining either side of a long room, strewn with various pieces of the gray poly- mer suits. Scanning around, I didn't see any of my team among the dozen or so techs working, so I continued through to the test facility. I spotted them immediately, a mismatched group, the heavyset Putty standing to one side in his regular uniform while two techs worked on the tall, wiry rookie and the diminutive Chang, both of whom were encased in armor. Chang had a standard in- fantry suit, fabricated smaller to fit her frame. It gave her a little bulk, but mostly hugged her form except for bulges at the joints.

Rookie wore a heavier suit, thicker armor with more power and able to haul extra weaponry. Whereas my suit weighed sixty kilos, the heavy version clocked in closer to a hundred. It made for less mobility, and it couldn't fit into tight places, but it could take a hit from a heavy weapon and keep going. It had a psychological effect too. Since the heavy troopers carried Beasts, they could dish out serious pain. They looked like a carnival of destruction when they opened up, so they tended to draw the enemy's fire, focusing it on the person with the most survivable suit. That gave the rest of us the ability to maneuver. I could put one in each fire team, which would give us some extra firepower if we had to mix it up.

The tech, a dark-skinned man in muted green coveralls, told Rookie to take a step. The first step went well, but his second leg didn't bend right, and he ended up dragging it, sparks flitting against the deck.

"Gah! Stop!" The tech crouched and examined the knee, and then plugged his tablet into a hidden socket and moved his fingers across the screen. "Try it now."

Rookie took another lurching step forward, and this time the second leg reacted properly. He wobbled a bit in the big suit, getting used to the different stride.

"How's that feel?" asked the tech.

"A little sluggish," said Rookie. He had his faceplate down, so the voice came through his external communicator, loud and tinny.

"Try punching," said the tech, indicating a round device that served as a shoulder-high target. Rookie slammed his big gloved fist into it, and it rocked back. The tech glanced down at a readout on his device. "You're getting full power, so it's not the suit. Take your helmet off and we'll recheck the neural relays. That could be causing a slight drag."

I sidled up to the tech and glanced at his name tag, which read Doubrou. "We going to be good to go today, Doubrou?"

"Maybe," he said. "This is a common problem. The helmet tech probably rushed the job, which is why the suit is reacting slow for your man here. I'll bet you five credits I can tell you what tech did it."

"I'm sure you can, but I don't really care who did it. Can you fix it?"

"Like I said . . . probably."

"Tell you what. I've got a critical exercise tomorrow, and if I don't have a full team, I'm screwed. I'll give you the five credits you wanted to bet plus twenty more if he walks out of here with a working suit today."

Doubrou looked at me fully for the first time. "Consider it done."

"You'll find it in your account before you wake up tomorrow." I smiled. Doubrou was my kind of soldier, the kind I understood. I turned my attention to Chang.

The blonde tech adjusting the small woman's suit stood up from where she had worked on the knee joint. "That should do it. Go ahead and put the helmet on, power up, and give it a try."

Chang's grin didn't disappear until the helmet covered her face. "Power up," she said. She didn't really have to say it—thinking it with the helmet on would engage the function—but first-time users took a while to adjust to that. She probably also just wanted to say it—it *is* kind of cool.

We waited sixty seconds for her systems to come online. It would go faster in the future—the first boot-up was always a pain in the ass.

"Try taking a few steps," said the tech.

Chang took one step, her foot striking heavily against the metal deck, then another, more gracefully. She took off running, quickly picking up speed until she was moving at least twice as fast as she could without the suit. She ran right at the wall, leaped with one foot, planted the other on the vertical surface, and launched herself into a backflip.

"Holy shit, this is awesome!" Her amplified voice echoed as she jumped through the air, covering half the ground back to us.

"I'm going to say that's a good fit," the tech said, not cracking a smile.

"Why didn't you tell me about this sooner?" Chang grabbed me and almost crushed my shoulders.

"Easy, killer," I said, wincing. "You're stronger in the suit. You're going to break my bones if you don't let up."

Her grip slackened. "Sorry."

"Maybe dial it back a bit?" I cut my eyes to the tech. I didn't need word of this fitting getting around. There was no situation where a mechanic was supposed to be in augmented infantry armor.

"Right. Sorry, Boss."

I turned to Putty. "Once they get weapons fitted and tested, make sure you hook both suits to the charger when you put them in storage." Power readings on new suits were notoriously unreliable, and I wanted all the juice we could get when we hit the surface.

"Roger," he said, as if I had just told him how to find the mess hall.

I glanced back to the blonde tech—her name tag said Elspeth—and found her looking at Chang with a little bit too much interest. It wouldn't take a genius to know that the smaller soldier wasn't augmented infantry. I had forged an authorization due to a special mission where we had to recover a piece of equipment that required us to have a mechanic with us, but I wanted to be sure it held. "We going to have a problem here?"

"About her?" Elspeth glanced at her tablet. "Authorization is legit. No problem."

"Sure." I considered giving her the cover story, but something about her body language told me to be honest. "Maybe you still don't talk about it for a day or two. Can you do that? It would help me out a lot."

She smiled, and then winked. "Talk about what?"

"Thanks."

I HAD THE team in for a briefing that night—everybody but Dex, who was busy prepping the ship—so I could lay out the basics of the mission and make sure they were ready. I didn't give them all the details. For one thing, I didn't want to run the risk of compromising operational security. For another, I still didn't have a lot of the details completely sorted.

I told them where to be and what to carry, which sounds simple, but there's a lot to it when you're not going to get a resupply. We'd have to hump all our rations, and while our suits would print fléchette ammo as we needed it, we had to carry the base material cartridges. Since we'd all be in power armor, the weight wouldn't matter to us physically, but every kilogram drew more power to move it, and regardless of weight, we still had space constraints. Where we could save room, we would. But we did need, on top of our regular gear, to pack civilian clothes and hard currency. This wasn't a standard mission, and I couldn't be sure what might come up.

When the meeting broke and Erickson opened the door to leave, I noticed someone in the hall. Killer lived in the room right across from us, so it could have been coincidence that had her standing there.

But I doubted it.

I stood and pushed past the soldiers congregating in front of the exit. "Miller," I called to her back as she tried to duck into her own room. Sure. That wasn't suspicious at all.

She stopped, and after a few seconds, she turned to face me. "What's up, Gas?"

"Whatcha doing?" I spoke the words with a casual tone that we both knew for false.

"Just headed to my room. How about you?"

"So you weren't out here trying to listen in on our meeting? What's the matter? Need some pointers on how to run a squad?"

I think she almost laughed at my suggestion that I could teach her something. Almost, but not quite. "Why would I do that?" This time it was her putting on a false innocent front. She was so full of shit. She'd turned me in when I tried to stow away on the ship, which worked out, since it got me a meeting with Gwan. But now she was looking for a way to stop my real mission. I needed to find out what she knew, but obviously I couldn't come right out and ask. So I decided to bait her.

"Why do you do anything? Because you're a suck-up."

Her face pinched at that, but she didn't lose her cool. "Was there something you didn't want me to hear?"

"Nope. Just a routine meeting. But seeing how it wasn't *your* meeting, I have to wonder why you're curious. People meet all the time, right? Me, I figure you can't help yourself, and you have to stick your nose into everything, no matter how small. Otherwise, how would it get so brown?"

She didn't take the bait, instead glancing past me through the door. "What was Chang doing in there? Isn't she a mechanic?" And just like that, she had me on the defensive and searching for a possible answer. I pictured her running off to tell someone about it, and then I pictured me having to zip-tie and gag her until my mission was over. As entertaining as that would be, it wasn't a realistic option. One day, though.

"Hanging out," I lied. "I think maybe she and Martinez are a thing."

"Is that so?"

"Pretty sure. I didn't ask or anything. Not really my business." I left unsaid that it wasn't really *her* business, either. I had to get through another fifteen hours, and then Miller wouldn't matter. Unfortunately, I didn't trust her to keep out of the way for even *that* long, but there was nothing I could do about it at the moment.

"Cool," she said. "We good?"

"We're good," I said.

"Okay. I'll see you around."

The way she said it, she might as well have said, *I'll be watching you.*

And instead of me saying, *We're good,* I might as well have said, *We're fucked.*

CHAPTER 9

LATE THE NEXT MORNING, WE HAD OUR FIFTEEN-minute launch window. Dex's associate, who we code-named Juniper, was spoofing a command in the base's main system that would make the shuttle believe we had authorization. Dex and Chang had chosen a bay that had been malfunctioning recently and giving occasional false launch readings. We intended to hide in the noise. The idea made perfect sense, and it made me feel smart for recruiting those two.

I led the other seven members of the team, all kitted out in full mech-suits, toward our target ship. I tried to keep my pace steady but found myself continually increasing speed and having to consciously slow down. Fifteen minutes didn't give us a lot of time, and Dex told me that if we missed this window, it would be a day or two before he could get us another one. And I was done waiting.

Like when I tried to stow away, we were all on camera, for sure, so we had to make things look normal. But again, like my first attempt, the cameras only mattered if the AIs saw something unusual that triggered their programming. I wasn't worried about people watching, either. Only one person—Miller—had shown any interest in what we were up to, and we'd avoided her this time. I'd checked her squad's training schedule, and they had weapon maintenance, conveniently located a third of the way around the station. In front of me, the corridor lay mercifully empty.

I reached the drop ship and ushered the team forward. Putty stopped in the hatch, forcing the other soldiers behind him to bump into one another, battle armor and weapons rattling.

"Come on, Putty," I said. "We only have a short window."

"Sorry, just thinking about the space whales," he said.

"Don't start that crap again. You're a soldier. You've been on at least twenty drops, and you know there are no space whales. Stop trying to scare the rookie." I gave Putty my best pissed-off sergeant look.

I may have practiced it in front of a mirror to perfect it. I didn't usually mind a little levity, but this was important.

Putty sighed loudly. "Fine. I'm sorry, Rookie. There's no need to worry about space whales. They don't exist."

Rookie looked at him, tension coming out of his face.

"Was that so hard?" I asked.

Putty continued talking to the rookie. "What you should really be worried about is Chang missing her entrance angle and us bouncing off the atmosphere and hurtling into deep space."

"What?" Rookie glanced around again, looking for someone to say something. "Is that possible?"

"No, of course not. The computer flies the ship," said Chang. She waited for Rookie to turn to look at me, and then shrugged her shoulders behind his back.

"We don't have time for this shit. Just load the stupid ship," I said. "Juniper can't hold off the security system forever."

The first person hadn't gotten through the hatch when a female voice rang out from behind me, clear and authoritative. "What are you ass-clowns doing?"

Miller. Of fucking course. Why wouldn't it be her? Everything was running too smoothly.

I turned to face Miller. "Hey, Killer. What's up?" She had on her power armor like she was on duty, emblazoned with the same rank I wore on mine. Clearly she hadn't just stumbled across us. Not that I ever thought she had these last few days.

She made an exaggerated gesture of peering around me at the drop ship. "Seems like you've got something going on. Anything I should know about?"

I looked over my shoulder to where the soldiers stood, staring at the two of us. "What? This? Practicing loading and unloading drills with my squad."

"Chang isn't in your squad," said Miller. "What's going on, Chang? I thought you had more brains than to get involved with this idiot."

Chang shrugged again, her armor exaggerating the motion. Thankfully she didn't answer. Keeping silent beats a bad lie.

"I heard you might be headed to the surface," said Miller, fixing her stare back on me.

Shit. My mind raced, trying to figure out a way out of it. Coming up with nothing, I stalled for time. "Huh. Where'd you hear that?"

"You're not the only one with people who tell you things, Gas."

"Who told?" It was pointless to lie about it. She knew. My mind whirled. Technically we hadn't done anything wrong yet. Nothing major anyway. I could still back away, but that would end the mission and leave Kendrick down there, stranded. I'd never have another chance to set something like this up. We didn't leave our people behind.

"Does it matter?" Miller held my gaze.

I blew out a big breath of air. She had me, so it was her move. "So what do we do now?"

"I'm going with you," she said.

I started to speak, then stopped. Of all the things I'd expected her to say right then, that hadn't even been on the list. "What?"

"You heard me. You've got eight people; the ship has ten seats. Adding me still leaves room for Kendrick on the way back. I'm going. Either that or I get on the comm and let Operations know what's going on."

Something in the way she said it grabbed at me. Something off in her tone. She was pushing a little too hard, which made me wonder: *Why?* If she wanted to turn me in, she could have done it without showing up to tell me. In fact, she *wouldn't* have shown up. That way she could deny being the rat, like she did last time. She was bluffing, which meant I didn't need to necessarily give in to her demands without a fight. I decided to push back without letting on that I knew. "You understand we don't have a pilot, right? We're using a mechanic."

Miller rolled her eyes, feigning nonchalance, but it came off a little too stiff. She was a bad liar. I liked that about her. "The ship flies itself. Besides, it's Chang. I trust her."

That felt so out of character for her that it confirmed my suspicion. Miller didn't trust *anybody*. She didn't want to stop us—I'd been right in seeing that as a bluff—she wanted *to go with us*, and she wanted it bad. She also wouldn't risk court-martial, which she'd be doing the minute she entered the ship. Unless she had top cover, like me. I'd liked to have grilled her on it and gotten her to slip, but I was running out of time. I had to get to the heart of it. "What's your game here?"

"What do you mean?" Her voice hitched slightly.

"Either you tell me what's going on with you, or I'll scrap the whole thing and claim it *was* a training exercise. It'll be your word against mine. Mine and these others." *And probably Colonel Gwan as well.* I didn't break eye contact. I had her.

"You wouldn't leave your man down there," she said.

"As you keep saying, I already did it once. Try me." I was bluffing too, and she probably knew it. But when it came to playing chicken, I had way more experience than she had. She was a better sergeant than me, except when it came to this exact type of situation. Which is probably why Gwan reached out to me in the first place.

She stared a few seconds longer. "I don't trust you

and this band of misfits not to get yourselves killed. With me along, maybe you'll survive."

I still didn't buy it. She didn't care about us. "Time is running out. How about we cut the shit and you tell me the real reason or this all becomes moot?"

She hesitated. "Fine. If you have to know, I care about Kendrick too."

"Hah! You and Kendrick. I knew it!" Putty interjected.

"Shut the fuck up, Putty," Miller said. Say this for Miller, she had the pissed-off sergeant's voice *down*.

Just in case, though, I held up my hand, adding to her order.

"Why are you bringing him along?" Killer nodded at Rookie.

"I wanted another Beast." I tapped on the heavy automatic pulse weapon that Rookie carried slung over both shoulders. "Don't change the subject."

"What about Dex?" she asked, ignoring me. Dex stood a head taller than everyone else loading the ship.

Was she kidding? "Dexill's our tech guy," I said. Dex smiled.

"You've got a tech guy?" she asked.

"Welcome to the present, Killer. You can't do anything without a tech guy."

I have to admit, it made me happy to see her look even remotely abashed. I did something better than her, and she knew it.

We stood silent for a moment after that, until it grew awkward and Miller said, "So, are we going to do this thing or what?"

Fuck. I didn't have a choice.

"You have your basic load of ammo?"

"And then some," said Miller. "Spare B pack too."

I hesitated for a second, then nodded and overexaggerated a gesture toward the door with my arm. "Fine. Lead the way."

She only hesitated a couple seconds before boarding.

"Putty, Rookie, load up," I said. We were going. I didn't want her along, but I didn't have any more time to argue, and I really didn't want to scrap the mission. I was taking a team on a stolen ship with the biggest straight-lace in the whole outfit riding along to find Kendrick, who she claimed she cared about. It made for a good story, I had to admit, and one that might be believable to the rest of the team. Everybody loved Kendrick, especially women. Nobody would question her word on it. I had to hand it to her—it's exactly the kind of story that I'd have made up if I was trying to hide my real purpose.

And just like a lot of my stories, it was total bullshit.

I pulled Patel aside before he boarded and spoke to him quietly enough that nobody else would hear. "Monitor Sergeant Miller's comms without her knowing, and suppress any transmission she tries to send from the ship."

"Roger that. What about when we hit the ground?"

"Check in with me. I'll let you know."

Once I figured out what to do myself.

CHAPTER 10

WE STRAPPED IN, THREE ALONG EACH SIDE WALL
and Miller and I against the back with an empty
seat between us, all facing forward, locking our armor
magnetically to the points built for just that reason to
keep us from bouncing around on entry into the atmosphere. Chang, as the pilot, had her own tight compartment forward of us. Gallia's atmo rating logged in at
1.04, meaning it had a bit more oxygen content than
standard. Combined with its 0.95 standard gravity, that
would give us a pretty easy time of it if we had to cover
any kind of distance. That wasn't the plan. We intended
to land near his beacon, in an undefended portion of the
enemy wilderness, cover the six or seven kilometers to
Kiergard where we'd find him, take care of some business there, and pick him up and get out.

Those were the basics. And while I hadn't fully decided everything, I allowed for the chance that it might
not work. So I had backups. We had extra ammo and
extra B packs, because you could never have too many
bullets or too much power. Patel had a high-powered
satellite communications array, Erickson had a full

med bag, Martinez had some surprises of the explosive variety, and I had brought along the best tech guy I knew and had a brain full of ideas. I'd accounted for everything I could, and knew we had the ability to wing it if things went south.

"Helmets on," I told the team, and I put on my own. We didn't technically need them on the ship, which had its own air system, but it was SOP, and I saw no reason to change. "You ready, Chang?" I said on a channel that I had open to only her and Dex.

"Sure thing, Boss. You sit back and I'll have you on the ground in thirty minutes. Nothing to worry about."

"We good to go, Dex?"

Dex held up his hand, asking me to wait as he concentrated on something. "Window opens in one minute," he said finally.

"Roger."

You never really appreciate how long a minute can last until you're sitting with your own thoughts, worrying that at any second, the door will pop open and you'll be face-to-face with a squad of heavily armed SPs. I glanced at the others, but I couldn't read their expressions through their helmets. I almost opened a channel to Miller but decided against it. She was along for the ride, and there was nothing I could do to change that now.

Dex's deep voice broke the silence of my thoughts. "Window is open. We've got three minutes."

"Three?" I asked. "I thought we had fifteen."

"Time's wasting," he said. He was right. I could ask about it later.

"Chang, you're clear to launch. Don't waste any—"

I cut my transmission when the ship lurched as the mechanical lock detached from the base. I waited for some sort of alarm to sound, even though that was ridiculous. We'd never hear it. Either Juniper and Dex's plan worked, or we'd triggered an alarm in Ops. I had to trust my team. Even if Ops caught us, we might not know it right away, unless they tried to communicate with us. They couldn't send ground troops after us now—they'd have to scramble something to go after us in space, and that would take time. Still, I monitored the Ops net on one channel, even as I kept the private comm to Chang and Dex open on another.

For a moment, everything was quiet, which kind of sucked, because it gave me time to consider the worst-case scenarios. What *would* they do if they saw the launch in Ops? If the spoofed launch malfunction wasn't working, or if we didn't fool the watch officer? I couldn't predict what they'd do. It would depend on the specific watch officer, and I mentally kicked myself for not checking who that was, figuring out their tendencies. I was sure that Dex knew—after all, that was his job—but I should have known too. I'd tried to prepare for everything, and already I'd missed something. For a second it flashed through my mind that they could shoot us down. The base had defensive turrets, even though they never used them except to shoot apart incoming space debris. They could blow us to pieces with the quickest command.

They wouldn't do that, though. It didn't make sense. More likely they'd call first and order us back. We wouldn't answer, and they'd try to take over control and return us that way. Maybe they'd launch fighters after that to run us down and force us to turn back, but hopefully they'd be overconfident in their hackers and not do that right away. They shouldn't be able to catch us until after we'd started entry into the atmosphere. In theory.

This mission had a little too much "in theory" for comfort.

The scenarios didn't stop spinning in my head until Chang's voice broke in on my comm almost fifteen minutes later. "Thirty seconds until atmosphere." She said it over the private channel where the rest of the crew couldn't hear, so I relayed the message. Like me, they were alone with their thoughts, and that was another failure on my part. Instead of wallowing in my own worry, I should have been talking to them, even though I had no doubt that Putty and Erickson were yakking with someone on private channels. Putty was probably telling Rookie about some sort of imaginary alien dragon monster on Gallia.

Around the cabin, the squad reacted to my news in silence, but there were little tells. Miller checked her magnetic seat connections, and Rookie fidgeted, unsure what to do with his hands.

I contacted Dex on the private channel. He'd been busy with his screens since we left, working hard to keep us beneath the notice of the station. But the part that mattered most for him still remained. If he couldn't hold off the enemy cyberattacks, we'd be burning in within five minutes. "Almost your turn. You ready?"

Dex remained totally still, focused. "Nothin' but. Bring it."

Entry into the atmosphere marked the most dangerous moment of the journey—a window of just a few seconds. If we failed, we'd never know it. Unless we skipped off the atmosphere and out into dead space. In that case, we'd all have plenty of time to think about it until we ran out of oxygen and died.

A lot was riding on my faith in Chang, and Chang's faith in her own abilities.

I held my breath, and then consciously let it out, trying to project calm to the rest of the team. The spacecraft bumped and started to shimmy.

"Atmosphere entry complete," Chang announced on the team channel. Nobody cheered openly on the comm, but tension came out of more than a few shoulders. "We've got to bleed off some speed. We're going to make some turns. It's normal."

Sitting in the back, I didn't feel the turns, but the deceleration pushed me toward the front of the craft. I closed my eyes and tried not to think.

The ship lurched.

"Shit! The controls are dead!" said Chang.

"Rebooting," said Dex. "Shit shit shit. It's too early for this."

"I'm back," said Chang. "Nope. Fuck. Dead again."

"What's going on?" I asked.

"Working on it," said Dex in a way that meant, *Stop talking right now.* I shut up.

"I've got some control, but the ship is fighting me. We're flying like a brick," said Chang.

"I'm having to repeatedly reboot," said Dex. "Yank

us as hard as you can to the west. We need to get away from the enemy computing power."

I cursed under my breath. I waited as long as I could, trying to give them time to work, until I couldn't stand the silence. "Can you get us down safely?"

"Uh . . . I think so," said Chang. "But I can't promise you where. Our guidance system is toast, and the steering isn't much better. It's going to be everything I can handle just to land."

Shit. "Okay, do what you have to do." I wasn't going to argue with the closest thing we had to a pilot, especially when I couldn't affect the outcome anyway. "Dex, what have you got?"

"They're still fighting me, but we've drifted out of enemy airspace into friendly, so I've got it under control."

That seemed like the grand prize in a mixed blessing tournament. "You've beat them?"

"Apparently," he said. "But that was a lot harder than I thought it would be. I wouldn't want to try it again."

"Twenty seconds," said Chang. "Better buckle in. We're coming down a bit hot."

That got my attention since Chang wasn't one to worry without a significant reason. I flipped back to the group net. "We're safe, but we're off course. Not sure where we're setting down, but I'm going to try to get a read before we land. Be ready for anything. Hang on for a rough landing."

It was a credit to my team that nobody asked any questions. They grabbed their armrests and held on tight. It wouldn't do any good if we crashed, but instinct is instinct. I tapped into the ship's nav system with my wrist unit and tried to get a fix on our location, but it was hard to concentrate given the impending landing. It didn't help that the ship kept updating the landing data every two seconds while blaring crash warnings in my ears.

When we hit the ground, my teeth slammed together, and my stomach tried to launch itself out through my throat. I swear we bounced. Sparks flashed behind my eyelids, which I'd clamped shut. The wind whuffed out of me for a second, and I gasped for air. The acrid smell in the cabin spoke of burning electronics. When I opened my eyes, red emergency lights bathed the cabin in a hellish glow.

At least the hull seemed intact.

Fire is inspirational, and nobody needed aid or encouragement to get out of the spacecraft. We all started moving at once. The door didn't open on its own, so Putty hit the emergency release when he got there first, and it swished open with a slight squeal of protesting hydraulics. He kicked the manual ramp out and hustled through the hatch.

I waited for the rest of the team to exit, counting them one by one on their way out. When Chang came from the pilot's cabin, she made eight, and I followed her out, making nine.

I grabbed her shoulder and pulled her around to face me once we both stood on the solid ground of Gallia. "Good work."

She nodded, though I'm not sure she believed me. I'd

never seen her shaken before. Behind us, black smoke wafted up and curled in the slight breeze.

"You okay?" I asked.

She seemed to regain her composure at my question. "It won't fly again. Not without some serious repairs."

"Can you fix it?" I asked.

She shrugged. "With the right tools and parts? Maybe. Without them, not a chance."

"What the hell happened?" Putty came over to join us.

Chang shook her head. "The ship went to shit, dying and restarting every half second or so, but somehow Dex got control back. After that, I just did what I could to recover it."

"What do you think, Dex?"

The big man took a few seconds to think. "The enemy hackers came in way harder than I expected. Sorry."

"But you got it back. I didn't think that was possible," I said.

"It shouldn't be. Someone on the other side must have messed up. I threw some offensive stuff at them, and maybe they got nervous. Or maybe they thought we were a decoy, and a big wave is coming next. Either way, we'll take it. I got just enough of a break for Chang to pull us away from their source and into friendly airspace, and they let it go. Bottom line, I got lucky."

"Good work," I said.

Much like Chang's, Dex's face said he didn't believe me.

"What now?" Putty asked, turning to me.

"We need to get away from this ship. It's a beacon to our own forces, and given that we're in friendly territory, they'll be on the way soon. I think it goes without saying that we don't want to be here when that happens." I walked over to the rest of the team. Miller had put them into a hasty perimeter by the time I reached them, and for a moment I was glad she was along. She was a rat, but she was a competent rat.

"What've we got?" She opened her visor so we could speak directly, and I copied her.

"Chang says the ship's done." I flipped open the computer on my wrist and brought up a map, and then brought up our original landing zone. "We got off course on the way down. We're about fifty klicks from where we intended, behind our own lines."

"That's good, right? We're safer there than with the enemy." Killer looked at me with confusion on her face, perhaps noticing something in my look.

"Not exactly. The front line itself is the most defended space in the area. If we had landed behind the enemy, we could have moved to Kendrick without much resistance. Now we've got to find some place to break through. And we then have to find a way off planet, because it's not likely going to be on that," I said, gesturing to the smoking drop ship.

Lines on a map didn't mean too much when both sides had access to space, but the stalemate on Gallia had remained mostly static for several years, with neither side able, or more likely willing, to commit enough resources to dramatically change things.

Miller put her armored hand on my shoulder. "So that's it. We're done. We hike it to a lift point, throw ourselves on the mercy of our leaders, and beg forgiveness, right?"

I turned away from her gaze, back to the map, while considering what she said. Less than an hour ago, she'd been gung ho to find Kendrick. Now she wanted to pull out, and that change didn't make sense. She'd been lying when she said she cared about Kendrick. I'd thought so, but now I had confirmation.

"Right?" she prompted again.

"Take a look at your map. There might be a weak point in the enemy line, here."

She shook her head, then took a moment to tighten her helmet. "No. There's no weak spot. If there was a soft spot in the enemy line, don't you think someone besides us would have found it by now?"

"They weren't looking," I said.

"Of course they were."

No, that's the thing—they weren't. But I was. I pointed to the map. "Look."

"It's a swamp," she said.

"It's probably not very heavily defended."

"That's because it's a fucking swamp. It's impassable."

"Sure, to a heavy force," I said. "But it's perfect for a team like ours. We'll sneak right through."

"Do you know what lives in a Gallian swamp?"

"Is this some sort of philosophical puzzle? Does it matter?" I asked. "We need a way in."

She stared at me for a moment, and I tensed, thinking she might take a swing at me. I wouldn't mind if she did. I needed to know if I could count on her to follow my lead or if she was going to be a problem. One benefit to landing on our own side of the line was that I could safely leave her here. It was time to put her to the test.

"Look," I said, trying to keep my voice calm. "We're not quitting, so we have to improvise. I've made my decision."

She considered it for ten or fifteen seconds before she finally sighed, then responded. "Famous last words."

"Let's move," I called to the team.

Miller swore under her breath.

I swore back at her under mine.

CHAPTER 11

WE'D COVERED SEVENTEEN KLICKS WITHOUT much talk or fuss when we reached the edge of a forest. The slightly lower gravity helped a little, but more important, it eased the power drain on our suits, which was our most critical resource. The sun reached the horizon and cast a purple glow over everything.

"Why is everything purple?" asked Rookie.

I didn't know, but after waiting to see if I answered, Miller jumped in. "It's caused by trace gasses in the upper atmosphere."

That's right. They'd told us during our orientation to the planet, but that was months ago, and I hadn't paid much attention even then. I never really cared what color the sky was when I was in the middle of a firefight. Of course Miller remembered shit like that.

We'd made slow progress, mostly because we'd had to hide from one of our own supply convoys as it wound its way along the broken road we loosely followed. We didn't get too close to the highway itself, but it cut through the only flat ground, and it beat humping over seven-hundred-meter-high hills. Even with power armor, that sucked.

Now we'd reached a forest made up of local trees that looked like evergreens, but were actually deciduous, shedding all their growth yearly. The needles made the ground spongy and dampened sound, giving the whole place a serene feel.

When we'd gone about a kilometer into the forest, Miller called me on a private channel. "You want to think about calling a stop? It's only six klicks from here to the swamp."

I'd have liked to push on farther, but she had a point. We didn't know exactly where the swamp started, and we didn't want to overnight too close to it. "Yeah. Good call." I still didn't trust her, but I could at least be civil. I hadn't been thinking about bedding down for the night, and she'd helped me out.

"Find a good place to stop," I called on the squad net, giving Putty, as the point man, the authority to pick the spot. A few minutes later we were setting up camp in a flat clearing with reasonable visibility in all directions.

"I hope it doesn't rain. I bet it will, though," said Putty.

Rookie tapped on his wrist unit. "I can't get the weather to pull up on this thing."

"I shut connectivity down, idiot," said Dex. "When you access the net, it pings the system with your location."

Rookie's eyes got big. "Sorry. I saw the sergeant using his, so I thought it was okay."

I shook my head. "I pulled up a map at the crash site, but I saved it locally. After that I disabled net access. They'll have the ship's location anyway, so I wasn't giving anything away."

"The ship," said Putty. "No way to hide that. They know we're gone."

"No doubt," I said. A recovery team probably had it already. I wondered if they'd sent a tracking team as well.

"Should we keep moving?" asked Miller, publicly second-guessing her own private advice to stop. "We're what, eighteen klicks from the crash site? Once they find the ship, they'll have drones out looking for us. Even the most rudimentary search pattern will find us."

"No, I don't think so. If they were coming to get us, they'd have found us already."

That was more worrying than Miller's scenario. They *should* have found us by now, but they hadn't. I could guess at what that meant—Gwan had our backs at least to some extent—but I couldn't be sure. I hadn't shared all my secrets with him, and he certainly hadn't shared all his with me.

"You think?" She sounded more curious than doubtful.

"Like you said, it would be reasonably easy to find us once they had the ship, if they wanted to dedicate assets to the task. Either way, I don't want to move in the dark. With the sun going down, we'd burn more power because we can't use our portable solar to recharge. We've got a long way to go, and I don't want to get in energy debt."

To check my point, I pulled up the charges for each

of the team's suits onto my display. Putty's and Rookie's suits used the most juice, and they were at seventy-five percent and seventy-three percent, respectively. "Conserve power while we're stopped," I said to everybody.

"You want me and Rookie to recharge from our spare B packs?" asked Putty.

"Save them for an emergency," I said. "We'll find a time to stop tomorrow and deploy our main solar collectors to recharge." Those required us to be stationary, but they provided about fifteen times the charging rate that we got from the built-in units we could use while mobile.

"So we can't move forward, but if we stay here, they're likely to find us," said Dex.

"But they haven't, which means they probably won't."

"We're so fucked," said Putty.

"Agreed," said Erickson.

"There's still time to turn ourselves in," Miller said to me on a private channel.

"Is that what you want?" I asked. I tried to keep the anger out of my voice, but I'm not sure I succeeded. It was more frustration than anything else as I saw the whole squad starting to turn on the mission. Dex's assessment wasn't wrong. If they wanted to find us, they would. It was understandable for the others to be worried, but I knew things they didn't. The problem was, I didn't want to tell them my thoughts on Gwan. Not yet. And definitely not everybody. I had to convince them without using my true argument. I looked around to find everyone staring at me.

"Listen up," I said, looking around to make sure I

had everyone's attention. I figured that I might as well address it with everybody at once and get it out in the open. "As I see it, we've got two choices. One: we can flip on our devices, light up the net, and go turn ourselves in at the nearest lift point. I'll claim that none of you knew what I had planned. Chang, that probably won't cover you since you flew us, but it might do for everyone else." I left unsaid that Miller was on her own. She knew that, and I figured she already had a way to wriggle out of whatever jam we might get in.

I paused for several seconds to let what I said sink in. I wanted to push on regardless, but without the support of the team, I couldn't—I was too far out, and there were too many obstacles for me alone. So I needed to find out where I stood. "Or two: we can try to get to Kendrick. I know you didn't all serve with him, but for me, Putty, Patel, Martinez, and Erickson . . . he was part of our team."

After a several seconds when nobody spoke, I continued. "Everyone gets a vote. Majority rules. Whatever the group decides, we all live with it, no complaints. Got it? We all support the decision of the group."

Putty spoke first. "This is the military. We don't vote on things; people tell us what to do. That's why I signed up. Nobody should be making decisions based on what I think. You're the boss, and I trust your judgment more than I trust my own. *Everybody* trusts your judgment more than mine. I drink vodka slushies for breakfast. You decide."

"I'm the boss, and I say we vote. Go after Kendrick or go home. Erickson, you vote first."

"Kendrick's family," she said. "I'm in."

"Putty?"

"Kendrick," he said. I knew they'd be with me, which is why I asked them first. After that, it got a lot less sure.

"Chang? How about you."

"You know I'm in. Not much of a choice in my view," she said.

Rookie would vote however I did, so I had the five votes for a majority, but I needed more than that. If the team didn't commit, we wouldn't make it. "Miller, how about you?"

She looked at me for a moment, unblinking. I might have surprised her by asking her next. "Let's do it," she said, after drawing out the silence. I didn't know whether she really agreed or if she'd simply done the math like I had and saw the inevitability, but it still helped to have her say it out loud in front of the others.

"Martinez?" The short, quiet man nodded his head.

"Dex?"

"I'm not a quitter," said the big man.

"Patel?"

The commo specialist didn't answer right away. "Yeah. I'm with the team."

"Okay then, so it's decided," I said.

"Hey, don't I get a vote?" asked Rookie.

"It's eight to zero, dumbass. Your vote doesn't matter," said Putty.

Rookie sulked. "I just wanted a chance to say I was in."

"I knew you were with me. That's why I didn't ask. But I appreciate you speaking up—you're part of the team too," I said. He seemed to perk up a bit with that.

"Now, if we're done, we'll set three shifts for watch tonight and move out at first light tomorrow. We could make more ground if we kept moving right now, but we'll hit the swamp in a few more klicks, and I'd rather not bed down there."

Everyone nodded, and that was that.

I took the first watch along with Rookie and Patel. I walked a long way from camp, all the way out to the edge of the woods, so I could scan the open area with the thermal sight built into my helmet. I expected to see something. A heat signature. *Something*. They weren't coming, but I couldn't get over the thought that they would.

Everything stayed dark.

THE SWAMP STARTED at least half a kilometer before the map said it would, the ground turning soggy and pulling at my boots, causing the joints in the legs of my armor to whine with the strain. All sorts of flying insects sprung up at about the same time, some so small they were invisible and others as big as a plum. They bit and stung any exposed skin they could find, drawing a course of curses from the group until we broke down and fully sealed our armor. We could stay buttoned up as long as we needed to since we could breathe the atmosphere and the suits could replenish oxygen stores as needed, but staying closed up long-term made things uncomfortable. We'd sweat a lot and be miserable, or we'd burn extra power to run our cooling units full-time.

On the plus side, putting on the extra gear cut down on a lot of the chatter. Something about talking by comm shut people up, like you somehow needed something important to make it worth broadcasting. We used the low-powered internal transmitters, so there was no chance anyone would pick up on our comms from long range, but I guess we didn't have much to say.

Until Putty yelled.

I rushed to the front of the wedge to see what had him spooked, my boots sinking into the mushy ground with every step. Rookie had Putty by one arm, pulling; one of Putty's armored legs was buried in mud almost up to the hip, and the other was sinking fast. I hurried to help, but Dex got there quicker, adding his strength to the task, and soon they'd extricated Putty from the goop. He slumped back—brown sludge coating one leg and half of the other—collapsing in a bed of moss. His chest heaved, and he breathed hard enough to fog his faceplate slightly.

"Holy shit, that smell!" said Chang. "What did you do in your armor, Putty? Do you need some wet wipes?"

"Har har," said Putty. "I almost get sucked into a man-eating swamp, and you're making poop jokes."

Chang shrugged. "That's what I do. It's part of my charm."

"What happened?" I asked. Stupid question, but nothing better came to mind.

"I didn't see it," said Putty. "It looked the same as every other step. Then, all of a sudden, it yanked me down."

"Fucking creepy," said Patel, walking over toward where Putty had been stuck, testing each step before he moved.

Something screeched in the distance, and everybody froze. Given how large it sounded, it wasn't far enough away for comfort.

"What the fuck was that?" asked Killer. We all spoke over the squad net now, so everybody could hear. But if Killer didn't know, none of us did.

I glanced around to see if anybody had thoughts but got only blank faceplates. "I'm sure it's nothing."

"Are you fucking kidding me?" Erickson said. "It didn't sound like nothing." She hurried to join the group of us clustered around Putty. "I think it came from above. Maybe a bird? Birds don't usually make noises like that, but it definitely sounded like something in the sky."

"Can I change my vote?" Putty asked. "I feel like nightmare birds and murderous mud add a new dimension to the decision."

"I told you about wildlife is in the swamp," said Killer, this time using a private channel to me. "You really didn't check?"

"We weren't supposed to have to go through the swamp," I said. "We should have landed well beyond this. So, no, this didn't make it into my intel-gathering in the limited time I had to put this together."

She really couldn't argue with that, but that didn't stop her from commenting. "Shit, I'm going to have dreams about some giant flying snake-bird biting me in half at the waist." She exaggerated a shudder.

I didn't have to look around to sense the apprehension of the group. They'd charge an enemy trying to kill them with high-tech weapons. They'd steal a drop ship and go on a mission that could get them all court-martialed. But alien wildlife that sounded like something out of a horror vid . . . that was a whole different thing. And I didn't blame them one bit.

I turned to Killer and used the group channel. "What do you think?"

"That mud is what worries me," she says. "At best it's going to slow us down because we'll have to watch every step. At worst—"

"Yeah." I cut her off. "But what choice is there?"

"There's got to be another way." Putty sat up and wiped mud from his armor as best he could. "How much of this swamp is there?"

"At least six klicks," I said.

"Fuck that," said Dex.

I thought about it. "The line isn't fortified everywhere. It's more like a series of checkpoints. We'd only have to fight our way through one."

Killer shook her head. "We don't have the firepower for that. They've got fortified positions with at least twenty to thirty troops, plus heavy weapons."

Somebody has done her homework.

"Could we sneak between them?" asked Chang.

"I doubt it," I said. "They'll have optics and other sensors covering any dead space, and some sort of force to react to an incursion. Not to mention rockets and air cover. Unless . . ."

"I don't like when he gets that tone," said Putty.

"Hear me out," I said.

"Yep," said Putty. "We're all gonna die."

I ignored him. "If we could cause a distraction at the checkpoint, we could use that to slip through out of sight."

"They have redundant sensors," said Miller. "We can't distract everything."

"Sure," I said. "We'll have to take some of them out. Plus, they're probably attuned to larger forces than ours. But . . ."

"I see where you're going with this. A lot is resting on that 'probably,' though." She knew as well as I did that I was making that up, but I was in full sales mode now, and I never let facts get in the way of a good pitch.

"You have a better idea?" I asked. "If it doesn't work, we lay down covering fire and fall back." I waited for her to protest, but she stayed silent. "We can always turn ourselves in to our own side later if we don't get through. It's not like we're going to get in *more* trouble for taking another day. What are they going to do, court-martial us twice?"

"With my luck, they might," said Putty.

"So we need a distraction," said Patel, who had winced at my mention of that particular potential consequence. "Something that can occupy a force three times our size long enough for us to slip by an unknown array of sensors before we all get fried to a crisp."

"Exactly." I ignored the sarcasm in his voice. "We need a bot tank."

"I do like tanks," said Putty.

Miller turned to him, and I imagine she was glaring under her visor. "Where are we going to get a tank?"

Putty pushed himself up to a sitting position. "No idea. But any plan with a tank is better than any plan without one."

"You're an idiot," she said.

"Maybe he's not," said Dex.

"Let's not be too hasty," I offered.

"Well . . . maybe he's not in this case," said Dex.

"Thanks," said Putty, confused.

Dex continued, "If we need a diversion, we could hit one of *our* maintenance points. Maybe hack a bot tank or something and take it with us."

Miller's voice rose. "You can't just hack a bot tank."

Dex snorted. "Maybe *you* can't."

"I told you, he's our tech guy," I said. "You really think you can do it?"

"Sure," said Dex. "I'll need a couple minutes alone with it, but if you can get me that, I can make it happen."

"I think maybe you should have led with that," said Putty. "I don't know when, but at some point, I think 'I can steal a fucking bot tank' should have come up."

Dex turned his huge palms upward, a gesture exaggerated by his armor. "I didn't know we needed one."

"Can we get back to the point that we're essentially attacking our own people?" Miller asked.

"Not attacking," I said. "We're putting in a complicated requisition."

"Like the drop ship," Chang chimed in.

"Exactly. Like the drop ship." I looked around to check for any other major dissent. Finding none, I cut off discussion. "So it's settled. We make our way back to a maintenance area, appropriate a tank, and use that to create the distraction we need to breach the enemy line."

"Anything that gets us out of this fucking swamp," said Erickson, who had been uncharacteristically quiet.

As if that was all the confirmation necessary, I started walking back in the opposite direction, not wanting to give anyone else a chance to reconsider.

CHAPTER 12

MILLER, DEX, AND I LAY IN PRONE POSITIONS ON top of a rise overlooking a series of prefabricated maintenance bays surrounded by a barbed-wire-topped chain-link fence. Each side measured about a half kilometer, which was a large area to cover for what appeared to be only two dedicated guards. The number didn't matter much, since we weren't going to fight them, and it only took one to sound an alarm.

The lack of defense didn't seem negligent since we were twenty or so kilometers behind our own front line, and the enemy was another five to six kilometers away on the other side of no-man's-land. Besides the guards, a few other people—probably mechanics—appeared and disappeared between wide-spaced vehicles in a gravel lot. They parked vehicles far apart so that they didn't make a good target for enemy rockets, even though three towers spread across the base had recessed pulse turrets that would shoot down ninety-eight percent of incoming indirect fire. It never hurt to have redundant protection.

The vehicle spacing made our job both easier and harder. On the one hand, the spread would give Dex extra time if we picked a tank away from everybody. On the other hand, it made sneaking around the lot much more difficult. I needed to turn something else to our advantage.

Four large rectangular bays ran parallel to each other on the far side from our position. Those were the actual maintenance facilities, which would be mostly automated, with only a few personnel to oversee the robots. That's what made our mission possible. I estimated maybe fifteen to twenty total humans on the premises, mostly for security, administration, programming, and facilitating movement of repaired systems to the units that needed them.

It wasn't going to be easy, but it wasn't nearly as complicated as getting off the space station.

"What do you think?" I asked.

"We need to get something that's already come out of the shop," said Dex. "No sense stealing a broken vehicle."

"That's probably the group over there, on the back wall, set apart from everything else," said Killer, indicating seven armored vehicles parked toward the back of the compound. "We've got plenty to choose from."

"That's good. They're in the back, away from the command shack and the barracks," said Dex. "Maybe we can cut the fence."

I shook my head. "No. If we cut the fence, it will draw too much attention. It only takes one sensor, or one person seeing us, and we're caught."

"So what's the plan, then?" asked Miller. "Don't tell me we walk in the front gate."

"We walk in the front gate."

I did my best not to smirk.

"Brilliant."

I ignored her sarcasm. I was getting good at that. "What? Don't you trust me?"

She laughed in spite of herself. "Come on. What've you got?"

"We walk down like we're a squad who got detached from our unit, blown off course by enemy fire as we tried to drop in."

"That sounds familiar so far," she said.

"Right. The best lies have part of the truth in them. We give them a story about how our ship went down, and we humped it over here, and we need to use their communications."

She thought about it for a bit. "They'll know there was no official mission."

"Why?" I answered. "This is a rear logistics area. How closely do you think they're following the events of the war? Do you think they're paying attention to updates? As long as the broken machines come out fixed, I don't think much else matters here."

She considered it some more. "You're probably right. Okay, but if we're doing this, *I'll* go into the command center and ask to use the comms. You work the stuff outside."

I started to respond but stopped. She was asking for the lead on the mission, but it would also put her out of my sight with access to communications. If she wanted to turn us in, I'd be giving her a perfect chance. On the other hand, all she had to do was cut on her armor's beacon. She wasn't part of my squad, so I couldn't override it, and I wasn't a hundred percent sure that Patel could jam it. She hadn't done that yet, but even so, I wasn't quite ready to trust her. "Why you?"

"Because I'm the perfect person for this task. I'm the most officious, bureaucratic person that we've got. Who's going to question me?"

I choked back a laugh. She was looking at me, deadly serious, but I couldn't help it. I'd never considered the possibility that she knew that about herself and used it as a tool. That was some serious self-awareness. "Okay. You're on. Take Patel with you as an underling. It will make you look more official." *It will also give me eyes on her, just in case.*

She nodded, then frowned.

"What now?"

"What do I do if I get in there and there's an alert for us? For all I know, my picture will be posted on every screen on the planet. What happens then?"

"You improvise."

She snorted.

"You said it yourself: you're the most bureaucratic person any of us know. That's a *good* thing here." *Mostly.* "If anyone can baffle the folks in charge, it's you."

I left unsaid my reservations. She wasn't a good liar, and if anybody pressed her, I didn't have a lot of confidence that she'd handle it well. But once she offered, I saw the benefit of me being outside where I could see everything in case we had to *really* improvise.

She hesitated, and then nodded. "I can't believe I'm going to do this. What are the rest of you going to do?"

"Chang, Putty, and Erickson are going to make friends with the staff on the ground—distract them and draw them away from the area where we need to work. Dex, Rookie, and I will get to the tank. Martinez will stay here and keep eyes out to warn us in case something else approaches." Martinez was our sniper, and because of that, his suit had upgraded optics.

"And that's it?" asked Miller.

"That's it," I said. "In and out. Simple."

"When is anything simple with you?"

I smiled. "What could go wrong?"

I STOOD BEHIND a bot tank that was just tall enough to hide me, peering around the end to watch for problems. When it fired up, it would hover half a meter off the ground, but in dormant mode, it sat on six cylindrical feet, a few centimeters off the packed gravel. I was on edge, not just because I was worried about getting caught, but because even if we didn't get caught, if we failed in any way, the team would fall apart. Everything had gone wrong so far, and we needed a win. Even the best team would crumble if they did nothing but taste defeat.

Chang was out of her armor and inside a personnel carrier with one of the local mechanics, looking at an electrical failure, and Erickson's voice carried across the compound as she asked another poor mechanic a seemingly unending series of questions. Dex knelt a few steps away from me, hidden from general view. A two-meter cord snaked from a device he carried to a port near the front of the bot tank.

"Anything your way, Rookie?"

"No, Sergeant."

"How's it coming, Dex?"

"It would be a lot better if you didn't keep asking that," he said. "I know I made it out to be easy, but this is some complex shit."

"Got it. Remember, though, you told me not to lie to you, so I'm going to be honest here: I really want you to hurry up." I glanced around the corner of the vehicle, acutely aware of everything that could go wrong. It was all I could do not to tick them off in my head.

"I hate you, Gas," Dex said. I could understand that. "Thirty seconds," he said.

I could understand that even better.

My mind wandered to Killer, and what her deal was. She'd disappeared inside the command building and hadn't come back out. That was good. If there were cameras covering the yard, the monitors would be in there, and anyone paying attention to Miller wouldn't be looking at those feeds. I had no idea what she was doing in there, though.

That was bad.

I needed to trust Patel. If something was off, he'd have messaged me.

"We're good," said Dex. "Next vehicle."

I passed by Dex and Rookie and led them around the back of the bot tank, down the row past three more vehicles to a PC—personnel carrier. It had lighter armor than a tank and had a smaller gun turret, and could carry nine personnel, though not with the heavy gear we had. It would carry most of us, though, and that would speed us up and save power. We had twenty klicks to cover to reach the front line, and we'd burned a lot of time. Every hour that passed made it more likely that someone decided to come after us.

We'd been at the new vehicle for maybe four minutes when an unfamiliar voice spoke from behind the vehicle. "What are you doing back here?"

"Uh—" Rookie stammered.

I hurried past Dex, trying to shield his huge form with my own so the speaker wouldn't see him. "There you are." I glanced at the rank of the soldier who walked up. "Sorry, Corporal. I was showing Rookie here some armored vehicles up close. This is his first time down on the planet, and he hasn't seen them outside of simulation."

The corporal chuckled. "Pretty impressive, aren't they?"

Rookie nodded, plastering a stupid look on his face. That may or may not have been intentional on his part, but it worked.

"I'm going to have to ask you to move, Sergeant. These here are ready to roll, and I've got to get them on their way back to their units."

"No problem. Where are they headed?" I needed to stall to give Dex time to finish his work.

"Four are going to Kilo battalion. They took some tough fighting earlier in the week and need to refit before they get back to action. Two to Delta, and one to Echo."

"I'm glad we're not out there with Kilo," I said.

"No lie, right?"

Dex appeared behind the corporal. He must have finished and walked around the other way.

"Thanks, man. See you around." I grabbed Rookie by the arm and pulled him with me before he could say anything else and hurried to catch up to Dex.

"You hear that?" I asked.

"We've got to hustle if we're going to get our vehicles out of here before they move," he said. "Can you get the rest of the squad moving?"

My brain spun. "Change in plan. We're not going to take control of the vehicles here. That was always the weakness, right? You couldn't drive them out of here without someone noticing. Too obvious."

Dex hesitated, thinking. "What do we do?"

"You're in the system, right?"

"Yeah. I can control them as long as they're in range."

"Perfect. He's sending them out the gate to their forward locations, saving us the trouble of figuring out how to break them free from here. We just have to stay close enough for you to control them once they're out of sight of the maintenance facility."

"That will work," said Dex. "But we can't let them get more than a few klicks away. Theoretically I can control them up to about ten klicks, but I wouldn't want to test that. There are too many factors—like terrain—that might shorten the range."

"We'll be in place, and I'll have Patel send a hornet drone after them so we can keep eyes on. You sure it will work?"

"Pretty sure. We'll see when they get outside the gate," he said.

"That's all we can hope for," I said, clapping him on one of his massive arms. "Good job."

"I don't understand how we get through the enemy line," said Rookie.

"We use the bot—"

"I get that part," he said, cutting me off. "But doesn't the enemy have stuff that will stop it? It would seem to me that if they couldn't stop a single tank, there wouldn't be much point to their front line. Plus, how do we get past our own lines? We can't shoot them."

I looked at him with a little different perception. Fortunately, I had answers for him. "Rookie . . . Stimpson," I said, correcting myself and using his name.

"You know my name."

"Of course I do. I'm your squad leader."

"I don't know. I thought you called me Rookie all the time because you didn't remember."

"Nah, I . . . I tell you what. I'll explain the name thing later. We've only got a minute until the rest of the crew gets here, and I want to answer your questions. They're good questions."

He smiled. "Thanks."

"Getting through our own line is tricky, but they're not really looking backward. Plus, because all of their sensors are on our network, Dex here can access them and make them see something other than us."

There was a lot more to it than that—some of which even I didn't understand—but I didn't want Rookie to worry any more than he already was.

"As for the enemy, their checkpoints aren't actually designed to stop a large force. Any sort of full-scale attack we launch, they'd pick up with their sensors. The checkpoints would then delay the attack, retreat, or direct outside assets—mostly air and artillery—against the attacking force. They're there to buy time so that the bad guys can mobilize their own forces and get them into position to stop the assault."

"Like pawns on a chessboard?" he asked.

I paused. I hadn't thought about it like that, but he had it right. "Yeah. Pretty much exactly."

"Aren't we pawns too, though? We don't have a lot of firepower, either."

"Us? Pawns? Nah. We're knights. We're going to move fast and hit them from angles they don't expect."

"Okay," he said. "I feel better about it."

And that was that. Leave it to a newbie soldier to teach me a leadership lesson. Keep soldiers informed, and they'll follow you anywhere.

Even if your information is mostly bullshit.

WE LINKED UP with our two stolen vehicles after about a two-klick fast march, and from what I could tell, nobody was the wiser. It might have been my imagination, but as we loaded into the PC, everyone seemed to have a bit more bounce in their step.

As I noted, the crew compartment of the vehicle was designed for nine, but not people in power armor. And bot tanks didn't hold passengers at all. But we just needed a ride—we already had armor to protect us. So we jammed six people inside the PC any way they could fit, which included ripping out seats. Martinez and Rookie sat on the roof, and Putty hung on to the back. There was no risk of them falling off—their suits had magnetic capability designed for use in zero-G combat. Normally I'd have given one of my soldiers the inside seat and taken to the outside myself, but the two heavy suits wouldn't fit no matter how much yoga they did, and more important, I needed access to the vehicle's systems.

There was a small risk that somebody would notice the two vehicles' locators switch off, but we wouldn't know until we saw some sort of reaction. I had to monitor that. Bot vehicles went where they were told, so probably nobody would think about checking their progress, and the first time they figured out the vehicles had gone missing would be when they failed to show up at their assigned destinations. By that time, we'd be long gone, and depending on how the distraction went, the vehicles might be gone as well. I didn't really care what happened after that.

The PC lifted off the ground into a low hover and started forward, following the tank. They both drove themselves, and their AIs picked their routes, so it made for a common enough occurrence that nobody would think twice if they saw us.

I extended the cord from the recessed port on my wrist comp and plugged it into the vehicle. Slaving off that system gave me access to the net without giving away my personal location. I updated my map, and then checked priority force dispatches. I half expected to see some sort of warning to the force telling everyone to keep watch out for nine fugitive soldiers. I didn't find it.

Nothing in the system mentioned us at all.

I glanced across to Miller, who was accessing her own screen, but, as if sensing me, looked up and met my eyes. She was seeing the same data. She shook her head slightly, not understanding it any better than I did. For some reason, I found that comforting. If she couldn't figure it out, I didn't feel as bad that I couldn't either. I mean . . . they had to know we were gone. It had been too long, and our cover story of a maintenance failure causing the launch of a drop ship wouldn't hold up to any sort of scrutiny. Plus, they were missing a fucking ship. One possibility was they knew about it, but whoever was in charge of that bay didn't want to admit that it had happened. Getting a drop ship stolen was, after all, a bit embarrassing. Or someone higher was covering it up. I almost opened a private channel to Miller to talk the situation through but chickened out. I still didn't fully trust her.

I didn't have long to consider the implications anyway. Traveling at a hundred twenty kilometers an hour, we covered the ground to the border in under ten minutes, and I wanted to brief the team on the plan before we got there. They knew the basics, but my recent conversation with Rookie had reminded me to read them in to as much as possible.

"Listen up," I said over the squad net, and I waited for a second until everyone inside the vehicle looked at me. "We're going to drop off about two-point-five klicks from the enemy line, about three-point-five clicks north of their checkpoint 17. We'll be in no-man's-land. I picked that spot because it's got a natural rise that protects us from line of sight from the checkpoint, and because it's still six kilometers from the checkpoint to the north, checkpoint 18.

"We'll hunker down there for a few minutes while Dex circles the two vehicles back and to the north. Once they're in position, we'll move out. The goal is to move as fast as possible, but to prioritize stealth. The two vehicles will hit the enemy line about two kilometers *north* of checkpoint 17. If all goes well, everyone at the checkpoint will be looking that way as we slide through to the south.

"Priority is going to be taking out sensors," I continued. "Patel, your focus is locating them and confusing them. Martinez, you take them out."

I got two rogers in response.

"If we get split up, far-side rendezvous is here." I sent a point to their maps about five klicks behind the enemy line almost due west from our breach point. "Save this to your offline files, so you have it without connecting to the system." More rogers. "If things go totally to shit and we don't make it through, make your way back to the maintenance facility. We'll turn ourselves in there. If *I* don't make it back, make sure to pin it all on me." I was pretty sure Miller wouldn't hesitate to do that, but it would help her that I gave permission in front of the rest of the team. I didn't intend to fail, but then, nobody ever did. Still, better to be prepared than go in blindly optimistic. Maybe Miller's diligence was rubbing off on me.

The vehicle's computer gave me access to all friendly unit locations, so it was easy enough to avoid our own checkpoints, especially since they weren't really look-ing for us. I figured we had another forty to fifty min-utes before anyone noticed the missing tank, based on its destination. I intended to be on the enemy side of the border by then.

I almost let myself get caught in the trap of thinking it was going *too* well. Especially for an improvised plan. But missions *did* work, so I tried to remind myself this was just another mission.

Which, of course, it wasn't.

We dismounted at our designated spot and went to ground. Trees dotted the low-lying area around us, pro-viding some measure of concealment, though we didn't need it with the distance and the rolling terrain. We kept a tight perimeter while Dex reprogrammed the two vehicles to circle back around to hit the enemy position from the other side. I had a lot of confidence that he could make that work. What I didn't know—the wild cards—were how much of the enemy's attention they would draw and how well we'd be able to detect their sensors. I took hope in the fact that most sensors are only as good as the people watching them. So far, I'd based a good portion of my decisions on that very thing. Tech was amazing, but it could only do so much without operators. People. People made mistakes, though, and I was putting a lot of my chips on the enemy doing just that. Dex's remote control vehicles upped the odds of that mistake. An attacking tank would provide them a direct threat, and I can say from experience that when tanks are shooting at you, they hold your full fucking attention. That gave us two chances for success: the sensors not finding us or people not watching them if they did.

How it would turn out? We couldn't know until we tried.

I checked the feed that Patel forwarded me from his hornet drone to make sure I had video, and I set a timer for three minutes and fifteen seconds, which was how long it would take the tank to get in position and open fire. The timer didn't matter much, since I had video and we'd hear the world explode with all kinds of firepower, but it gave me something to do besides think about all the ways this could go wrong.

The distraction didn't really work.

"Last chance to turn back," said Putty, coming up beside me. The bulk of his heavy suit dwarfed my lighter version. Each suit, just like each person in the team, had a specific purpose. Putty's was to smash things.

"You think we should?"

He turned his palms faceup. Inside the suits, we had to exaggerate gestures to make them understood. "Fuck it. What's the worst that could happen?"

I chuckled. "Want to know what's weird? There was no notification in the system about us. About the fact that we deserted."

"We're about to invade the territory of a hostile enemy, and that's what you're worried about? You're what's weird, Gas."

"It doesn't make any sense."

"Of course it doesn't," said Putty. "But what in the war does?"

The screech of the tank's main gun broke into our conversation, followed quickly by a deep explosion, muffled by the small hill between us and the checkpoint. We couldn't see them, which meant they couldn't see us. Not directly.

"Let's move!"

We headed out in a double wedge, five in front forming an arrow point, four in the back wedge. I took point of the second wedge, which put me in the dead center, where I could see everything. Putty had point of the lead wedge with Rookie flanking him on the left and Martinez on the right. Patel had the left wing and Miller the right. I kept Erickson, Chang, and Dex in the back wedge with me, where they were less exposed. Dex and Erickson could fight if they had to, but they didn't have the same skills as those in the front wedge. Chang had no experience at all. Rookie was new too, but he had his basic training, and he was wearing a heavy suit. Heavy power armor compensated for a lot of shortfalls.

We trotted, and with the assist from our suits, it was more like the speed of a regular human sprinting. I kept my eyes and sensors on full alert, and I trusted the rest of the group to do the same. Each soldier in the front wedge had a sector, and everyone knew the job. Time to trust the training.

We'd covered about two klicks when Patel came on the net via whisper microphone.

"Remote sensor. Twenty degrees right front, three hundred forty meters."

"On it," said Martinez. He dropped to one knee from

his position in the right of the front wedge, and three seconds later his sniper rifle coughed. "Sensor down."

"Sensor down," agreed Patel.

"Confirm, sensor down," said Putty. "Moving."

We started moving again, slower this time, and I listened for any indication that we'd drawn attention from the checkpoint to our north. There was no way to tell what that sensor had picked up before Martinez drilled it or what would happen when it died, so I didn't know what might be headed our way. I checked the hornet drone video briefly, but all I could see was the flashes of gunfire and smoke. The distinctive whine of a bot tank pulse cannon followed by the deep chatter of a heavy conventional gun told me that the enemy still had their hands full, though.

Patel came over the net again, louder this time. "Hold!" But it was too late for Putty, who was at the front and had already triggered the ambush. A whine echoed through the thin forest, like a jet engine warming up, drowning out the sound of the distant battle between tank and checkpoint.

"Pop bot!" I yelled, even though my microphone would pick up a whisper. Most of the team hit the ground in practiced unison as the spherical bot shot from the ground, leaves and dirt flying in every direction as it popped up to four meters and hovered, instantly searching for targets. Chang remained standing to my right but got the idea after a couple seconds and grabbed dirt with the rest of us.

It wouldn't take long to find us. I hadn't assessed the model yet, but most pop bots had motion detectors, infrared heat sensors, and half a dozen other ways to find a target. "Patel, get countermeasures on those sensors!" I said. He didn't need me to tell him, but it gave me something to say to feel like I had control of a shitty situation. Patel's suit had technology built in to fool radars. We all had it to some degree, but nothing as sophisticated as his. It flung flares out to the front between us and the bot to confuse the heat sensors, and it would be projecting electronic spoofing as well. Patel's armor would fight its own high-tech battle with the sensors of the pop bot, playing out some elaborate game preprogrammed by people millions of kilometers away. Lucky us, we got to be the tokens on the game board.

Martinez fired a test shot, but the powerful sniper round ricocheted off the bot's force shield. I sighted through my rifle but held my fire. The fléchettes wouldn't penetrate, and the pulse function would burn out on the energy shield. The only things that had a chance were Putty's and Rookie's heavy guns, and even those would have to pound on the bot for a while to break through.

"Fuck!" said Patel. "Countermeasures aren't working. I don't know what's wrong."

As if to punctuate his point, the pop bot swiveled and targeted Patel. Not only were the countermeasures not working, they were painting a target on him. Four guns slid from the bot's spherical body and snapped into place with a metallic clack. My HUD identified the bot as a Mark 14. The Mark 14 pop bot had two pulse weapons and two that fired projectiles.

"Putty! Hit that thing with everything you have. Now!" I yelled.

Putty pushed himself to a kneeling position and lit up the bot with his Beast. Sparks and dirt flew all around it, but destroying a pop bot was tough. This one was solid metal and polymer with all the sensitive bits safely ensconced deep inside. It was pure engineered death.

All four of the bot's guns jumped to life at once, screaming and popping at the same time, pouring pulses and bullets from the cloud of smoke and dust kicked up from Putty's fire. The ground on the left side of the front wedge churned into a burning volcano around Patel. I fired three measured pulse shots into the center of the bot, and several others added their fire to mine.

"I'm hit!" yelled Patel.

I panicked for a second, and before I could give an order, Rookie had leaped to his feet and sprinted three mechanically assisted steps to put himself between Patel and the pop bot. Flashes sprayed from his armor, but he kept his feet, and after a second he added his Beast fire to Putty's.

"We're wearing it down!" said Putty.

"Martinez, rocket!" I called.

"On it."

"Patel, you with us?" I asked.

"It's bad." The strain in his voice confirmed his assessment. "My suit's running diagnostics now, but most of my systems are dead." That was bad in more ways than one. Not only did I have a man down, but Patel's suit contained most of our countermeasures, and its loss left us vulnerable.

Martinez's rocket whooshed forward, trailing smoke.

The force of the explosion rocked me and made me close my eyes even as my face shield darkened to dim the flash. I opened them again to find the bot spinning, blown back several meters from its original location, lower to the ground.

It wobbled, but hung in the air, then righted itself.

"Engage! Don't let up," I yelled.

A series of lights flashed on the bot, as if it were running diagnostics, trying to reset. A black hole smoked on the upper left side where Martinez's rocket had done its damage, and I sighted my weapon there. Hopefully the rocket had taken out the armor and made it vulnerable. I tried to control my breathing to get a steady shot, which was hard with my heart pounding in my ears.

The bot's guns retracted, and then extended again.

Shit.

I pulled the trigger, but in my haste, I jerked the shot wide, missing the hole, my pulse blast slamming into the bot's armored plating.

Light flashed, and my visor darkened again to protect my vision. When it cleared, the bot had disintegrated. Smoke and small pieces of debris hung in the air where it had been, and a small grass fire flared, churning black smoke into the air. Someone else had made the shot. I scanned our team to see what had happened. Right side of the front wedge. Killer.

"Rookie, check in," I said.

"Uh. I can't see. And I can't read diagnostics. That bot fried something in my HUD."

"Can you manually open your face mask?" I asked.

"Roger."

"Okay. Run a manual test to see what functions you still have. Chang, get up there and help him out."

"Moving, Boss," said Chang. Rookie's armor had at least kept him alive. That was good news. I scrambled to my feet and headed toward Patel to figure out what the bad news was. I reached him a second before Erickson, who dropped down beside us, already grabbing her med bag from a compartment on her armor. She removed Patel's helmet, being careful not to put pressure on the injured man's neck.

"Patel? Come on, buddy. You with us?" Erickson put her face directly over his to gauge his response, then grabbed her scanner.

"Fuck," said Patel.

"What hurts?" asked Erickson.

"Shoulder," said Patel. "Neck. Right side. My suit's toast. It's not even injecting pain suppressors."

Erickson plugged her device into Patel's pockmarked, scorched suit. "Projectile penetrated the armor. Likely broken collarbone. Ninety-four percent chance the bullet is still inside. He's got arterial bleeding. The suit is trying to seal the wound, but it's not functioning right, and there's too much blood."

I watched her work, trying to assess the criticality of the situation from her face, but she was pure business.

"Patel, I'm going to shoot you up with nanites. It's drastic, but we've got to get that bleeding under control, and this is the only way to do it and still save your arm."

"Do it," he gasped.

"How the fuck did you get nanites?" I asked.

"You didn't think I'd spend your money on anything but the best, did you?" She pulled a large needle out of a compartment on the thigh of her armor and concentrated as she put it into the meat of Patel's injured shoulder.

I almost smiled, despite the situation. The nanites would save his life, but they had another side effect. They made him ineligible for continued military service, meaning an automatic medical discharge. They were only used in high-end med facilities, and only as a last resort. But I'd told Erickson what I needed, and she'd come up with an innovative way to make it happen.

Miller's voice broke in over the radio. "Hate to rush you, but we've got to move. We made a ton of noise, and I don't hear the tank anymore."

"Roger," I answered. I tried to pull up the hornet drone video feed, but it had died with Patel's suit. "Any function in your suit at all?"

"I can move," said Patel. "Give me a minute for the pain meds to kick in and I'll be ready."

"You can't take him with us." Erickson fixed me with that glare that medical people always get when they think you're going to do something stupid.

"I'm fine," said Patel, struggling to rise.

"You're a moron," said Erickson. "You can't even get up."

"So. Help me."

"I'll—"

"That's enough," I said, cutting Erickson off before she could say anything else. "You're not coming with us; you'd slow us down. Rookie's suit is damaged. I'll have him go with you and help you to the rear. You can find a friendly patrol and tell them you got lost."

"You can't afford to give up a second soldier," said Patel. "I can make it on my own."

"Chang, what's the diagnosis on Rookie's armor?" I asked.

"It's just the HUD. Let me look at Patel's helmet. If we get a few minutes, I can probably cannibalize it for parts and get Rookie back close to a hundred percent."

I looked at Patel, skeptical.

"Really. I promise. I'll move until I'm clear of the enemy, then pop a beacon."

I stared at him for a moment. Sweat mixed with dust on his face, and the pain showed in his eyes. "Okay. Erickson, how long until the nanites take effect?"

"He'll be stable in ninety seconds." She continued to glare at me, but she had the decency to keep her thoughts to herself. It was a shitty thing to do, sending him off by himself, but we really did need every soldier we had. Even as I made the decision, I knew I'd regret it until we all made it safely back to wherever we'd see each other again. But as soon as he fired off a beacon, a rescue team would find him. He'd be safe. At least physically. It would take them some time to get him back to the orbital base, but once they did, he was going to face the full brunt of what the whole team had done. What I'd done. At least until I got back.

If I got back.

But I didn't have time to dwell on that. I looked at him, and our eyes caught. "Two orders. One: get back safe. Two: stick to the truth."

"The truth?"

"That I dragged you into this. You didn't want to go. Don't try to explain anything you don't know for sure. Tell the docs you got a nanite injection, but don't try to explain where it came from." If things worked, we'd get Kendrick, and Gwan would get what he wanted. In that case, a lot of our transgressions should be forgiven. But if Patel got caught lying . . . it wasn't worth it. They already knew we were down here, so no use hiding it. If he told the truth, hopefully Gwan would give him some cover. If not, I'd work on that once I got back.

Patel took my meaning and nodded. "I couldn't tell them where the nanites came from if I wanted to. For everything else, I won't volunteer information, but if somebody important asks, I'll tell the truth."

"Good man. What about the tracker for Kendrick? Can I get that?"

"It's incorporated into my suit, and it's fried."

"Shit." That meant we'd have to find him another way. Oh well, I'd worry about that when we got there.

"Let's move," I said, and we took off as one. I hated leaving Patel behind. Shit, that's why we came down here in the first place. We didn't leave our own behind. But what could I do? At least he was on the friendly side of the line. And while it hadn't happened the way I'd planned it, he was getting his discharge.

"What the hell *was* that?" Rookie's voice came across the comm, wavering.

"Pop bot," said Dex. "Mark 14."

"They're smaller in the simulation," said Rookie.

I wanted silence on the net, but it was better to let

the man speak. The first time a soldier sees live rounds fired in anger—the first time he sees another soldier get hit—you never know how he'll react. Better to let him talk than bottle it up and have the worry eat him from the inside.

And silence didn't matter at this point anyway. We'd given away our position. The only thing we could do was move as fast and as far as we could before the enemy found us.

"Hey, Rookie. What made you jump in front of that fire?" I asked.

"You say that everybody on the team has a purpose," he said. "I figured maybe mine was to protect Patel."

"You did good," I said.

CHAPTER 13

W E'D GONE ALMOST TWO KILOMETERS WHEN AN alert flashed in my heads-up. "Down!" I broadcasted to the squad. A moment later the low hum of a drone buzzed overhead, not directly above us, but within a few hundred meters. Of course they'd sent a drone. And based on the size, one with a lot of capabilities too. Their pop bot had engaged us—they might even have video from it, since Patel's suit was supposed to suppress that transmission, but he'd been hit. Either way, they wouldn't know which direction we headed after the pop bot died. We could have hit it and retreated. Hell, maybe we should have. They probably sent a drone into no-man's-land too, looking for us there. That started me worrying about Patel again, but I couldn't linger on it. We had our own problems in the form of a small disc, maybe a half meter across, flying a hundred meters up at about forty kilometers an hour.

The squad hit the ground almost as one this time, going motionless. Like with the pop bot, it wouldn't make us invisible to the drone, but it would at least defeat the motion sensors. It probably had three more redundant systems including visual, thermal, and IR, but motion sensing would always be the first trigger.

"Electronic camo," I called to the team, flipping my own suit into that mode at the same time. I couldn't see it, but my armor would generate a field that showed the same heat as the surrounding area, defeating thermals while becoming virtually invisible to IR too. It made us hard to detect, but it also used a shitload of battery power. It wouldn't have helped with the pop bot, because it had already seen us. This time, though, it gave us a chance. Still, we couldn't afford to do it for long with the power drain, especially with more distance to cover.

"You want me to take a shot?" asked Martinez.

I considered it, which spoke to how good Martinez was with his weapon. Hitting a target flying at that speed sounds easy enough, but it's extremely difficult for an average person. Add in that he'd have to hit it in a sensitive area the size of two fists, and it became near impossible. "What are your odds?"

"One in three," said Martinez without hesitating.

"Let it pass. See if it flies by," I said. If he shot and missed, it would lock in on us immediately. Even if he hit it, the enemy would get some indication of our location from the last known broadcast and any kind of homing device it had.

I found myself holding my breath, and slowly let it out, trying to calm down. The drone continued on its path, heading to the north, perpendicular to our route. I followed it, magnifying the view through my visor as it started to disappear.

"I think we're good," I said. "Let's move."

I glanced at the drone one more time where it had almost disappeared, only to see it start to grow again. "Get down!"

"Take the shot?" asked Martinez, no change to his voice.

"Yeah. Everyone else, whether he hits or misses, be prepared. We move. Five seconds after Martinez's shot, drop your camo to save power. Move at full speed." That would suck power too. We couldn't run at top pace for long. Neither our bodies nor our suits would handle it. But it wouldn't do any good to save power if the enemy brought in suicide drones or heavier ones with missiles.

As a wise drill sergeant once shouted at me: *You can't use power if you're dead.*

I checked my map and plotted a route. We didn't want to move directly toward our target, as any sensor that picked us up would give the enemy a good projection of where we were headed. At the same time, we couldn't head perpendicular because that would run us down the front line, and we'd hit another checkpoint before long. I decided to split the difference and head on a course thirty degrees north of our destination. Assuming Martinez made the shot. If he didn't, it wouldn't matter much where we ran. We'd be looking for a place where we could make a stand. Probably our last.

The drone continued to draw closer on a path that would take it maybe fifty meters to the east of our position at the closest spot. Martinez would fire before then, though. When it passed close it would be directly perpendicular to his line of fire, which would mean he'd have to lead it more. Firing from farther away gave him a better angle, as he'd be shooting closer to head-on. I resisted the urge to look over at Martinez, even though he held the survival of the squad in his steady hands.

Trust the team.

His rifle popped behind me, and almost instantly the drone lurched, dropping several meters before righting itself. It wobbled for a second, then slewed violently down and to the side until it crunched into the ground, kicking up dust and forest floor. It skidded to a halt against the trunk of a tree, and for a moment we had silence.

"Let's move." I spoke on the squad net. "Heading of fifty-five degrees." I took off at a run, not bothering to check that everyone was following. The trail person would take responsibility for that and call in if we had a problem. Right now we had to put as much distance as we could between ourselves and where the enemy thought we were.

Again.

Two fast-movers screamed in the sky a little to the north—I think it was two. I couldn't see them through the trees, and even if I could, by the time you look at the sound, the ships are gone. The distinctive hiss of an anti-air missile came right after. None of it seemed to be directed at us, which was a good thing. The anti-air missile hadn't been far enough away to be ours—it had to be enemy—which meant that the fast-movers were . . . friendly? Maybe they were flying cover for a rescue mission to pick up Patel. Maybe—just maybe—it was Gwan sending some cover for us. That was a stretch, but not out of the question. Whatever. Anything that distracted the bad guys helped us. I didn't hear an explosion, so I guessed the missile whiffed. But the ships didn't return, either.

We ran in silence for almost fifteen minutes, engaging the sensors built into our helmets to scan for enemy activity. Part of me expected a rocket strike on the area around the downed drone, but for whatever reason, none came.

The enemy had to know that their drone *and* pop bot went down, and they had to at least suspect the reason for it. They wouldn't have a perfect fix on us, but they'd be able to estimate based on where they lost contact. They'd know how long we'd had to run and about how much distance we could cover. Somewhere an intel tech would be programming a circle on a digital map, expanding it every few minutes to encompass our possible locations. All we could do was make that circle as big as possible.

A shot sounded from the south, and I almost went to ground before I realized it was too far away to be targeting us. It could have been random—a misfire or an antsy patrol—or it could have been something else. My heads-up didn't show anything, so I kept running. I tried to avoid the subconscious desire to speed up, keeping a steady pace at about sixty percent of the suit's max capacity, which was faster than a sprint for someone without mechanical augmentation. Dead branches and leaves popped and crunched as we plummeted across the forest floor, but there was no help for it. We needed distance more than we needed silence or to hide our trail.

After several more minutes, a whine came from the east, building, and this time I dove into a prone position, toggled my electronic camouflage to the highest level, and called for the squad to do the same. Two aircraft whipped overhead, drowning out all thoughts, loud enough to trigger the sound dampening in my helmet. Unlike the last set, I was pretty sure these were enemy. They passed in an instant, the echo of their engines still reverberating in my brain. I hadn't gotten a good look at them through the canopy of green above, but they sounded like GA-43s—they had a low-pitched rumble beneath the whine that stood out from other craft. Flying the ground attack fighters this close to the front without some sort of higher air cover would be risky, so they probably had other fast-movers in the area as well. My suit had the capability to scan the sky, but that would involve an active sensor, which would help them see us too. I kept it off. We didn't need to know that badly.

Curiosity and dead cats and all.

"You think they saw us?" Killer asked, once the sound of engines disappeared in the distance.

"We're still alive, so . . . no." I popped back to my feet and started jogging again, dialing it back to about fifty percent on the speed to save a bit of power, which was becoming an issue. They could build all the tech in the world into our suits, but it always came down to juice in the battery packs. Without a charging station nearby, we'd get only what we picked up from our solar chargers, which wouldn't be much in the shade of the forest.

After another six minutes we reached a pretty steep

slope, so I circled around to the right, which would put us closer to the ultimate destination. Something rumbled pretty far behind us, but the woods distorted sounds. I couldn't tell how far back or what it was, and it didn't seem like a good use of time trying to figure it out.

"Gas, I'm going to have to stop soon. I'm under forty percent on my power," Putty called over the comm. I glanced at my own gauge. Fifty-two percent. That made sense, because the heavier suits that Putty and Rookie wore used more juice, especially when covering long distances.

"Roger," I answered. "We'll start looking for a place to recharge." We had a little time, still, but not much. As a general rule I didn't like to get below thirty-three percent. The suits would still function, but the last thing we wanted to do was get into a firefight with our batteries running down. We'd have to use our emergency B packs if that happened.

But it's hard to recharge when somebody's looking for you. To employ our more powerful stationary solar chargers, we had to get into the sun, which meant no overhead concealment, so anything passing above could see us. We could use the low reflective remote solar arrays, which would help, but it was a trade-off since they wouldn't generate as much power as the shinier stuff. A lot of that was moot, though: we *needed* power. We'd have to figure out the rest once we found a place to recharge. I led the team farther uphill. If we were going to be vulnerable to stuff overhead, we could at least keep the high ground in case something came at us on the surface.

After several minutes circling around about two thirds of the way to the crest of the outcropping, I found our spot. "Dex, Erickson, take up outposts. Dex, you take thirty degrees, Erickson two-ten."

"Roger," they replied simultaneously.

"Putty, you and Rookie get the low-reflect chargers laid out in that clearing above us, then get yourselves back under the trees. Report once you're hooked up, and we'll get the smaller suits charging too. We won't need as long."

Putty gave me the thumbs-up and moved to comply. I turned to find Killer staring at me.

"What?" I asked her over a private channel.

"Nothing," she said.

"Come on. Spill."

She hesitated. "You're a totally different person in this environment."

"How so?"

"You're . . . efficient. More mature."

I shrugged, not sure how to respond at first. "I guess people shooting at you will do that."

"I guess so. It's a good look, though." She kept staring at me for a couple of seconds before turning away and digging into a suit compartment.

"How do you mean?" I asked.

"I never saw this side of you before. I saw all the slick shit and the lack of care for the rules, and it made me think you were a bad squad leader."

"You mean I'm not?" It was a sincere question. I found, unexpectedly, that I really cared what she thought. I don't know why.

"You recruited a good team, and you know how to get the most out of them."

"They're good, and they believe in themselves," I said.

"They believe in themselves because of *you*. You trust them, so they trust themselves."

My face heated, and I'm sure my embarrassment showed. "Thanks."

She hesitated, as if she had something else she wanted to say. Finally she spoke again. "I'm working for Dentonn—"

I started to interject, but she held her hand up to forestall me.

"Let me get this out," she continued. "I've been working up my courage, and if you stop me, I won't get through it. I'm working for Colonel Dentonn. But then, you knew that. That's why you had Patel watching me."

I almost laughed. Sometimes I forgot that other people could be smart too. "You caught that?"

"Subtlety is not his strong suit."

"You're right. I did know. At least I had a pretty good idea you were working for somebody."

"When did you figure it out?"

"When you showed up to go on the mission with us. There was no way you'd have gotten on that drop ship without top cover. You wouldn't have taken the risk to your career."

"Ah." She paused, as if considering it. "Yeah, shit. I didn't see that." She paused again, considering her next thought. "So what are we really doing here?"

"We're getting Kendrick back."

"There's more to it than that," she said.

I did some quick thinking about how much to tell her. "You're right. There is. But I'm not ready to tell you what yet. I hope you can understand that."

She nodded. "That's fair. I did just tell you I was a spy sent to watch you."

"I'll promise you this: when you need to know, I'll make sure that you do," I said.

"Deal. So about Kendrick. What's the plan there? Because what we're doing is getting close to the line of what's rational. We've been out too long, and we've got too far to go. The enemy knows we're here, and it's only a matter of time until they get a sensor over us. Hell, they might have a satellite looking right now."

"Not likely," I said. "We mostly push each other's satellites out of orbit as fast as we can seed them. They're super vulnerable up there."

She blew air out loudly. "So then another asset."

"What am I supposed to do about that?" I said it with a little more venom than I needed to. I wasn't mad at her, but I was frustrated with how things had gone so far, and Killer made a convenient target.

Miller took a few seconds before responding, keeping her tone measured. "How long can we keep going? We're off course, we've got to recharge, and who knows what the enemy has out there looking for us. We're rushing blind to get to a place that we don't even know Kendrick is."

"He's there," I said.

"You can't know that."

Except I did, even if I wasn't going to tell her the truth about how. "My whole team knows that. We have an SOP. I've drilled everyone on it. If you get left behind for whatever reason, go to ground in Kiergard and wait."

"That doesn't mean he did it."

"He did."

"I don't get how you can be so confident," she said.

"Because I drill it into my team from day one. Even Rookie knows," I said. And that was true, even if it wasn't the *whole* truth. I hadn't been inclined to change my mind about the mission in the first place, but her challenging me on it made me dig in my heels even further. "We're going to find him."

She shook her head slowly. "I wish I believed you."

"So what would you have me do? Quit?"

She shook her head. "Come on. You know it's not about quitting. Give me a little respect. There's no shame in abandoning an untenable position and saving the rest of your team."

"Untenable? We're winning."

She laughed at that. "You believe that?"

"If I don't believe, who will?" I asked.

She considered it. "Yeah, that's a good point. But do me a favor. Take a few minutes here to think. Whatever you intended when we started, this wasn't it. So make sure you've got your objectives clear, reset, and come up with a new way to get us from here to Kendrick and home again. Preferably one that doesn't get us killed."

I considered her words. On the surface, they were simple, and maybe even a little patronizing. But tone didn't bother me. What she was saying was smart, and it was exactly what I needed to hear from a peer. My plan *was* a bit off track, though it was getting better. And I *did* have a few moments to work on it. "You're right," I said finally.

She looked at me, stunned, as if me saying that had almost stopped her heart from beating. "Uh, okay then."

"I need to walk," I said. She narrowed her eyes, confused, so I clarified, "When I think, it helps if I move."

"Ah. Got it. I'll leave you to it." She paused. "One last question before you go."

"Sure."

"Everybody on your team has a purpose, and you said that you knew from the moment I showed up at the drop ship I was a spy. But you took me on anyway, and you've kept me along. So in your eyes, I have a purpose. What is it?"

I studied her closer now. She had a strong jaw, and her brown eyes didn't waver as she held mine. There was more to this woman than I'd thought. More than just a rule-following automaton. So I decided to be honest. "That's easy. Your purpose is to observe and to tell the truth."

"To tell the truth? That's it?" Her face and body language said she didn't believe me.

"Yes, that's it. Nobody is going to believe what I say happened. And they shouldn't. I'm a liar, and a lot of people know that. But you're not someone who would lie to a superior, and people know that too. And they'll know that you're not just parroting what I want you to say. Would anyone believe that I told you to lie and you just accepted that and did it?"

"Definitely not," she said.

"Right. They'll believe you. So that's your job. Observe everything, and tell the truth."

"Even if it doesn't help you?"

Even if you think *it won't help me, yes.* I nodded.

She thought about it. "I can do that."

I smiled. "I know you can. Or you wouldn't be here. Now. Since we're being honest, I have a question for you. You're working for Dentonn. Why?"

"He's a colonel. I follow orders."

"Bullshit. There's more to it than that."

The side of her mouth quirked up in a cute little excuse for a grin. "Okay. If I'm being honest, I didn't like you, and part of me wanted to see you go down."

"You might still get your wish."

"Somehow I doubt it," she said.

I WALKED THE perimeter of our little patrol base, checking the lines of sight for the sentries, talking to each person for a moment, seeing how they felt. Soldiers would hide little ailments, but if you asked, they'd tell you. And once you got them talking, they'd tell you what they thought about pretty much everything. I waited for somebody to tell me how fucked up the mission was, but nobody did. Erickson did talk for five minutes about a movie she'd been wanting to see, and she seemed pretty broken up that she was missing it, but other than that, everyone appeared to be okay with what we were doing. Chang didn't have much to say, because she was working hard to get Rookie's helmet functional, but she assured me she'd have it ready before we moved.

When I reached Dex, he had something more important on his mind. "You want to tell me what we're doing out here for real?"

"Yes, I do," I said without hesitating. I hadn't been ready to tell Miller, but I'd told Dex I wouldn't lie to him, and I was finally ready to hold to that. Plus, I needed his help. "We do have to get Kendrick, but it's not just that."

"That much I knew."

"And you have a big part in it. Don't tell the others, because not everybody knows." In fact, nobody knew, because I was only taking the truth thing so far. "I sent Kendrick to Kiergard on purpose."

"What?" Based on the look he gave me, he hadn't guessed. In some ways, that was good news.

"Kiergard is run by a mob boss by the name of Ma Ventnor. You might have heard of her."

"Sure."

"She's the reason that nobody hits the town. I learned that she's in bed with two different major defense contracting companies, and I believe that those companies then put pressure on the government and the military to protect the town."

"How did you discover this?"

"Let's just say that I used to work around some of Ma's organization before I joined the military. Not for her, exactly, but some freelance stuff."

"So this is personal," said Dex.

"A little," I said.

Dex stared me down.

"Okay, yes, it's fucking personal. I had to join the military to get away from them."

Dex nodded his head, probably without knowing it. "Where do I fit in?"

"Ma doesn't trust distributed computing. She keeps her records locally, in a facility—"

"In Kiergard," said Dex, finishing my sentence.

"Exactly," I said.

"And you want me to go in there and get something."

"Yes. While I cause a distraction. And maybe blow the fuck out of her facility and her goons as a bonus. I want to make her pay. And it's not just for what she's done to me. She's got a hand in this entire war. She keeps it going, because along with the defense companies, she's turning a profit from it."

"That *is* fucked up," admitted Dex. "But you're not altruistic. There's bank in this for you, right?"

"Yes."

"And I'm getting a cut."

"You are. Everyone is. Paid into untraceable off-planet accounts. Accessible to you as soon as you get out of the military."

"Why not now?"

"There's going to be too much heat for you to touch it while you're still in."

"That's the truth?"

"That's the truth."

"It better be a big number," he said.

"Dex, you know I don't do anything small."

WHEN I REACHED Putty, who was lying on his back in a patch of grass with his muted solar array splayed out flat beside him, he had questions as well, but as per his usual, he was a lot less serious about it.

"There's a reason why the enemy hasn't found us yet, isn't there?"

"Yeah, there probably is. You figured that out all on your own?"

He tapped the side of his head. "I'm not just a pretty face, even if that's why your sister is going to love me. You want to tell me the reason?"

"Do you want to know?" I asked.

He thought about it. "Not really. Just offering in case you wanted to get it off your chest."

"I'm fine if you are."

"That's good. You know I count on you to figure out the hard stuff and just tell me what I need to know. As far as I see it, we're soldiers. We don't get paid to think. We get paid to fight."

"Do you really believe that?" I asked.

"I don't know. It sure is easier to live that way, though. Thinking is hard."

"Yeah."

"Just tell me this," he said. "Are we doing the right thing?"

I met his eyes. "Are we ever?"

He laughed. "No, seriously."

"Seriously?" I paused. "Yeah, we're doing the right thing." And as I thought about it, I realized that I wasn't lying this time.

CHAPTER 14

AFTER CHARGING, WE HAD ABOUT FIFTEEN KLICKS as the crow flies to the town of Kiergard, where I expected to find Kendrick, but closer to twenty-five by the route Miller and I had chosen. We had to avoid the high-traffic avenues of approach, and that meant coming in from the northwest, which was almost the direct opposite of where we were now. My intel work had shown that there shouldn't be much enemy in the town—hopefully none, but my read wasn't perfect, and I couldn't rule out a garrison of some kind, in which case we could get there and find ourselves completely unable to enter. The town was surprisingly small, with about four hundred buildings, so it *shouldn't* hold a major force. Ma liked it that way. She thought it let her keep better control of things. Limited law enforcement to bribe, and a lot of the people who lived around there were quiet farmer types. Emphasis on the *quiet*. Whatever happened, we'd still have to find Kendrick when we got there, and while four hundred buildings doesn't sound like much, when you're looking for a person in only one of them, it's more than enough.

We moved out at 1800 hours, and the sun would set at 2034. With no swamp in the way, I intended to keep going and to enter the town at night. Whatever force the enemy had there, we'd try to take them by surprise—not that the enemy couldn't see at night. Of course they could. But it's still human nature to let your guard down in the dark. Circadian rhythms, or some shit like that. I don't know—I probably saw it in a training video somewhere. Or maybe I made it up.

I guess we'd find out.

We covered the first six klicks in no time. All the stray sounds of gunfire and fast-movers that had plagued us previously had disappeared. Finally, Putty put his hand up to signal a stop when we reached a horizontal danger area. That's fancy military talk for a road. I'd expected it. It was four lanes—the main east-to-west road in the area. That also meant it would be the most watched piece of terrain in the entire region. I'd have avoided it totally if I could have, but we had to cross it to reach the side of the town I wanted to hit.

Pretty much the same reason the chicken crossed, I figured.

It was a simple enough battle drill. Putty took a position to cover the road to the east—where we most expected traffic—and Rookie took up a spot covering the west. We maintained our cover and observed for five minutes. Four civilian vehicles passed—beat-up, older things. So old, in fact, that they were actually driven by people and not AIs. Very quaint. Two passed going in each direction, none of them within thirty seconds of the other. They weren't a threat to us physically, but we couldn't afford for one to spot us. You never knew who was in them. A lot of civilians wouldn't know one force from the other, so maybe they'd drive by and think nothing of it. But what if one carried a veteran? Or even an active Confed soldier. Or just a regular old busybody that was too nosy for their own good. Everyone had a comm, and with one call, we'd be in a lot of trouble.

With just the sporadic traffic, as long as we moved quickly, we should be okay. We'd cross in pairs: Miller and Dex first, then me and Chang. Once we established far-side security, Putty and Rookie would come over while Erickson and Martinez took their near-side duties. Those two would cross last. I'd set it up that way because I'd trained with them more than any of the others, and I knew they'd do it right. Plus, if somehow they got cut off, I trusted those two to handle things on their own more than the others except for Putty. But his role was determined by his suit: we couldn't get our heavies cut off.

I tuned my sensors as tight as I could to focus on sound, but it didn't give me much clarity with the background noises of the woods starting to come alive in the early evening. We couldn't wait forever, so eventually I gave in and signaled the first team to move. Dex and Killer sprinted across the concrete and disappeared into the woods on the other side. After thirty seconds, I called Chang and we moved out.

I heard the vehicle before I saw it, but not by much. It came from the east, from the town, fast—maybe two hundred klicks per hour. We'd almost reached the far side, but no way would it miss seeing us. I glanced over at Chang just in time to see her freeze between the road and the wood line.

No!

I thought the word, then I yelled it into the net as she raised her rifle to her shoulder and fired off a fléchette round. The vehicle—a flat red civilian thing with a small truck bed—swerved violently one way and then the other, skidding, before finally righting itself and coming to a stop on the side of the road, thirty meters from us.

"Everyone move now," I said. "Go!" I added, and finally everyone snapped out of their states of shock. The gig was up, and we had no choice but to make a run for it.

I didn't see the old lady get out of the vehicle until she slammed the door. She had to be at least eighty, and she stalked toward us. "What in the absolute *fuck* are you doing?" She spoke in a different language, but the translator in my helmet had no trouble parsing it for me.

Chang hadn't moved other than lowering her rifle, and she was the closest to the new arrival.

"Chang, move out. I've got this," I said. I didn't know how Chang would react, so I couldn't have her near the civvie. I didn't have a clue what I was going to do, but what we were *not* going to do was shoot an old lady. That's the *only* thing I knew. You don't really expect to run into a situation like this on a military mission. There's no training video for how to deal with a pissed-off octogenarian. "Everybody move," I broadcast again. "Get some distance. Rally one klick out. Miller, you pick the site. I'll catch up."

"Gas, you shouldn't—"

"Just fucking move, Miller!" I cut her off, and she was going to be pissed at my tone, but I had a short old lady stomping toward me, and I didn't have time to deal with back talk.

The old lady stopped four paces from me, all gray-haired one-point-six meters of her. She wagged her index finger at me. "You can't shoot at a fucking civilian vehicle!"

"Yes, ma'am," I said. What else could I say? She had a point. Plus, I didn't want her telling anyone about our position. "Sorry about that."

"Sorry. Pfft. You could have killed me. Dumbass soldiers, playing at war. Always getting your panties in a bunch and shooting at things you've got no business shooting."

I didn't know whether to be amused or scared. "Again, I'm very sorry, ma'am. My troops are a little bit on edge, that's all."

"On edge. What have you got to be on edge about? Nobody's shooting at *you*. I nearly shit myself."

People probably *would* be shooting at us if they knew we were here, but something told me she didn't want to hear that. She was going to like the next part even less. "Ma'am, I'm going to need to take your communicator."

"My . . . what the fuck are you talking about, dumbass? I'm not giving you—" I have to admit, I was pretty impressed with the accuracy with which my helmet translated her epithets.

"Ma'am, I'm afraid I have to insist—"

"And I'm afraid that you can kiss my old, wrinkled ass."

I stood there, unable to speak. I mean . . . how do you respond to that?

"Why do you need it?" she asked, probably more to get the conversation over with than because she really cared what I wanted.

I made the snap decision that my best option was the truth. What can I say? She intimidated me. "We can't have you calling in our position."

She looked at me like a teacher who had asked a question when I hadn't been paying attention in class. "Why would I do that? Who would I even call?"

"Our enemies?"

She looked up and rolled her eyes. "Sonny, I don't care which side you're on, though I do pity your commander, having such a moron for a soldier. I'm eighty-four years old. Seventy years of that have been in Kiergard. Do you know how many times my town has changed hands in my lifetime?"

"No, ma'am—"

"Nine! That's how many. I don't care which side you're on because you're *all* the enemy. Every last one of you gun-toting idiots is a danger to folks like me who are just trying to live their lives. You want my communicator? You shoot me and take it."

I couldn't form words. I believed her. Every word. If she was lying, she was the best actor the galaxy had ever seen. I tried to think, assess the situation. She'd come from Kiergard and was heading the other way. In theory, we'd be there and on them before she got back to town. "You said you're from Kiergard?"

"That's right—"

I cut her off before she could call me a dumbass again. "Are there troops there right now?"

"There are *always* troops there."

"Do you know how many?"

"What do I look like? A spy? I have no idea. More than ten. Maybe as many as twenty. I don't pay any attention to you assholes if I don't have to. Until your dumb asses *shoot at me*."

"Yes, ma'am. Again, very sorry about that. I'm going now. You have a good evening."

This time she stood speechless. "I can go, just like that?"

"Just like that."

"You're not afraid I'm going to give you away."

"You said you wouldn't."

She considered it, and then nodded. "Right. I won't. You be safe."

"I'll try."

"And don't shoot any civilians!"

"Absolutely not."

She hesitated another few seconds. "Okay then." She turned and stomped back toward her vehicle.

I headed into the woods.

I CAUGHT UP to the others right where I told them to rally. Miller had them in a hasty defensive position covering all directions. "Thanks for that, Chang," I said.

"Sorry."

I let it go. She knew she'd fucked up, so I didn't feel the need to dwell on it. Part of it was my fault for bringing a soldier not used to fighting on the ground. But we needed her, so there was nothing for it, and I didn't beat myself up too badly, either. "Let's go. Wedges. Move out."

We started moving again, and Miller contacted me over a private channel. "What happened?"

"She chewed my ass, that's what happened." I spoke the words a bit more harshly than necessary, but I was embarrassed.

"But what did you do?" From the tone of her voice, I got the idea that she was asking me if I killed the woman, which was pretty fucked up but not totally unreasonable. We both knew people who probably would have.

"I didn't kill her."

"I didn't think you did," she said, but I could hear the relief in her voice.

"Would you have?" I pushed some low-lying vegetation away with my arm so I could force my way through.

She thought about it. "No. But it's a tough situation."

I appreciated that she told the truth. "Yeah, it was. No book for that, right?"

She stumbled as one of her feet slipped out from under her for a second. "Nope. So what *did* you do?"

"I asked her for her comm."

"Oh, that's smart. I wouldn't have thought of that."

"Yeah, well, she didn't give it to me." I slowed my pace to keep my interval because Putty had to slow to work his way around some impassable ground.

"No shit? She . . . so she stared down a soldier in full mech gear and told you no?"

"Yep."

"That's kind of badass," said Miller.

"Yeah it is. She's eighty-four. You know what I want to be doing when I'm eighty-four?"

"What's that?"

"Getting drunk in bed with my thirty-year-old lover."

She stopped walking for a second. "You're such an asshole."

"Yeah, but I just got reamed by an eighty-four-year-old civilian, so cut me a break."

She laughed. "You can't make shit like this up."

"You really can't."

WE MADE IT to the outskirts of Kiergard under the cover of darkness with only minor incidents—we had to stop a couple of times and go to ground as aircraft passed overhead—but beyond that, it seemed like people had stopped looking for us, or they were looking in the wrong places. I didn't know if I should chalk that up to incompetence on their part or something someone on our side was doing without my knowledge. I didn't really care. They hadn't found us, and that was all that mattered. That, getting Kendrick, fucking over Ma Ventnor, and then working on an exfil and getting our asses out of here.

We deployed in a ragged line in the trees about half a klick from the outermost building in town. I'd picked high ground so we could see most of the town through our various night optics. Thermals showed heat from most of the buildings, as the evening was cool and the relative warmth inside bled through windows and thin walls. Only one building didn't. A large, dark building that took up most of a block on our side of town. Ma's place.

Our collective scans showed seven people outside. It wasn't late enough to assume that all of them were soldiers on guard, and I'd already made the decision to wait until the early hours of the morning to make our assault. I wanted to minimize—or hopefully eliminate—civilian casualties that weren't thugs for Ma.

That's when I noticed the bot tank.

I highlighted it on the squad display map and then contacted Killer. "Is this what I think it is?"

"Shit," she said. Apparently it was. Not that I had any doubt. I was just hoping she would give me some other plausible explanation.

"That's what I thought," I said. "The old lady said ten to twenty soldiers, but she completely forgot to mention the fucking bot tank."

"Maybe she didn't know."

"Maybe," I allowed. It was on the far side of town from us, which is why I didn't see it right away. Maybe she lived on this side of town. Maybe it was as much a part of the town as the bank or grocery store and she'd just gotten used to it, like the stink if you live near a factory. It didn't matter why. This changed everything. Being on the far side of town, while it seemed helpful on the surface, was now the worst possible position for us. Sure, it made it less likely that it would spot us here in our observation position, but it also made it impossible for us to attack it and take it out before entering the town unless we circled to the other side.

We had *some* advantages. Stationed here in town, it would have a higher filter than the one we'd set for our tank when it went against the enemy checkpoint. Being in town, it had to be *sure* something was a target before it could engage. It couldn't randomly fire and risk taking out the old men's yoga club. Or hitting something that belonged to Ma. But a lot of that advantage evaporated once we showed ourselves.

Once it ID'd us, we were pretty well fucked. It would have a chance to maneuver on us and fire from a distance, maximizing its advantages. On top of that, we'd end up fighting it in the middle of town, which would cause a ton of collateral damage, and not to the part of town that I wanted. Even before the old lady yelled at me, I'd wanted to avoid that. It would suck to win a battle and find Kendrick only to end up with an entire town full of pissed-off civilians coming after us with torches and pitchforks. Without knowing the enemy bot tank's thoughts on civilian casualties, I couldn't risk it.

Putty's voice came over the squad net. "So, are we going to talk about the bot tank, or nah?"

I laughed to myself. Leave it to Putty to put it out there. "I'm working on it. I don't suppose you have a plan?"

"How many times do I have to say I'm not much of a thinker?" he said.

"I've got three rockets left," said Martinez. "Two HE and one armor-piercing." That was good to know, but the HE—high explosive—wouldn't do much more than explode against the tank's armor while simultaneously drawing a direct line to him for the tank's targeting array. It would be like one of those fancy desserts they make in high-end restaurants . . . it would look pretty, but not be very satisfying. Give me a plain old warm brownie with ice cream on top any day. But I digress.

The armor-piercing at least had a chance. But with a bot tank, he'd still have to hit some critical piece of electronics inside what basically amounted to a solid piece of metal. And he'd have to do it while the tank was trying to kill him. It might come to that as our only option, but I wanted to consider alternatives first.

"Okay," I said. "We'll put that one in the bank. Dex, can you do anything?"

"Against a bot tank?" he asked.

"You were able to hack the other one," I offered.

"Sure. But it wasn't trying to kill me, and I had to plug into it directly for several minutes."

"So we have to get close enough to plug in," I said, hopefully.

"First," said Dex, "no. I'm not doing that. It's suicide. And second, even if I could get to it, I can't physically jack in. It's not our equipment, so it would take a *lot* longer."

"Roger," I said. "That's out. Martinez, how much hyper-nitrate do you have?" I'd had him bring it along to blow a big hole in Ma's building and provide a distraction for Dex, but the bot tank changed that plan. We had to make the tank a priority, and if that meant scrapping the rest of the mission, so be it. Revenge isn't particularly rewarding if you're too dead to enjoy it.

"Enough. Probably. Four kilograms," said Martinez.

That was a lot of explosive power. It would be enough if we put it in the right place. But it wasn't a shape charge, and we couldn't deliver it from a distance. Someone would have to get either on top of or under the tank, place the charge, and then get out of there before detonating it. That made Martinez's rocket sound good by comparison. But it could, in theory, limit the collateral damage, depending on where the charge went off in relation to buildings. We might not have a choice, though, because we definitely had to hit the tank.

"You're not really thinking about doing this, are you?" It was Miller, speaking on a private channel.

"We're here. We can't quit now." And we couldn't. I could scrap my revenge, but I'd put Kendrick in there, and we weren't leaving him. No way.

Silence. I could almost hear her saying that we absolutely *could* quit. "So we sneak in, find him, and get out. We don't engage."

Yes, we could do that. If, you know, we *could* do it. It was a long shot. But if we snuck in and found him without alerting the enemy, it gave us the best chance to protect the town. And more important, it gave us the best chance to protect *ourselves*. The problem was, we couldn't sneak in wearing power armor. Every sensor the enemy had would pick that up. It meant someone going in wearing street clothes. No weapons. Someone posing as a civilian could probably sneak past the enemy sensors, which meant they were only at risk to a

Confed soldier or one of Ma's people getting a visual ID. The old lady hadn't known their numbers, and she certainly hadn't told me about their patrolling patterns.

I was also pretty sure that dressing like a civilian was illegal, but that didn't really bother me. It wasn't the bad kind of illegal. (For the record, you know something is bad-illegal if other soldiers look down on you for it. Killing civilians, prisoners, or torturing people—those were bad, and every soldier worth anything would turn on you if you even considered them. But sneaking around out of uniform? Nobody cared. Mostly. Certainly nobody in my crew.) Yes, it was dangerous, and in a different way than doing battle with a tank. Fighting a tank, even though it had us outgunned, gave us at least a slim chance. If we lost, we'd die, but we'd die facing the enemy. Doing something we knew how to do. If I sent someone into the town unarmed, though, they risked death, sure, but they also risked capture. They were going in essentially green, too—none of us were trained for espionage. Which meant I couldn't ask any of the team to do that.

"You're right," I said finally. "I'll do it."

"You?" Miller's tone might as well have said, *What are you, an idiot?* "You can't do it. You need to lead the squad in case something goes wrong. Shit, you need to be here to lead them home in case something goes *really* wrong."

I couldn't argue with her. Going into the town alone wasn't my job. None of this was my job—but this particular task wasn't anybody's job. So who else was there? Putty and Rookie were out. Dex and Chang weren't the right kind of soldiers, though I could imagine Chang volunteering. I could also imagine her taking ridiculous risks, and I wasn't having that. Martinez could do it, but he was our sniper and our best chance at cover if things *did* go to shit. Erickson . . . she wasn't suited to sneaking around. That left me. "I've got no—"

"I'll do it," said Miller.

"What?"

"You don't have another fit. Martinez could do it, but then we lose our sniper." She'd thought it through the same way I had. "That leaves you or me. It can't be you, so the remaining choice is obvious."

She said it in such a calm, logical way that she almost convinced me. "You take the squad," I said. "We'll go to them together and put you in charge right now. They'll handle that."

"No they won't," she said. "Without you, there *is* no squad. Everyone who is here is here because of you . . . that came out the wrong way. I'm not blaming you. I'm saying that we're all here because you convinced us."

I noticed that she said *we*. Except I hadn't tried to convince her. I didn't have time to unpack that at the moment. She was serious in her desire to do it, despite her reasons for coming along originally. "You know you'd have to go in without armor," I said.

"Yep. So you better start working on what you're going to do about that bot tank if they catch me."

"We'll have to wait for morning." I couldn't believe I was agreeing with her. "A civilian moving around late at night would be too suspicious, and we don't know if the enemy has established a curfew." A new young

HAD HALF OF THE SQUAD POWER DOWN AND SLEEP while the other half kept watch so that when the sun came up and the town lurched to life, we were ready to go. Everyone had their part, depending on what happened, but it started with Killer. She stripped out of her armor and left it with Martinez, who was going to hold his position no matter what and observe from the high ground. He could engage from there if things went wrong. Scrounging through our civvies, not much would fit her—since she wasn't part of the original team, she hadn't packed clothes like the rest of us—so we incorporated her undersuit and decided that we'd try to sell the story that she was out for a morning run. That would also allow her to cover ground quickly without drawing suspicion. It wasn't perfect. She was still an attractive young woman nobody had seen in town before, and her square shoulders, muscular arms, and rigid demeanor almost screamed *soldier*. But hopefully the tight bottoms would distract any Confed soldiers from thinking about that. Not that they distracted me.

I barely noticed.

She planned to run a zigzag route through the town that would let her pass every building in hopes that Kendrick would see her and make contact. Then we'd just have to figure out how to get him out. Dex wired her up with a subvocal microphone but didn't have anything invisible where she could hear us. She could broadcast but not receive, which was better than nothing. We'd hear everything going on around her.

She ran the first road, and it was . . . anticlimactic. Yep. We all sat there on edge, ready for anything, and all we heard was her breathing, her feet slapping against the pavement. Running. It's hard to imagine anything more boring than running yourself, but up until then, I'd never tried vicarious running. I stifled a yawn. On the third street, a man in uniform came out of what looked like a guesthouse—a combination restaurant and hotel—just as Miller approached.

"Martinez, you see that?" I asked.

"Yep."

"Wait for my word." Miller had a code if she thought she was in trouble. I'd let her call it. She could provide a much better perspective face-to-face than we could via optics. But if she said, *Drop it*, I'd have Martinez open up, and we'd deal with the consequences after. In retrospect, I probably should have thought that through a little better.

Story of my life the last few days.

"Morning." The male voice came from Miller's feed. The soldier.

Miller waved in response. Nothing out of the ordinary. We could all speak a few words of Confed, but she wouldn't want an accent to give her away.

"Stand down, Martinez," I said. "Find your next target."

"Roger."

She passed two people, an old man and woman, walking on the next street, then went down two more roads before running into another soldier who didn't even seem to look at her. He wore a utility uniform with a rifle slung over his shoulder as if he wasn't expecting contact. So far, so good. We didn't have any more information about Kendrick, but nobody seemed suspicious about a strange woman running through town. She jogged down the last three streets in our plan, leaving the last one untouched. Disguise or not, I didn't want her that close to the bot tank. Even from a street over, I could hear the whine of its engines through her feed. Kendrick wouldn't have hidden there anyway unless he got pinned down and had no choice. If that was the case, so be it, but I hoped he was somewhere safer.

Miller took a right on the street that circled the outside of town and started back toward us. She'd come about two thirds of the way when she spoke subvocally into the net. "I'm going to try one more thing."

She took another right, heading down the third street, where she'd originally passed the soldier. It was a street of shops, and five civilians were out now, four of whom—two groups of two—had taken tables at an outdoor café across from the soldier's guesthouse. He had gone back inside—or somewhere. He wasn't visible.

What the hell are you doing, Killer?

When she reached the café, its tables separated from the street by a waist-high fence of black iron bars, she stopped.

What the fuck *are you doing?*

"Excuse me," she said, talking to one of the tables in their language, which my helmet translated for me. I didn't even know she could speak it that well. "I'm looking for a friend who said he'd recently come to this town. Have you perhaps seen someone new?"

"Other than you?" joked the man. He was older, maybe fifty. The woman he was sitting with looked younger than that—maybe thirty-five? It was hard to tell through optics from a distance, and she had one of those ageless faces.

Killer tried to laugh, but it came out fake-sounding. "So . . . nothing?"

"Why are you asking?" The woman spoke this time, her voice grating, louder than the man's.

"Like I said—he's my friend."

Behind Killer, the door to the guesthouse opened, and two uniformed soldiers walked out, both carrying pulse rifles at the low ready.

"You seem nervous," said the man.

"Not at all," said Killer, but the quaver in her voice put the lie to it.

Get the hell out of there, Killer.

"I think you should leave," said the woman in a loud, piercing voice.

I think that too.

One of the soldiers stopped and turned their way.

A second later his partner turned, and then stopped as well. They said something, but the microphone didn't pick it up. Maybe they were talking to each other and not Killer. The first soldier took a step toward the café, and then another, his weapon still low, but in his hands.

I'd seen enough. I wasn't waiting for Miller to get into an impossible position. "Martinez," I said. "Take him out."

A second later Martinez's rifle—a slug thrower—barked, and instantly the soldier's head exploded, spattering blood and brains all over the other soldier. Killer and the café patrons flinched away. The blood-covered soldier whirled, looking for the source of fire. That was a mistake. She should have moved. Martinez fired again, and she went down. A chest shot this time.

Run, Killer.

I hadn't even said the words out loud, but she was smart enough to take off at a sprint.

Four seconds later, everything went to hell.

Soldiers poured out of three different doorways on the street. Martinez's rifle popped again, and a second-story window of the guesthouse shattered.

The enemy soldiers were disorganized—we'd taken them by surprise—but there were a lot of them, and that surprise wasn't going to last for long. Too many. Way more than the old lady had mentioned. Killer wasn't going to make it out on her own, and we couldn't leave her there—I wasn't leaving a *second* soldier on their own.

"Putty, Erickson, Chang—with me. Martinez, cover us. Dex, we're about to create one hell of a distraction. Be ready if your chance comes. Rookie, you stay with

Dex. Blow a hole in the building for him if you need to, and fuck up anybody who tries to get in his way: soldier, civilian, or whatever."

"Roger, Sergeant," he said.

I was moving down the hill at full speed before finishing my orders. Across town, the bot tank started moving.

"Keep going," I told the others. "Weapons tight . . . make sure you've got a clean shot before you take it. There are civilians down there. But if the civilian has a gun, consider them a combatant." Ma's people would be armed. I stopped, still high enough on the hill to observe the bot tank. There were two logical ways for it to reach us: the road through town and the road that skirted around it. If it took the outside route, that would bring it closest to our initial position, and we'd be able to engage it without buildings in the way.

It took the interior road.

Because of fucking course it did.

And it wasn't taking any time about it, either, quickly accelerating to what had to be eighty kilometers an hour. I felt bad for anything that got in its way—the tank wasn't going to stop now that it had found a threat. I had about a second to make a decision: help Miller or take on the bot tank and hope she made it out on her own.

There was only one real choice. It wouldn't do any good to get to Miller if the bot tank killed us all anyway. I took off at full speed, carrying all four kilograms of our hyper-nitrate in a pack that I held by its straps in my left hand. I had to beat the bot tank to the spot I'd picked out, which was going to be a close thing.

I headed for the road that ran by the west side of Ma's building. I couldn't think of a better place in town for a firefight, and it was only one street from Miller. If she came through the building, she'd be right there with us. I couldn't tell her that, obviously. But hopefully she'd figure it out.

Fucking hopefully again.

Putty, Chang, and Erickson fanned out at the end of the street with Putty in the center of the road in his heavy armor, pretty much daring people to shoot at him. Chang and Erickson were spread to either side, using stairs and alcoves as cover. Chang had moved forward farther, and watching her for a second, I could see why. She put her hands on one rail and, with a mechanical assist, vaulted herself up and over a set of stone stairs, disappearing on the other side. Someone fired at her, too late, and Putty used that to target the shooter with his heavy pulse weapon—the Beast—turning them into a spray of smoking meat.

"I need to get to the other end of the street," I said. "Cover me."

All three members of my team began firing at once, picking their shots. We were trapped on the street with nowhere to go. If I didn't get to the bot tank and it turned the corner, we'd all end up as smears on the pavement.

I ran down the middle of the street, forcing Putty to stop firing behind me, since I had him screened, but I couldn't help it. I needed speed. To my front right, a soldier popped up and got off a pulse rifle shot that slammed into my shoulder, spinning me back and making me stumble. A quick check of my diagnostics said they hadn't gotten anything vital, but he did piss me off. I pushed off hard with my left foot, changing direction sharply, and fired my own, larger pulse weapon one-handed into his unarmored chest. He flew backward, smoking, and slammed into the stone face of a building as I rushed past.

A shot caught me square in the back and threw me forward and to the street, where I skidded for a few seconds at high speed, throwing up sparks, before I could right myself and scramble back to my feet. I didn't look back. One of my team had to get whoever did it. The whine of the bot tank's engine cut through the rest of the noise, and I focused on the end of the street, expecting it to appear at any second.

I stopped as I passed a set of concrete stairs headed down into a basement on the right side of the road. It seemed like as good a place as any to hide, so I jumped down, letting my suit absorb the shock as I landed. The bot tank would have to slow down to take the corner, which would give me my best chance.

"When the tank turns onto our street, I need you guys to distract it," I said.

"You want us to *what*?" asked Erickson.

"On it," said Chang. Her enthusiasm worried me for a second, right until the tank came into view thirty meters in front of me and I forgot about her.

Come on. Just a little farther.

Time slowed. When you consider attacking a bot tank with an explosive, the theory seems good. Get on top and blow it up. Theory is best saved for briefing rooms, far away from live fucking bot tanks. This close, pure terror overwhelmed theory.

Shit.

Its thrusters pushed down into the street with such violence that everything around it vibrated. It crept forward, slower now, searching for targets. Its main gun slewed, and I risked a look in the other direction in time to see Chang running up the side of a building at an angle and launching herself into a flip through the air at least five meters off the ground. The *fwap* from the tank's main gun was so loud that my helmet cut off sound for a second to protect my hearing.

Heavy pulse fire bounced off the front of the tank— that would be from Putty—but it cut out as the tank fired again.

And then it was right in front of me.

Forcing myself out of my paralysis, I ran up the stairs and launched myself into the air. It was moving too fast. I was going to miss. Shit. I dropped my rifle, transferred the pack to my right hand in one move, and reached with my left hand for the back of the tank. I hit it with a clank and activated the magnetic grip, securing myself to the back of the machine. It dragged me for a second until I took two running steps and used the strength assist in my arm to pull myself onto its back deck. The temperature sensor in my suit binged an alarm at me from the heat of the engines—I'd passed right through the back-blast. I'd worry about that later, when I wasn't on top of the tank.

An enemy in a mech-suit appeared at the opening to

the street behind the tank and drew a bead on me. I went for my rifle, forgetting that it was lying in the street. I froze. I couldn't dive off the tank without placing the bomb.

A blast took the mech-suited enemy in the chest. Then another hit it in the face.

"I got you covered," said Chang. "Do it, Gas!"

"Get the hell out of here!" I shouted in reply. I peeled the back off the industrial sticky tape and slammed the pack down on the deck right behind the turret. "Everyone, bug out. Try to draw the tank down the street, but get the fuck away from it." I had the bomb planted, and I knew where I wanted to detonate it. Right where it would cause Ma the most pain. But I wouldn't risk the lives of my soldiers to do it.

I leaped from the back of the tank, which was starting to pick up speed. My feet went out from under me as they hit the pavement too fast for my stabilizers to compensate, and I rolled, trying to protect my suit from damage as much as possible. Coming to a stop, I scrambled to my feet and sprinted toward my weapon. The enemy mech-suit reappeared—apparently Chang hadn't finished them off. I dove just as they fired, the pulse blast passing above me as I sparked along the pavement. I grabbed my rifle and fired back, but they disappeared behind the corner of the building again.

That was going to be a problem. Not as big a problem as the bot tank, which I hoped was still focused on Putty and not about to shoot me in the back, but enough that it would screw up what was left of my plan. Now that we'd engaged, we had to take out every single enemy in town, and we had to do it before reinforcements arrived, which wouldn't be long. That put us at a serious disadvantage. The enemy could afford to sit down in defensive positions and wait. We couldn't. The only thing we had working in our favor was that they didn't know that.

Regardless, I charged.

I reached the corner and instead of slowing down, I went to my knees in a full-speed skid. Sparks flew up from my leg armor as I raised my rifle and fired up, catching the unsuspecting enemy mech in the helmet under their chin, snapping their head back in a way that heads—and necks—aren't supposed to move. They tumbled backward, hitting the ground hard and going ass-over-head until they ended up in a heap. I ignored them and scanned for more targets but came up empty.

"Yo, Gas, a little help?" Putty's voice sounded like controlled panic. "Pissed-off bot tank over here." As if to punctuate that sentiment, the tank's main gun *fwap*'ed again, far enough away from me now that my suit didn't have to dampen the noise. In front of me, Chang lined up a shot at the tank's rear.

"Chang, no!"

She lowered her rifle, thankfully having heard me in time.

"We need the tank to chase Putty just a little longer."

"We need the tank to do *what*?" asked Putty.

That was good. If he was pissed at me, he was still alive. "Dex, move now. Chang, get to the café. Find Miller."

"On it, Boss."

"Is anybody else being chased by a bot tank? No?

Well, I am! So can we focus and revisit that part of your plan? You know, the stupid part," said Putty.

"Just a little farther."

"Easy for you to say," said Putty. "You don't have a tank trying to blast a basketball-sized hole in your ass."

"A little farther." I grabbed the detonator from its compartment on my thigh.

The bot tank fired.

"Mother fuck!" called Putty. "I'm down. Three seconds." That's how long it took the tank to recharge its main gun.

I waited two seconds and hit the button. A white-out flash engulfed the far end of the street, and my helmet blacked out my vision for a second to protect me. A split second later, the shockwave and sound slammed into me like a sack of dirt hitting my chest. My suit compensated, and I kept my feet, but just barely. I headed down the street toward the wreckage at a jog. "You okay, Putty?"

The net stayed silent for a couple of long seconds. "Yeah. I'm good. Holy shit, you blew the turret right off of that thing! And man, did you fuck up that building."

"Erickson?" I asked.

"I'm here," she said.

I reached the tank, which was a flaming heap of metal, and scanned the smoking hole that encompassed the middle third of Ma's place. Hopefully I hadn't destroyed all the equipment that Dex needed, but he'd entered from the far end away from the blast. I looked for movement inside, but didn't find any, and no heat sources through my thermals other than the things on fire.

"Miller isn't in the café," said Chang. "But the guy who owns the place is really pissed about his window."

Shit.

Not about the windows—I could give a fuck. But Miller was gone . . . one of the enemy must have grabbed her. I thought we'd taken them all out, but everything happened so fast, it was tough to tell. "Martinez, you see any bogeys?"

"Nothing," he answered. "Nothing moving in the town right now but us. Civilians have all gone to ground."

That made sense. When things started shooting and exploding, people hid. More important was that Martinez didn't see any enemy. That didn't mean they weren't around, but it did mean that if they *were*, they'd gone to ground as well. Most likely they'd be holing up in buildings, and from the pattern, it looked likely that it would be one of the buildings a street over from where we'd just fought it out with the bot tank. That was not good, as they'd be calling for reinforcements, but we had other problems and couldn't take the time to root them out. At this point, all we could do was find Miller and Kendrick and get as far away as possible while being wary of someone taking a potshot at us on our way out of town.

"I've got eyes on Miller," said Martinez.

"What? Where?" I asked.

"Leaving town and headed my way."

"Roger. Erickson, get to her and give her cover." A sniper taking a shot at one of us in armor wouldn't necessarily matter, but if someone took a shot at Miller . . .

"Moving, Gas." She took off at full power-armor speed.

"Chang—fall back to Martinez's position. Putty, come with me. I'm going to try one more thing before we get out of here." I got a chorus of rogers in return, and a minute later Putty walked up, his oversized suit thudding with each step.

"What's our move?"

"Give me access to your external speaker." We all had them, but Putty's heavy armor had a more powerful one, and I wanted to make myself heard.

Once he complied, I cranked up the volume and made an announcement. "People of Kiergard, we mean you no harm." *Well, we mean most of them no harm. But we've already established that I lie a lot.* "We will leave your town in peace momentarily. We're looking for a lost soldier named Kendrick. We'd like anyone with information about his whereabouts to come forward. We will ensure your safety."

Nothing moved. I almost expected a piece of paper to blow down the street to show how dead things were. That's how it would have happened in a vid. If there were any soldiers left, or any of Ma's people, they wanted no piece of two dudes in power armor.

"Let's try one more time on the other side of town," I said. Even if it didn't work, it would give Dex more time to do his thing. "Dex, how's it coming?"

"Found a terminal. Rookie had to wax a couple guys with guns. Working now."

"What's that about?" asked Putty.

"Remember what you said about not wanting to know?"

"Got it. But the faster we get out of this place, the

better. Somewhere there's a pile of reinforcements headed our way, and I don't think we're going to like our odds very much when they get here."

"Then let's run." I took off at seventy percent speed, taking the route that circled the outside of the town and kept us most visible to our own team. I was definitely putting the team in danger, but we'd go soon. I had to find Kendrick, and then all I had to do was get us to a safe spot, have Dex connect us to the net, and call for help. That was the deal. Colonel Gwan said if I could prove he was alive, they'd send a team.

But we had to find him. Not going to lie, without Patel to track him down, I was starting to lose hope. He would have heard the battle, but he wouldn't have known it was us, so he might have gone to ground with everybody else. At least, that was what I told myself. This was my last try. After this, I couldn't in good conscience—now that we'd had a gun battle that would definitely bring attention—do anything but try to get the rest of my squad to safety.

I picked a random street somewhere near the middle of the other half of town and repeated my broadcast. Nothing. The same silence as last time. "Okay," I said to Putty, after giving it a minute. "Let's head out." I flipped to the squad net. "We're moving out. Link up at checkpoint four-oh-one. Circle around the town."

"I need more time," said Dex.

CP 401 was on the far side of town from the over-watch position, back in the original direction from which we'd come. More important, it was back toward friendly lines. "Roger," I said. "Martinez, maintain your overwatch until Dex gives the word. Chang, stay with him. Everyone else start toward four-oh-one."

"Movement in town," said Martinez. "One street south from you. Civilian. Male. No weapon."

"Roger. We'll check it out."

"Hey, over here!" a voice called. Given the direction, it might have been the guy that Martinez saw. A familiar voice.

I looked at Putty, and he looked back at me. "No fucking way," he said.

"Let's go." I cut between two old-style houses via an empty drive and a thin strip of grass. Based on his reaction, Putty had heard the same thing I had.

Kendrick's voice.

We cleared the houses and I looked around. The man was a hundred meters to my right, walking down the middle of the street toward us. I upped the magnification of my optics.

"No. Fucking. Way," said Putty again.

I didn't even have words.

Kendrick started running toward us. "You came for me!"

We met him halfway, and he jumped around. I would have hugged him, but that's a really bad idea when we were in power armor and he wasn't. "Did you think we wouldn't?" I asked.

"I was beginning to have doubts, especially when the bot tank showed up yesterday."

"Yeah, I can see how you might," I said. "Come on. We've got to get out of here. I don't suppose you have your power armor stashed somewhere."

"Had to scrap it. I set it to burn itself. I've got the location, just in case. Yours looks like it has seen better days too."

I glanced down to where I'd scraped the crap out of my legs and chest on the pavement. "We had some action on the way in."

"I heard. Everyone okay? You get what you came for?"

"So far everyone's fine. We got you, and that was key. But we're working on the other thing. We'll catch up on all that later. Right now we need to move. I hope you're ready to run."

"You know I've been prepping for this. I can do a 20K."

"You'll need water," I said. For the rest of us, hydration wasn't an issue. Our suits condensed it out of the air, and we could drink as needed. Kendrick didn't have that luxury. Keeping up was going to be tough as it was—he was going to slow us down—so water was a must.

"I'll grab some from the lady I've been staying with. She won't mind. It's back this way." We headed in that direction, and he disappeared into a nondescript wooden house, just like the others on the street.

"I can't believe this shitty-ass plan worked," said Putty.

"Thanks for the vote of confidence," I said.

"Come on. You didn't really think we were going to find him. You can admit it now."

"Never a doubt," I lied.

I was saved from Putty's surely sarcastic answer when Kendrick reappeared carrying two one-liter bottles of water. Understanding the urgency, he hadn't wasted any time. A woman appeared in the door behind him. "Good luck," she called.

It was the old lady we'd met on the road. I almost said something to her—she didn't seem to recognize me. But then, as she'd said, all soldiers were the same to her. That she'd taken care of one of us might have put the lie to that—obviously she cared—but I wasn't complaining.

Dex came to me over a private channel. "We're out. I got it."

"Fuck. Yeah."

"Which way?" asked Kendrick.

"West."

"Let's go." He turned and took off at a jog.

CHAPTER 16

COVERING THE GROUND TO THE LINK-UP POINT was easy enough for Putty and me as we kept pace with Kendrick. We didn't get a chance to talk to him since he was running and he needed his air, but more significant, he didn't have comm, so with our helmets on, we didn't have a great way to communicate anyway. I pulled us up short so I could speak to him before we reached the others. "Fair warning. Killer Miller is with us, and she kind of implied to the rest of the squad that she hooked up with you."

"What the fuck?"

"Yeah, I'm serious. It was bullshit—I know that—but some of the team might believe it."

"Dude. You've got to be kidding me. Miller is here? Does she know what we're doing?"

"Well . . . not everything. Let's just say that things got complicated."

He shook his head. "I knew this was too ambitious."

"Come on," I said. "It's working. Mostly."

"I hope so. What are we going to do about Miller, though?"

"Not sure. Shh. Here she comes."

Miller was back in her armor, and she approached with Chang, Erickson, and Martinez. Miller ignored Kendrick and stepped close to me.

"I can't believe this worked," she said.

"It was tight there for a minute." I flipped open the squad net. "Let's go. We'll debrief later. Stick to the woods. We'll try to get ten klicks, then call for extraction. I don't want to be near Kiergard when enemy reinforcements show up. Remember: Kendrick doesn't have armor, so the mission is now protection, got it?"

Rogers all around. Kendrick took off and we fanned out around him.

"At least in the woods, they can't send more bot tanks after us," said Putty. And he was right. The trees made it mostly impassable for vehicles or would at least slow them down to the point that they wouldn't catch us. But they could—and most likely would—send soldiers in power armor. In town, we'd faced regular soldiers, with the exception of the one mech, and had a relatively easy time of it. But we'd had surprise. Now? They'd know what they were up against. Eight soldiers in power armor running away. Whatever they sent now would be more than enough to handle us, so we had to do whatever we could to avoid that fight. I had what I needed, and all I wanted now was to get the team home.

WE STOPPED AFTER about ten klicks to call in a rescue force and to give Kendrick a needed rest. We had traveled northwest to disguise our location at least a little bit. I'd have liked to go in a random, unexpected direction, because it would have made us harder to find, but I wanted to give us at least a chance to reach our own lines in case we couldn't get timely exfil. The team set up solar chargers, and Dex began work on a comm link up to base. I checked on Kendrick.

I slid my visor up so we could talk. "You doing okay?"

"Not bad. I'm glad I'd prepared for the run for the last few weeks."

"How was it in town? Having to hide out?" I asked.

He looked at me, confused. "Gas . . . they knew I was there."

"Say what?"

"Yeah. They caught me on the way in. I went to Kiergard, like we planned, to wait for you and to scout out Ma's facility. I had ditched my armor and weapon, so I tried to blend in . . . you know, walk in like a civilian. It didn't work. A couple of soldiers stopped me pretty much immediately. I tried to lie to them, but without knowing the language, they saw through it pretty quickly."

"So you were detained?" I asked.

"No. That was the weird thing. They spotted me as a soldier, but then kind of shrugged it off. They noted that I didn't have a weapon, and they asked me if I was going to cause trouble. I told them I wasn't. I lied a little and told them that I just wanted somewhere to ride out the war. Obviously I didn't tell them you were coming for me."

"So they didn't care?"

"I don't know," Kendrick admitted. "There weren't

any officers there. It was maybe a half squad of grunts
and some supply types, and they were all paid off. Their
army put them there, and they had a mission to hold
the town. But they'd cut a deal with the mob to basically
not do anything."

I nodded. "So Ma's got her hands in on both sides.
I believe it."

"What? Our side too?"

"Pretty sure. I'll know more once we get back and
I can go through what Dex has. But there's a colonel
up on our base that's pretty sketchy, and I think it's all
connected."

"Do we have a plan for that?" asked Kendrick.

"We've always got a plan."

"Hey, Gas, we have a problem," Dex cut in over the net.

Of course we did. "What's up, Dex?"

"I can't get a link established. Still working through
it, but I think we're being jammed."

"But you're talking to me over the net right—"

"Do you want me to take the time to explain the
difference to you, or do you want to accept that I know
what I'm talking about? Trust me, this is fucking *bad*."

"Right. Give me a second to think." Miller came
up to me, and Kendrick faded back, giving her some
space.

"Tell me you have a plan," she said.

We've always got a plan. Should have knocked on
wood or something when I'd said that. "I did. This is
where Gwan is supposed to bail us out."

"*Colonel* Gwan?" she asked. "What's he got to do
with this?"

"Everything," I said. "Gwan wants this fight. We're his excuse to get it. Our side can't afford to have us get caught behind the lines—too much negative press in that—so he has to come for us. And my bet was that they'd be coming in a big way. Because Gwan thinks we're not fighting the war to win, and he desperately wants to change that. We're his chance."

"Except he's not here."

"Except he's not here, and I can't get in touch with him." I'd miscalculated something. Our side had to know that we'd hit Kiergard—which meant Gwan knew. We'd made too much commotion there for them to miss it.

And then it hit me like a punch in the gut.

Gwan was running a game—a big game—that was for sure. The key to every big game, every big con, was that you had a blow-off. To get away with it, you had to get away clean. What if Gwan's blow-off was having me and my squad killed? We were still behind enemy lines, so he still had to come for us. But if we were dead, then we couldn't tell our side of the story.

I didn't know if Gwan was capable of that, but then again, I didn't know what it took to become a colonel, either.

Fuck.

"What?" asked Miller. "You look like you saw a ghost. What do we need to do?"

"We need to run," I said. "Dex, any chance you can get us unjammed?"

Dex replied without hesitation. "It may be targeted to a certain location. That's especially true if they know where we are. We need to move to find out."

"How far? And what's the chance that that solves the problem?"

"I don't know. And I don't know. All I can say for sure is that it's *not* going to work here. Maybe another ten klicks and try again."

"Roger." I flipped to the squad net. "Switch over your solar arrays. Drop the muted and use full absorption." That would help enemy sensors pick us up, but it would charge batteries three to four times faster than the muted arrays we used last time. I didn't want to stay here any longer than we had to, so the risk seemed justified.

A chorus of rogers responded.

"Miller, you and I will take watch while the rest charge. Use your built-in charging systems." By staying still, our suits would gain charge naturally, as long as we didn't use the big power-draining systems like camouflage. We wouldn't get much power compared to the others, but I trusted Miller and myself to be able to manage our resources better than anybody else, and we couldn't all go offline at once in hostile territory. As a last resort, we could use our emergency B packs.

I still didn't want to dip into those just yet. I had a feeling we were going to need them.

"Kendrick, you ready to run some more?"

"If it's that or dying, then yeah, I'm ready."

I moved closer to him and spoke so nobody else could hear. "If I don't make it back and you do, get the info from Dex. Make everything public." Gwan thought he was going to give *me* the blow-off? Fuck him. I'd burn everything down. "Take off now and get a head start. Head due west, directly for friendly lines. If we can't figure out comms, that might be our only chance. We'll suck up some power and then catch up to you."

"Anyone got a spare weapon?"

"Go without it," I said. "If you run into the enemy, being unarmed will be your safest bet. You'll look like a noncombatant, and maybe they'll just let you go again."

"See you soon." He turned and jogged away, his feet crunching across the forest floor. I watched him until he disappeared. It was 1222 hours. We'd move at 1252. By that point, he'd have covered about half the distance, and we'd be able to travel at full speed in our suits to catch him.

I turned my attention to my sensor suite and took up a position looking west. Miller was already focused to the east.

At 1228, everything went to shit.

"We've got company." Miller spoke to me softly via private channel.

"Specifics?" I asked.

"Not much. Something's coming, but they're using countermeasures, and I can't break through from this distance. They're moving toward us, though, about four klicks out."

"Roger." I took a couple seconds to think. With his six-minute head start, Kendrick would have covered about a klick. I assumed the enemy was in mech-suits. If so, they'd be closing at about twenty klicks per hour— maybe a little less, given the trees. If they had our location, that would put them on top of us in twelve minutes. That was worst-case. They probably *didn't* have our exact location yet. If they did, we'd have aircraft or missiles on top of us already. But they'd have it soon. We were stationary, which would make it harder for them to see us than for us to see them, but we didn't have the power to run significant countermeasures and they probably had drones. And the solar chargers were a signature to lock onto. I estimated they'd pinpoint us in three minutes. Which meant we had to be moving in two. Even that was a risk, but every joule of power we could get might make a difference.

"Keep charging, but listen up," I broadcasted to the squad. "We've got enemy inbound. In a minute, on my command, stow your power gear and move due west. Putty, you and I are going to stay here and delay the enemy. We need to give Kendrick time to get away. Sergeant Miller, you're in charge of the group moving west. Dex, you advise her and keep working to get us a link for exfil. If anyone gets separated, keep making your way west and try to get to our lines."

Miller came on over a private channel. "You can't stay here. Our best bet is to run for it."

"Negative," I said. "We've got too far to go, and while we had a head start on the enemy, Kendrick doesn't have armor. Eventually they'd bring in air or indirect fire to slow us down, and then we'd be hard-fucked. We need a diversion. You go, and get the squad out. When you make it, Kendrick and Dex will explain everything."

If they made it.

Miller hesitated before responding. "Okay. We'll go. But, Gas?"

"Yeah?"

"Don't die."

"Right." I didn't want to. But I was in charge, and I'd fucked up. I'd obviously misread the situation with Gwan, and there was no way I was letting the rest of my team pay for it. Not without a fight. From the start of this thing, I was out for myself—I'm not pretending I wasn't. But I always expected to bring the team inside once it was all sorted. Now they were in serious danger. That took precedence. Those were the rules.

I flipped back to the full squad channel. "Go as hard as you need to. If you run below fifteen percent power, use your spare B pack." I hated to do that, because it left us without an emergency stash, but extra B packs wouldn't do us any good in the grave.

I switched to another private channel. "Putty, you stay on the charger when the others leave. Get as much juice as you can."

"Roger."

Over the general net I said, "Martinez. Leave me your rocket launcher." I needed something to distract the enemy, to slow them down, because there was no way that Putty and I were going to survive a direct firefight against the force I expected to meet.

I turned my sensors to the east to see if I could pick up what Miller had spotted. After about fifteen seconds, I got it tuned in. I couldn't get a perfect read, but it was a group, it was bigger than ours, and it was getting closer. At 1230 I gave the order: "Mount up and move out."

The squad moved fast, like the pros they were. Even Chang, but then, she was a natural with a mech-suit. Rookie took the longest, but Miller got the others moving and waited for him before taking off herself. Just like she should. They might be okay, as long as Putty and I could buy them some time. He and I . . . our odds weren't as good. He knew that, and he hadn't said a word. Because of course he didn't. That was Putty's role. He did the shit that nobody else wanted to do.

"You ready for this?" I asked him.

"Pfft. The question is, are *they* ready for this? We've got them outgunned."

"How do you figure?"

"Well, I'm worth more than ten men," he said.

"Are you?"

"That's what your sister says."

I laughed. "Asshole."

"These guys aren't going to know what hit them."

"Which is what your dates usually say when they wake up," I said.

"Nice," said Putty. "If we live through this, there's hope for you yet."

"We'll live through it."

"You think?"

I paused, considering a joke, but deciding against it. "Yeah. We always do."

"There it is," said Putty. "There it *fucking* is. Works every time."

"Works every time but one."

Putty laughed. "Today's not the day. I can feel it."

I tried to soak up as much of that confidence as I could. "I'm going to range out ahead of you a bit. Get another two minutes of power, then come after me."

"Wait . . . you're going *toward* them?"

"A little bit. We can't stay here. They'll have our location soon, and if I was them, I'd blow the shit out of this entire hill with rockets."

"And yet you want me to stay here . . . I think I'm beginning to understand your plan." The humor came through in his tone. He knew I wouldn't do that. But I'm not sure if he realized that by moving forward, I'd be easier for the enemy to see, which would create the exact opposite effect. They'd find me first, and I'd be sacrificing myself. If I told him, he'd argue with me. And he'd be right. He'd have a better chance of surviving a barrage in the heavy armor. But we needed his firepower if we had any chance of slowing the Confeds down, and that was the job.

"Two minutes," I said, and with that, I scooped up Martinez's rocket launcher, checked its load to find one in the chamber, one in the ready rack, and took off directly toward what I thought was the enemy's current location. I left the third rocket on the ground. I needed my hands free, and it was armor-piercing anyway. Not much use for what I intended. I covered two hundred meters in about thirty seconds, stopped, and let the first rocket fly at a spot that I expected to be about a hundred fifty meters in front of the enemy. I was guessing, but in theory, they'd run right into the explosion, but even if they didn't, I didn't care. If it hit in front of them, or even near them, it would cause them to react. That could buy the squad some precious seconds.

I didn't wait to see what happened. Instead, I randomly turned right and sprinted fifty meters. The enemy would have traced the trajectory from my launch and pinpointed my location. I couldn't be there when they responded. My rocket wasn't going to take them out—not by a long shot. If they were in mech-suits, I'd have to hit one of them directly to kill them, and the odds of that—well, let's just say that Putty had a better chance of getting laid in a room full of educated women than me hitting an enemy mech with a blind shot. The rocket had some internal guidance and would home in on them, but the mech-suits would counter that. We liked to think that soldiers won battles, but really, this shit was being fought by engineers way before I ever landed on Gallia.

That wasn't the point of the rockets. Again, I was just trying to buy time.

I stood for a couple of seconds and let my sensors work. They'd function while I was moving, but I had to toggle off their displays. Trying to focus on your HUD while running full speed through the woods was something that you tried once in your life and then learned better. I got a more precise read on them this time. A couple of the sensor hits faded in and out, but it looked like they had about twenty soldiers in power armor. Against our eight, that was more than enough, especially when you factored in that they'd have air power and missiles available, and we'd have nothing. At least, not until Dex made contact.

I wondered why we hadn't seen anything in the air yet.

An alarm buzzed—incoming rockets. "Putty—" I started to tell him to move, but he already was. I fired my other rocket at a location a hundred meters offset from my first one. Then I started running. Enemy rockets riffled through the trees and crunched into the ground with a deep, chest-compressing bass. Dirt and wood splinters blew past me, and the force of the blast threw me into a makeshift dive into the soft ground. My helmet dug a furrow that obscured half of my vision until I raised my head. My heads-up put my suit integrity at eighty-one percent—one percent lower than when I'd completed my street dive in town. They hadn't hit me, but that wasn't for lack of trying. I'd counted six individual explosions, and they were big—probably two-hundred-millimeter as opposed to the fifty-millimeter shoulder-launched munitions I'd fired at them. That was hardly fair. Theirs wouldn't have to hit me to do damage. They just had to get close. My only hope was that with us as outnumbered as we were, they wouldn't bother with much indirect fire.

Checking my sensors, I saw they'd slowed. Not quite stopped, but they were walking, at least for now. I checked my power—forty-two percent—and flipped on my spoofing. It would make me look like multiple different targets unless their sensors were able to cut through it. Impossible to say. It was going to drain my battery, but at this point, I had to do it. If they dialed in on me, having battery wouldn't matter. And if they thought there were than two of us, maybe they'd approach more cautiously. I didn't have Putty trigger his. I wanted him to channel all his extra energy into firepower. His Beast would be the only thing we had that would take out a mech-suit cleanly. A couple of casualties would slow them down even more and buy Miller and crew extra time to get to safety.

After about thirty seconds, they picked up speed again. "When we open up, fire and move," I told Putty. "As much fire as you can, and as fast as you can without running into a tree. We'll head south. We can't let them pin us down and flank us. Hopefully we'll cause them to reorient and take them off the trail of the others."

"Roger," he said. "Hey, Gas?"

"Yeah?"

"It's been good knowing you. You're a great squad leader."

"We're going to make it through this," I lied.

"Yeah. Well, you know. In case we don't."

"I hear you. I love you, man."

"You're going to make your sister jealous."

"Tell you what. We make it through this, I might actually introduce you."

"Fuckin' A. That's all the motivation I need. Time to make these guys pay."

I considered that thought, making them pay. Pay for what? They were pawns in this stupid war just like us, and that should have mattered. Except it didn't. Not here, not now. Later it would. But now? Now we were engaged, and whatever their thoughts on the matter, these Confed soldiers in their power armor were here to kill me unless I killed them first. I'd started it by hitting Kiergard, but not really. Some nameless, faceless politicians started it more than two decades ago. They were the ones who should pay. But I couldn't make that happen unless I lived. And for me to live, that meant some Confeds had to die.

That was a long way of saying that, at a certain point,

motives really didn't matter anymore. It was them or us. When you're facing death, what you *want* to do goes out the airlock, and there's nothing left but animal instinct. Survival.

I'm sure they felt the same way.

"Here they come. Fire 'em up." I let Putty fire first. He had the range and the power. I waited for him to move, then followed. I'd cover his back as best I could. I flipped my dual-purpose rifle to armor-piercing fléchettes. I'd empty my magazines before switching to pulse. My weapon had a separate battery pack, but it didn't hold much. After that, I'd slave it to my suit and fire until I had nothing left.

If somehow we lasted that long, then I'd try to think of something else.

Putty's heavy pulse weapon screamed in a continuing blast, hitting everything and nothing. I didn't have visual on the enemy yet, and with the mess Putty was making of the forest—dirt, heat, and wood hazing the air—even flipping to max magnification, I couldn't pick out any targets. They could definitely see us. Putty was lit up as bright as a star. Small fires burst to life in his kill zone, and a tall tree, the diameter of a man's waist, snapped off at head-high and crashed to the ground, taking branches from neighboring trees with it. That would give them something to think about.

A few sporadic bursts came our way—lighter weapons—not really in range yet. They'd have to keep coming into the maelstrom if they wanted a piece of us. If they were smart, they'd wait it out. Putty could only keep it up for another minute. Ninety seconds max.

Chunks flew from a tree a meter in front of me. High-velocity slugs. They were getting closer. I kept running while trying to pick out a target, but Putty's fire still made it impossible.

"Start conserving," I said. "On and off."

Putty didn't respond, but his fire cut off for a couple of seconds before resuming for a three-second burst. He varied his pauses, so the enemy couldn't time him, but even still, pulse blasts and fléchettes started to find their range, ricocheting off his heavy armor like tiny shooting stars. Something smashed into my foot while I was in the middle of a step, spinning me around, and then I was on my back. I rolled over without hesitation, taking up a prone firing position and sighting in on a target. I fired a burst of armor-piercing rounds into the chest of a mech soldier about five hundred meters away. They dropped. I doubt I killed them, but I sure as shit gave them something to worry about other than shooting at me.

I checked my status on my heads-up, and finding my armor still intact, I scrambled up. While I was sprinting to reach Putty, a broken transmission came in. "This is . . . we . . . contact . . . west . . ." It cut out for a couple of seconds. It had been Miller's voice. "Large for . . . fren . . ." Another pause. "Contact."

What had she said? I used a precious second to check the messages in my HUD. Nothing. Just the voice transmission. From her distance, the jamming was having an effect. I could have almost sworn she said large force of friendlies, but maybe that was wishful thinking, and I

was hearing what I hoped to hear. "Say again, Miller."
I took the time to fire a burst blindly toward the enemy.
It was a waste of ammo, but I couldn't take it with me.

"Friendlies!" said Miller, coming across clearer for a
moment. "Get the fuck out of there!"

"Did you hear that, Putty?"

"Nope. Kind of busy getting shot to shit. Suit integrity is fifty-six percent."

"We've got reinforcements. Let's run for it."

"You go," he said. "I'll stay here and hold them off."

"No way. We both go. All or nothing."

"Gas—"

"Now! That's an order! Fucking run!" I waited for
his weapon to cut off and for him to turn before I took
off running myself. He was slightly in front of me,
giving me a good view of the pulse weapons ripping into
his back, throwing heat and light. Now that he wasn't
blasting them, the enemy could aim and concentrate
fire. "Faster!" I stumbled as pulse blasts struck me too,
knocking me off course like a drunk man trying to run
a straight line. One hit hard, feeling like someone had
beaned me in the back with a rock. Putty slowed some,
and I passed him. His pulse weapon opened up with a
steady whine. My heads-up buzzed, and a red warning
light flashed. Suit breach. I flipped open the diagnostic
tab to find the damage, even though I assumed it was
that shot to my back.

I almost hit a tree, braced with one arm, slid around
it, and kept going.

Putty wasn't with me.

"Where are you, Putty?"

"I'm done, Gas. Too many hits to the legs. I'm going to hold them. Keep going."

I tried to respond, choked up, tried again. I stopped and turned, brought my rifle up.

"Aaaaaaahhhhhh!" Putty yelled through the net as he unleashed a stream of hot death. Sparks flew from his armor, slugs bouncing off, maybe some penetrating. He dropped to one knee. "Run." His single word came out as almost a gasp.

I turned and I ran.

I couldn't save him.

Not by myself. And that meant I had to stay alive long enough to get help. Miller had said there were friendlies. Hopefully I could get through. "Miller, I need a strike. Max ordnance." I plugged in targets in a hundred-eighty-degree arc two hundred meters from Putty's position.

No response.

I repeated the transmission. I ran, and I kept repeating it.

Putty had stopped firing. I stopped running, dove behind the largest tree I could find, and came up into a kneeling position. I scanned back the way I came. Putty was down. The only way I could see him was by the incoming fire still searching him out. I picked out the highest density and fired a burst at the source. It stopped. So I picked another one and fired again. Pulse blasts slammed into my tree, and I ducked behind it. Two seconds later I popped out and fired again, this time only aiming for a split second. Wisps of smoke came off the now scarred tree. Slugs ripped into it, throwing bark and splinters, and I ducked behind again, and then came around the other side.

A lone figure approached Putty, maybe fifty meters from him, approaching cautiously. I put a three-round burst into their faceplate. From this range, I couldn't miss. I didn't. The mech dropped like a sack of wet clothes.

"Inbound, ten seconds!" A voice on my net—not Miller—a man's voice I didn't recognize. "Mark your position and get down!"

Reflexively I flipped on my locator beacon. A series of pulse blasts slammed into the right side of my chest, spinning me and throwing me to the ground where I landed on my side.

Ow.

I should have gotten down first, flipped my beacon on second.

Lesson learned, I rolled from my side to a prone position, wincing as something tore in my rib cage. I'd lost count, but it had to have been almost ten seconds.

Shit. Putty couldn't flip on his locator. I scrolled through my squad leader interface, and when I found the right tab, I lit up the whole squad. It was faster than trying to pick out an individual.

The forest evaporated in thunder and dust and flaming tracers. Waves of concussion shook me even in my prone position, and I squirmed, trying to wiggle my way deeper into the forest floor. A second later, the screams of multiple fast-movers ripped the sky, their ordnance having beat their sound to the target. I tried to count them, but a second wave of explosions thundered around me, drowning out their cries.

Red warning lights—more than I could count—plinked at the corners of my vision, blurry, and I realized I had tears in my eyes. I pushed down with my arms, trying to get up, but my right side gave way, and I yelled in pain, slumped back to the ground. The injection from my suit pinched my shoulder, sending in the welcome burn of painkillers. But painkillers weren't superdrugs, and they didn't give me any more strength. I kept going, tried to roll to my left to get in a position to stand up without my arm, but my suit wouldn't move. Something in the hip had locked up. I went back to my stomach, pushed with my feet, inched forward. It was stupid, drawing attention. Even with all that firepower we hit them with, the enemy almost certainly still had some combat effectives.

But all I could think about was getting to Putty. I pulled with my good arm, scrabbling at the dirt and burning underbrush. My other one wouldn't function. It started to throb even when I wasn't moving it. It was all I could do to lift my head. My sensor suite had blacked out—that was one of the flashing warning lights—and I was bleeding power even though I wasn't doing anything. Eleven percent. At least three . . . no, four figures moved through the lingering smoke and dust, which glowed in the rays of the sun now streaming through the canopy in bigger swaths.

Fast-movers applying ordnance tended to add holes to the tree cover.

I couldn't hold my head up any longer—something

was wrong with the mechanical assist in my suit—so I sank back to the ground. Lucky I did, as a bolt struck the top of my head. If it had hit my face, it might have snapped my neck. As it was, my ears rang, and my vison fogged at the sides. A new warning from what was left of my suit's medical monitoring told me I had a concussion. *Thanks, suit.* I wouldn't have figured that out my own.

Pulse shots ripped over me, and it took me a couple of seconds to realize that they were coming from behind me. I'm not precisely sure how I figured that out. Things were fuzzy. Then someone was standing over me, and even through the fog in my brain, I recognized the beautiful sound of a Beast whining away at full power.

Rookie. I slid in and out of darkness. If it was a dream, it was a good one.

The next thing I recall is someone kneeling next to me.

Miller.

"Hey, Gas . . . you okay?"

"Gwan didn't give us the blow-off."

"What? What are you talking about? Gwan? No questions about why our side launched like twenty thousand soldiers into an attack to save our asses, except not exactly when we needed it? No? You just want to talk about Colonel Gwan?"

I tried to laugh, but it hurt. "In my defense, I probably have a concussion."

Another woman spoke. It took a second to register, like I was underwater. Erickson. "That's it. Out of my way." Miller disappeared, and Erickson hooked into my suit to access its medical diagnostics. "The good news is that you're going to live. The bad news is that it's really going to hurt for a while."

"I can deal. Where's Putty? Is he okay? You've got to treat—"

"I don't know," she said. "If he's alive, they'll find him. Now, I'm going to give you a big 'ol painkiller and then a sedative. We'll get you evacuated, and they'll put you back together in no time."

"No drugs," I said.

"Shut up," said Erickson. Gone was her normal talkative, friendly demeanor. "This is my call."

"I have to be able to answer questions . . . they're going to ask about why we stole a ship."

Erickson popped open a plate on my armor, exposing my arm. "Nobody is going to ask you anything. You're going to be unconscious."

"I have to talk to—"

"Besides," Erickson continued, cutting me off as the drugs kicked in. "Haven't you heard? We're heroes."

CHAPTER 17

I DIDN'T IMMEDIATELY KNOW WHERE I WAS WHEN I woke, which is never good, and in this situation was especially bad since I didn't know how far things had gone off track. Certainly they'd been pretty far gone when I had to make an impromptu stand against the enemy, and there was no reason to think things would have gotten *better* since then. Who knew what kind of trouble I was in?

I was in a medical facility—that much I could tell from the beeping monitors, astringent smell, and other associated indicators—but whether I was on the planet surface or back on the station, I couldn't say. After a quick self-assessment, I figured that I'd probably been out for quite some time. My shoulder and side, which I remembered hurting immensely during the battle, now only ached in that dull way that happens after you've been injured but started to heal. I'd probably been sedated and in a rejuve tank.

And I had no idea what had happened to Putty.

The door to my small room whooshed open, and a dozen images came to mind of who might walk through.

Everything from the military police to Kendrick to Miller. Or even Putty. The heart monitor projected the increase in my pulse rate, so I couldn't ignore it. Traitor.

It was only the nurse. "Welcome back, Sergeant. How are you feeling?"

"Where am I?" The words came out in a croak, my throat feeling like it had been cleaned with a bore brush.

"You're on the military station orbiting Gallia." He stepped into the room, came closer, and spoke in a nurse voice, seemingly concerned. "Do you remember your name?"

I tried to nod. It didn't hurt, but I was stiff. "I'm fine. I remember everything. How is Putty? Putkin. Did he make it?"

"Your name first. Please."

"Gastovsky. C'mon—tell me about Putty—"

"I'm sorry, I don't know. He's not one of my patients. I can check for you. Is there anything else I can do?"

"I could use some water."

"Absolutely. I'll bring that right in. Some irritation in your throat is normal with the intubation required for the rejuvenation treatment."

"Thanks." I looked for a name tag, but his green scrubs didn't have one.

"No problem. The doctor will be in soon, and there is someone waiting to see you. Do you feel up to it?"

That depends on who they are. "Sure."

Might as well bring it on. Lying here thinking about what might happen would only stress me out. I'd done what I'd done, and now I had to deal with it, see what I could salvage and how I could get things moving the direction I wanted them. Hopefully Kendrick would come in first so I could find out the lay of the land, maybe determine how much trouble I had coming so I could plan my lies. I vaguely recalled Erickson mentioning us being heroes, and Miller talking about a huge offensive, but despite what I'd told the nurse, my memory from the last moments of my time on planet skittered away from me, almost like trying to remember details after waking from a dream.

The next person to enter was, again, not who I expected. It was a woman with a fancy camera, which immediately marked her as some sort of media specialist. Who else would have an actual camera? "Hi, Sergeant Gastovsky!" She had a cheery voice that made me think of a teacher of young children. Like she thought by being excited, she'd make me excited.

Spoiler alert: I wasn't.

"You can call me Gas."

"Okay, Gas! I just need to get a few pictures, if that's okay."

"I really don't think . . . I'm sure I look like shit."

"It's fine. We want to capture you in your natural state."

"Who's 'we'?"

"I'm Sergeant Stephanie Segula from public affairs." *Public affairs?* "What is this about?"

She paused for a moment, as if considering her next tack, and then her tone changed. Gone was the overcaffeinated cheerleader, replaced by a no-bullshit sergeant. "Listen. My boss told me to get pictures. I'm getting pictures. You can ask all the questions you want, but I have no fucking idea. And since you're stuck in a bed, you're not going to stop me."

I sat there for a couple seconds, stunned, and then I started laughing. It didn't hurt, which seemed like a good sign. "Well, why didn't you say that to start with?"

"I—" She started to respond, but then stopped, and she started laughing too. "I never really thought of it as a viable approach before."

"You don't deal with many infantry soldiers, I take it." Say what you want about the infantry—and people did. They called us dumb. Knuckle draggers. But we were direct, and there was a certain beauty to that.

She brought her camera up and started clicking, the flash pointed upward and away from my face. I never understood how that was supposed to work.

"You want me to smile?"

"You can if you want. The more variety I get, the more options my boss has. I don't know if he wants to see you happy or stoic."

"I'm in the hospital. What would I be happy about?"

She lowered the camera. "What do you mean?"

"I've been unconscious for a while. I have no clue what's going on."

"We've had the most successful offensive in, I don't know . . . forever? It's still going. The stalemate is broken."

"What's that got to do with me?"

"Seriously?"

"Seriously."

Her eyes narrowed, as if she didn't believe I was

asking the question. "What, you want me to say it? You don't seem like a guy who needs that kind of pat on the back."

I didn't respond, but my look must have convinced her that I didn't know what she meant.

"You really don't know," she said, bemused.

"Care to fill me in?"

Again, she looked like she couldn't believe what she was hearing. Finally, she said, "Your mission started the whole thing."

"Oh. Right. My mission. I didn't know how many people knew about that, so I wasn't sure if I was allowed to talk about it." It was a quickly constructed lie, but she smiled like she bought it. She'd helped me a lot. If public affairs knew about me and there'd been a huge offensive, that meant that I had probably read Colonel Gwan right after all. He *had* wanted a fight, and he'd gotten it. It had come a bit later than I'd have appreciated, but there was at least a chance he hadn't been trying to get me killed in the process. And now it seemed like he'd publicized our role in things, though I didn't know to what extent.

"Everybody knows about it. You're a hero," she said. There was that word again. I wasn't sure I liked that word. It hadn't been part of the plan. But you play the hand you have, not the hand you wish you had. Now I just had to figure out the players, the stakes, and what game we were playing. Minor things. What I needed in the short term was to get out of bed and find out what the Jim Bob fuck was going on. But I couldn't. I couldn't control who I talked to; I couldn't even control who took my picture. So I used what I had available: my charm and Sergeant Stephanie Segula.

Which meant mostly using Segula. Yes, I use people. I'm an asshole. I get it.

"I didn't know that," I said. "Really." I let my voice trail off, trying to sound humble. Just a guy caught up in things bigger than himself.

Her face softened.

"Sergeant Segula—"

"Call me Steph."

"Steph. How much do you know about . . . uh . . . my mission?"

"Not much. Nobody does. It was top secret, obviously. I know that you were the lead for the offensive." She lowered her voice. "Can you tell me anything about it?"

I pretended to consider it. Of course I couldn't tell her, since I had no idea what lies others had already told about it, and I *certainly* couldn't tell her the truth. But I couldn't come right out and say that. "I wish I could. But you know . . . classified."

"I understand." She twisted a little, back and forth, both hands on her camera. "Well, I've got what I need. I'll let you get some rest."

"Thanks for making me look good," I said.

She smiled and turned to go.

I waited until she had almost reached the door. "Hey, Steph? Can you do me a big favor?"

She turned, smiling. "Sure. What can I do?"

"There was another soldier on my mission. His name was Kendrick."

"Kendrick? Sorry, that doesn't ring a bell."

"He was—" I stopped mid-thought. She didn't know who Kendrick was. That was *not* good. "Who *have* you talked to?"

"Sergeant Miller. She's an absolute pain in the ass."

I laughed. "Yeah, she is." And the fact that she was the one who had talked to public affairs meant something. The problem was, I didn't know what. She worked for Dentonn, but the offensive suggested that Gwan had prevailed in the battle of the colonels. But if that was true, why was Miller still involved? Unless the two colonels were still going at it. Which meant I *really* needed some intel. "Steph . . . if you could . . . get a message to her from me? Tell her that Gas is awake and needs to talk to her?"

"Sure, absolutely."

"Thanks, Steph."

I slumped back into my pillow and waited to see if that tiny bit of charm had any juice in it.

EVERY TIME THE door opened, my heart sped up, hoping it was Miller. I needed information, and while I had my differences with Miller, I trusted her to shoot it to me straight.

First the doctor came. She told me I was doing well and that she would discharge me tomorrow. I pushed to see if she could speed that up, but she insisted that the healing accelerators needed another night, and it's hard to argue with a doctor, especially when she's a major and I'm not. Not that I didn't try. And the nurse came by and gave me the good news and bad news on Putty. He was alive, but they weren't sure he was going to stay that way. The nurse, after much cajoling, said that privately the docs gave him a ninety percent chance of surviving. That sounds high, but with our medical technology, only ninety percent meant you were in bad shape. Yes, he'd probably live. But what would that life look like?

That sent me into a bout of depression, which the medical people noticed. It's kind of their job after all. And *that* led to a psych consult, where a well-meaning doctor made me open up and share my feelings about Putty, my mission, my status as a hero, and even my parents. I lied, of course—you don't make it as long as I have in the infantry without knowing how to tell psych what they wanted to hear. All except for my thoughts on Putty. Those were pretty straightforward. If they'd wanted to save some time, I could have helped them out: I felt like shit about the whole thing. I'd fucked up, and Putty had paid for it. He had basically sacrificed himself to save me. I told all of that to the shrink, and he gave me some bullshit about mission and tough decisions and honoring the sacrifice. Easy for *him* to say. He'd probably never seen a live firefight. And it wasn't his friend in the rejuve tank.

All this meant that clearly I was going to need more time with a shrink. He surely saw that. Wisely, he didn't mention it. There would be time to deal with that later, after I knew the situation better. Until then, I wasn't giving the full truth to anybody. Not even a shrink. In theory, we had doctor-patient confidentiality, but I didn't trust that for a minute, given my situation.

I wondered if they monitored how my stress level went down *after* the psychologist left.

Finally someone I knew arrived. Erickson slipped through the door before it fully opened and had it closing again almost immediately. She was dressed in blue scrubs instead of her regular uniform—something was up.

"Listen, don't talk. I can't stay long." Her words came out rapid-fire, even for her. "Miller got the message that you were awake, but they won't let her in to see you. Me either, but I have a lot of friends who work in the med facility, so they were able to sneak me in. Very long story short, they're calling us heroes and said if we mentioned anything about what really happened, we'd be in a lot of trouble. Patel is fine. He was in the brig for a bit, but now he's out, and he's not supposed to talk about that, either. Putty is—"

"I heard about Putty."

She hesitated, wasting several seconds. "I'm sorry."

"Yeah," I said.

"Kendrick is missing."

"*Missing?* What?"

"I've gotta go."

"No, wait . . . what about Kendrick—"

"Nobody has seen him since we got back to the station. Miller will get to you as soon as she can so she can give you the story," Erickson said, already moving toward the door. "She told me to tell you this . . . she was very clear." Her voice changed in an impression of Miller's stick-up-the-ass sergeant voice. "Don't. Do. Anything. Don't. Say. Anything."

Despite the strange situation, I laughed at her imitation.

"Tell her I won't." I didn't fully trust Miller or even know where she stood on things, but we could agree on not talking until I knew what was going on.

"See you soon," said Erickson. With that she was gone, and I found myself more troubled than before she came.

They were putting us on parade. So why were we being silenced?

And why the hell was Kendrick missing?

FOR THE REST of the day, I saw nobody but medical people. Two different nurses came in from time to time to check on me, and the doctor came in after dinner to check on the integrity of my collarbone, which she pronounced not a hundred percent yet, but good enough that she'd still discharge me the next day.

I had a tough time sleeping, which happens when I get things on my mind. I start to rehearse what I'm going to do, what I'm going to say, how I'm going to react. The problem was, in this situation, while I knew something was going to happen, I couldn't fathom what. I'd come up with too many possibilities, and there were probably even more that I hadn't considered. I was running a big game, but I wasn't the only one. Gwan for sure had his own, and almost certainly Dentonn. And that just accounted for the players I knew about. Hell, I half expected one of Ma Ventnor's goons to show up and smother me with a pillow. Though I really hoped she didn't know I was involved. Some people might be that kind of petty, wanting their victim to know it was them. Not me. I'd prefer to get away clean and for Ma to never even think of me again.

Miller was the wild card. She'd sent Erickson in to talk to me, which seemed to mean she was at least nominally trying to help me, unless that was a ruse trying to get me to trust her. She could still be working for Dentonn. Somehow I didn't think so. As I've mentioned about Miller, she was pretty straightforward. She wouldn't stab me in the back.

She'd look me in the eye and stab me straight in the heart.

The guy I needed to talk to was Colonel Gwan. Until I did, I wouldn't have a clear read on where I stood. But Miller didn't want me to say or do anything. Why? What did she know? Had she seen the information Dex had obtained, and did that change things? There were too many variables, and every time I worked through them, I started the cycle again in my overactive brain.

My first thought—the reason I would tell someone to keep quiet—was that she'd told a version of the story, and she wanted to make sure that when *I* talked, I told the same lies. And I'd have believed that if it had been anybody but Miller. Because when I thought about how *she* would handle it, I believed with a lot of confidence that she'd have told the truth. I'd flat-out told her it was *her job* to tell the truth. But if it was that simple, she could have had Erickson simply tell me that. But she didn't. She said don't talk. Period. The implication was clear. She needed to tell me something before I talked to others, and it was too complex for Erickson to pass it in a message.

That alone added to my questions. Was the idea simply too complicated, or was it something that Erickson didn't know—or something Miller thought she *shouldn't* know? That thought turned in my mind for hours. I'd get away from it, but it kept coming back. I got maybe two or three hours of sleep. I should have asked for a sedative or something, but I didn't know what would happen in the morning, and I wanted a clear head. When they released me, I'd find Miller, figure out what she knew, and then find Gwan and get to the bottom of Kendrick missing and everything else. After I checked on Putty.

Whatever the emergency, that came first.

CHAPTER 18

THE START OF THE DAY DIDN'T GO AS I'D HOPED. I got released, but they wouldn't let me see Putty. He was still in intensive care, and no matter how much I bitched about it, they wouldn't let me in. And I *did* bitch, loudly and to anyone who would listen, right up to the point where a master sergeant first threatened to write me up if I didn't stop complaining, and then, when that didn't work, threatened to beat my ass.

They did let me talk to Putty's doctor, who informed me that Putty was out of the woods—he'd live—but that he was going to need serious work, including the loss of part or all of an arm. Which sucked. They'd give him a cybernetic arm, so he'd have a reasonable quality of life, but it meant the end of his career in the augmented infantry. Power armor relied on nerve and muscle impulses to work. Prosthetics were practically identical to their biological counterparts in terms of movement, and they could surely design a mech suit that reacted to an arm that was essentially another machine, but that would mean a custom job, and the military didn't do that. Putty would get a new assignment. One that didn't involve combat. And unlike Patel, Putty didn't want out.

That was going to hit him hard. I really needed to talk to him, to see how he was doing.

The doctor promised that I could see him in two days, though the treatment would last longer than that. Two fucking days. And that was on top of the three I'd already been in bed.

As a leader, it was brutal not to be able to talk to one of the members of my squad for so long. Worse, not to talk to my friend.

The second surprise came when I tried to leave the med facility. Two SPs stood waiting for me just outside Putty's doctor's office, as if they'd been afraid to come in, but were absolutely not letting me slip past. One of them I knew—a tall, dark-skinned corporal named Ramia, who was leaning against the counter of the nurse's station, trying to look casual. I couldn't remember her first name, but I knew I *should* know it, which bothered me, because I don't usually forget things like that. I hadn't slept with her or anything. Contrary to rumors about me, I hadn't had enough partners to forget. Seeing the SPs, I figured that my rant about not letting me see Putty, which turned into a rant about the relative worth of medical people in general, had gotten me in trouble. So while I was surprised, I wasn't *that* surprised. I'd been an asshole. Trouble comes with the territory when you're me.

"I didn't mean that stuff about the medical types," I said. I wanted to find some answers, and being in D Cell was going to make that difficult. "I'm really sorry."

"Sergeant Gastovsky?" asked the SP who wasn't Ramia—a shortish, freckly guy whose name tag said Pasternak and who looked eighteen but had to be older since he wore sergeant stripes like me.

I looked from him to Ramia while pasting an exaggerated questioning look on my face. Did he not know? His partner knew me, and he'd been waiting outside for me to emerge. And I had on a clean uniform, complete with name tag, just like him. Sometimes I hate SPs. "Yes?"

"Come with us, please."

"What's going on?"

"Our orders are for you to come with us."

I looked to Ramia, but she shrugged. There wasn't much she could do since the guy outranked her, even if she wanted to. "Okay, I'm coming. Can you at least tell me where we're going?"

The guy didn't respond, which pissed me off. He could do his job without being a dick about it. I almost said that but restrained myself. Who says I can't learn?

That said, I can only learn so much. I kept pressing.

"Are we going to D Cell?"

"No," he said.

Okay. That was something. Clearly he wasn't going to say any more than that, so we walked in awkward silence. People passed us in the hall, but if anybody looked at us, it wasn't more than you'd expect to see for someone being escorted by two SPs. That would always draw attention on the station. Someone getting arrested made for good gossip. I hoped that we'd pass someone I knew, someone from the squad especially, but we didn't.

WE ENDED UP the last place I expected—a recording studio, complete with a high-tech camera rig, operated by a corporal I knew named Dicontenza—Deeko for short—and a reporter introduced to me as Sergeant Todd LaChance, who, despite the uniform that marked him as a soldier, was too pretty to actually be one. The guy probably got to intake training, and they took one look at him and said, "Nope. No soldiering for you. You're going to be on camera." Or maybe I was still just a bit loopy from the hospital. They also had a makeup artist, but she wore a smock over her uniform, so I didn't get her name. While she covered me in thick foundation and a bunch of other stuff I didn't know anything about, LaChance gave me a rundown.

"I'm going to introduce you, and then I'll have a series of questions for you. This is for recording, not streaming, so if you stumble over an answer, just stop, and we can cut and start again."

"I hate to break it to you, but I don't know anything. Really." It wasn't true, but it seemed more prudent than saying I had no intention of talking to him.

"That's okay. I've got a briefing here with your responses." He held a tablet out to me. That immediately pissed me off, but I didn't argue, because knowing what they wanted me to say would give me valuable information. So I played along and looked at his proposed answers.

It was all bullshit. My mission—that's what they wanted me to call it—had been developed in order to rescue Kendrick, after I'd taken the initiative to push the command to let me do it. Along the way, I'd discovered a critical weakness in the enemy, but not before getting pinned down and unable to extricate myself and my team. So I called for help and provided critical intelligence allowing our side to win a decisive victory. It made me look great, and it was a good story.

If you were Colonel Gwan.

That much was clear. This was Gwan's story, and he wanted me to tell it. He could have at least had the balls to come look me in the eye and say that himself. But he didn't have to do that. He had people to do his dirty work for him. Unfortunately for Gwan, the story didn't work for me. I had a plan too, and this didn't fit it. Having my face plastered all over the news where people like Ma Ventnor would see it *definitely* didn't fit it.

I handed the tablet back to LaChance. "Yeah. I'm not saying any of this shit."

"Colonel Gwan's orders." He said it like that closed the subject. Which, for most sergeants, it probably would have.

"I don't see Colonel Gwan here."

"Don't be a dick," he said. "I've got no reason to lie about it."

"I don't think you're lying. But if the colonel wants me to do this, he's going to have to come tell me himself."

"He told me you might say that."

"Yeah?" I asked.

"He said that your choice is do it, or I call the SPs and you go straight to the brig."

Huh. So that's how we were going to play it. LaChance wasn't bluffing. I'd have bet a lot of money on that. And

Gwan had me in a tough spot. I didn't want to be on camera, but I couldn't get any answers if they locked me up. And there was still the matter of Kendrick's disappearance. To finish my game, I had to be able to move. I think Gwan was counting on that.

I was debating my next step when Deeko, the camera operator, helped me make my decision by winking at me behind LaChance's back. That probably doesn't seem like much, but Deeko and I had done some business in the past, and while the wink didn't promise anything, it gave me some belief that we could handle things after the fact. It wasn't at all a good solution, but it beat the brig.

The filming itself went by in a blur. The camera faced me while LaChance remained off-screen, asking me questions. They told me they'd film him later, which meant they could change the questions and plug my answers in, but it didn't matter. They were going to keep filming until they got what they wanted, regardless.

When we finished, I washed my face in the sink of a small latrine to get the makeup off of me. I didn't need the ribbing that everyone would give me if I went back to the barracks area wearing it. I half expected the SPs to show up again and take me away, but they didn't. They let me just walk out. I guess having me on film talking about the mission meant that Gwan had won and I was no longer a threat.

Go ahead. Keep believing that.

I WANTED TO find Kendrick, but I didn't have any leads, so I decided to talk to Miller in order to decrypt Erickson's message and to figure out where she stood on everything. I headed to her squad room and knocked on the door. Erickson opened it.

"Is Sergeant Miller here?"

Miller appeared behind Erickson. "You made it."

"Can we talk?" I asked.

"Yeah. Let me put my boots on," she said, correctly understanding that I didn't want anybody else listening. She joined me, and we started down the corridor. I probably could have found an empty room, but people would talk if we went somewhere alone. I didn't understand our situation—professionally or personally—so I definitely didn't want people talking.

I decided to keep things general until I could suss out her role in things. "The message you had Erickson deliver was pretty confusing."

"Was it?" she asked. "Seemed pretty straightforward to me."

Her attitude brought me back in time and made me want to punch her, but I played along to see what I could learn. "Don't say anything to who?"

"To anybody. They're going to try to use you as propaganda."

I snorted and rocked to one side as I walked. "They already did."

"But you didn't do it. You kept your mouth shut, right?"

"What does it matter?" If she wanted to keep talking, I was going to keep giving her the chance.

She stopped walking, forcing me to stop as well, and stared. "Really?"

"They put me in front of a camera crew and told me that either I told their story or I went to the brig."

She stared, and something in that look let me know that she wasn't *totally* against me. "Oh, shit."

"Yeah. Let's keep walking." I started off again, and she matched my stride. "What made you warn me?"

"There's something off with Colonel Gwan. He's telling a story that's not true."

"That he is," I agreed, without elaborating.

"And now you're part of it."

"I'm going to level with you, Miller. I was always part of it."

She looked at me for a second and nodded. "I think I knew that. There was always more to this than Kendrick."

Surprisingly, I found myself appreciating her. She was smart, and she was a good soldier, and she didn't deserve to be caught up in this mess. But like me, she was going to have to play the hand she had. Still, I made a decision right there—and I can't even say why, for sure, other than a gut feeling—if she would be straight with me, I'd help her play it. But that required a test.

"What about Dentonn? Has he tried to pressure you since you've been back?" I asked.

"Oddly, no. He hasn't even approached me. I've been wondering why. I know he and Colonel Gwan don't get along, so maybe because Gwan is having success, Dentonn is pulling back? But I've had darker thoughts about it too."

"Yeah? Like what?"

"He told me to do something illegal. Maybe he's trying to distance himself from that and hang me out to dry."

"Interesting. Maybe." In truth I had no idea, but it seemed plausible, and I couldn't rule it out.

"Somebody is following us," she said.

"What? How do you know that?" I started to turn my head.

"Don't look, dumbass," said Miller. "Haven't you ever watched a spy show? You don't let on that you know they're there."

"How did you notice?" I kept walking, stiffer, fighting the urge to look back.

"I'm a woman. We've got to notice these things." That was a sad commentary on life, but I understood what she meant.

"Do you recognize them?"

"No. It's a skinny guy, light skin, civilian clothes but a soldier's hair. Could be anybody."

"What do we do?" I asked.

"Act natural."

"Cool." I reached out and took her hand. She flinched, but then relaxed, her hand warm and dry in mine.

"What are you doing?"

"Acting natural. You said someone's following us, so I'm giving them something to look at."

"What are you talking about?"

"I'm talking about two soldiers walking together. A moment ago, we were talking about conspiracies, but if you look at us now, what do you see? Just two young people looking for a place to bang."

"You're a pig," she said, but her voice had a smile in it, and she didn't try to pull her hand back.

"I'm really not," I said. "I'm a con man. And one of the first rules of a con is that you've got to give them something to look at so they don't see the truth. Because if they don't see *something*, they'll keep looking until they do."

"Okay. Let's say I buy that." She swung our intertwined hands, pretending to get into it. "So this is the show. What's the truth?"

I walked with her a bit longer before answering, deciding what to share, deciding how much I could trust her. "How much do you want to know?"

"You said something to me down on the planet. You told me my job was to tell the truth. If I'm going to do that, I want to know everything."

"Everything?"

"It's the only way I can help," she said.

"Okay—but why are you helping me?"

She thought about it, hesitating before speaking. "I'm not sure. I think it's because down on the planet, I saw a different side of you. Don't get me wrong; most of the time you're not a good soldier."

I laughed. "Thanks."

"Really, though. You know that."

"It's a fair assessment."

"But you care, Gas."

"About the military? I don't think you quite hit that one."

"No, not about the military. You care about your squad. And down there? I was part of your squad."

And she was right. I did care about my squad, and however it had happened, she was part of it now. I stopped walking and turned her to face me, still holding on to her hand. "Okay. I'll tell you everything. But not here. Not where people can see us."

She nodded, and bit her lip, and damn if it wasn't kind of cute. I didn't know what to say next, which left me flustered. I had to visit Dex and see what information he had extracted from Ma's system, and I had to find Kendrick, and I had to check on Putty, but at the moment I couldn't figure out how to let go of Miller's hand.

Then she kissed me. It was a quick thing . . . she put her other hand on my forearm, stood up on her toes, and kissed me on the lips. Mouth open, but not too deep. We were standing in a public corridor after all. I went to put my hands on her waist, but she had pulled away, and it was too late. And whatever I was about to say fled my mind like rats when a light came on. Not that we had rats on the space station. Which was a dumb thing to think about, but that's what happens when someone kisses you and your brain turns to mush. "Give them something to look at so they don't find the truth, right?" she asked.

"Huh?" I stammered. "Oh. Right."

She smiled, and for a second I thought she might kiss me again, but instead she turned and walked away, intentionally swaying her hips from side to side. This time I definitely was watching.

CHAPTER 19

THE NEXT MORNING, RIGHT AFTER BREAKFAST, I checked the news to find that our offensive was still ongoing, and the rout of the Confed forces on Gallia seemed imminent. Thankfully my name didn't appear anywhere, and my role in the whole affair remained anonymous, though it did make me wonder why they'd insisted on getting me on camera, and why public affairs had called me a hero. Why have that information and not use it? Another name *did* appear over and over.

Colonel Gwan.

It was time for me to confront the good colonel and see where we stood. None of my squad had any clues that might solve Kendrick's disappearance, and if anybody knew his whereabouts, Gwan would. Beyond that, I clearly didn't understand his game, which meant that I didn't know how it affected mine—or if mine was even still viable. Regardless, I wasn't ready to give it up, so I headed to his office.

In the command group, I found the desk of Colonel Gwan's admin, and I smoothed my uniform a little as I approached. "I'd like to get on Colonel Gwan's calendar. I have some things about the recent mission to discuss with him," I said.

"Sorry, he's not available today," said the corporal with the perfect uniform and soldier-poster-model black hair.

"He's expecting me." It wasn't really a lie. He probably *was* expecting me. That didn't mean he wanted to see me.

"I said he's not available." The corporal looked at me and cut his eyes hard toward the exit, reset, and did it again. Was he trying to signal me? Something was off.

"I need—"

"Get the fuck out of here," he said in an exaggerated whisper. It took me a second to piece it together, to read his emotions. He wasn't trying to blow me off. He was trying to warn me about something. I didn't know what, but it didn't matter. I needed to get out of there and reassess.

"Thanks for your help," I said, a little louder than necessary. "I'll try back tomorrow."

I'd almost made it to the door when a voice boomed across the room. "Sergeant Gastovsky!"

I had a bad feeling about it, and for a second, I considered hustling the last ten paces to the door. Instead, I stopped and turned back toward the voice.

"With me."

It was the base sergeant major. Fucking great. He was the senior enlisted soldier on the entire station. Not an officer, but a direct advisor to the commander, and probably the second most powerful person in and around the

Gallia system. Some enlisted soldiers would argue the most powerful. I knew this much: I was not at all happy to learn that Sergeant Major Kinsley knew the name of Sergeant Jared Gastovsky.

"Yes, Sergeant Major," I said when I entered his office.

"Shut the door."

I complied.

"The commander wants to see you."

"Yes, Sergeant Major." I wanted to ask why, but my voice wouldn't function. My mouth apparently had a sense of self-preservation.

"When you go in there, you do not speak unless she asks you a question."

"Yes, Sergeant Major."

He stared at me for a few seconds and shook his head. "You're in it now. You know that?"

"I don't understand, Sergeant Major."

He stared at me some more, almost like he was trying to read my soul. Trying to find an ounce of insincerity in me. "This is officer shit. It's no place for us. You hear me?"

"Yes, Sergeant Major." I really hated that type of rhetorical question from leaders. Of course I heard him. I had no idea what he was trying to communicate, but I heard him.

General Yaklin's office wasn't as impressive as I expected. In fact, it looked almost exactly like the sergeant major's, with the exception of it being in the corner and having a door that I expected led to a private latrine. I wondered if the general had a nicer toilet than the ones regular soldiers use. What can I say? I think a lot about toilets, and it seemed better than trying to puzzle through why the general wanted to see me, especially since she would probably tell me. I stood in the entry, Kinsley so close behind that I could hear his breath in my right ear. The general took off her reading lenses and stood up behind her desk but didn't come around. "Sergeant Gastovsky."

"Yes, ma'am."

"Stand at ease."

I did, moving from the position of attention to an only slightly more relaxed posture.

"What do people call you?" She had a soft voice, calming, like a doctor, and it seemed at odds with someone commanding a huge military installation.

"Excuse me, ma'am?"

"Other soldiers. What do they call you?"

"A lot of people call me Gas, ma'am."

"Gas. I like that. Do you mind if I refer to you by that name?"

"No, ma'am." It was weird, but what was I supposed to say? It's like when a girl's dad asks if you're going to treat her right. There's only one correct answer if you don't want him to murder you with an ax.

"Good. What are you doing here, Gas?"

"The sergeant major told me you wanted to see me, ma'am." It wasn't what she wanted to know, but I kept the smart-ass tone out of it to keep it safe. I had no idea why the commander had summoned me, and all I wanted was out of there.

She smiled, but it was a cold, killer's smile. "In the command group. Why are you here?"

"Oh, yes, ma'am. I came to see Colonel Gwan."

"Why? Did he send for you?"

That seemed like a loaded question, like it had more behind it, but on the surface it was easy enough to answer honestly. "No, ma'am, he did not." I wasn't offering any commentary on that, though.

"Do you usually make a habit of visiting senior officers?"

"No, ma'am. Colonel Gwan has called me to talk to him a couple of times, though. He had me doing some public relations work surrounding the current offensive, and I had some questions." That had enough truth in it to be safe without giving anything away.

"Colonel Gwan is busy, and as far as you're concerned, he will be busy forever."

That took me aback. "Uh . . . yes, ma'am."

Behind me, the sergeant major growled, my answer apparently having one too many words in it.

"It's okay, Sergeant Major." The general smiled. She either had great hearing or she knew him well enough to predict his reaction to the inappropriate stutter in my response. "Gas here isn't going to be a problem. Are you, Gas?"

"No, ma'am." I said it smoothly, not letting any attitude come through. I was lying, but if I showed any insolence, the sergeant major would pop my head off like the top of a beer. Once in rejuve was enough for this week.

"See, Sergeant Major?" she said. "Not a problem. Because if he is a problem—if he is a problem in even the smallest way—things will not end well for him. We have enough evidence against him to dishonorably discharge him—at a minimum—but more likely he'll rot in a military prison for years."

I have to say, I don't enjoy the phenomenon where someone talks about you in the third person like you're not there. But there was no denying its effectiveness in this case. I guess when you're a general, you don't have to be subtle.

"We understand each other, don't we, Gas?" she asked.

"Yes, ma'am." Again, what else could I say?

"Good. Now. If you should have any issues that require the attention of senior officers, you will report to my operations officer, Colonel Dentonn. Is that understood?"

"Yes, ma'am." *Dentonn. So he is still a player after all.* It left me with another enemy, but at least I knew it now.

"Excellent. You're dismissed. And remember, no problems."

"Yes, ma'am." I turned and walked out her door into the outer office, and then waited for the Sergeant Major to indicate that I should leave the command group. It clicked for me then. Back on the planet, I'd been worried that Gwan intended to blow me off by leaving me to the enemy, but I'd been mistaken. *This* was his plan. He didn't have to kill me. He had the command structure, and they had control of every aspect of my life. I didn't think that they were necessarily a homogenous group—I suspected Gwan was still at odds with the other leaders. But that didn't mean he couldn't use them to rid himself of a pesky sergeant.

I didn't meet anyone's eyes as I left, staying focused

on the door. I didn't want them to see me, because I was afraid my look might be transparent.

I had some bad news for the general.

I *was* going to be a problem.

I NEEDED TO see Dex and assess the information he'd gathered, but I got a message across my device that Putty was awake, and that took priority. I made my way there, keeping alert for anyone following me. The watcher from the previous night with Miller had me a little spooked, and while it didn't matter if someone was following me now—I wasn't doing anything wrong—it seemed a good idea to get into the habit of being aware.

A young-looking doctor met me outside of Putty's room to brief me before I went in, which I took as a bad sign. If everything is okay, nobody needs to prepare you. Putty had lost his right arm. His right femur was still in pieces, and he'd need another day back in the rejuve tank before he'd be able to stand on it. Between that and fitting him for the prosthetic arm, the doctor estimated three days before he'd be released. I could have really used Putty's help figuring out my current predicament, but his recovery meant more than anything. Three days was a small price.

His room was small but efficient, packed with machines and monitors, all beeping and blinking in reds and greens and blues. He had tubes running into his good arm and leg, and wires disappearing under the covers of his hospital bed.

"How are you feeling?" I asked.

Putty's eyes were open, but unfocused. "I'm high as fuck, Gas."

I laughed. He laughed too, which I guess hurt, because then he winced. "Sorry," I said.

"No worries. I lost my arm." He turned his head, looking at the bandage that covered his right shoulder.

"Sorry about that," I said. "It's going to be hard for you without your right arm. That was your only girlfriend."

"I hear your sister is still available."

That's when I knew he was going to be okay.

"Besides," he continued. "They're giving me a robot arm. State-of-the-art. I'm sure there will be some kind of attachment they can put on the end for me. You think I should ask my doctor about it? She's pretty. Ooh . . . what about a buzz saw blade?"

I laughed again. I'd have to warn the doctor. I wouldn't want Putty to suffer a medical accident. "You remember any of what happened?"

"Most of it, until the end. I have no clue how we got off the planet. I just woke up here."

"Our side launched a major offensive, and we're winning. It's a long story. You rest. I'll fill you in when you're better."

"So I guess we're heroes?"

"*You* are, buddy. That's for sure. *You* are." And he was. Regardless of the reason I had him down there, Putty did exactly what a soldier was supposed to do. He fought to protect the squad. To protect me. Whatever else happened, whatever the general said, that didn't change. I owed him.

"Thanks. I'm going to close my eyes for a minute. Being a hero takes a lot out of a guy."

"Okay. I'll stay here for a bit."

"Cool. Hey, Gas?"

"Yeah?"

"Thanks."

And that's when I might have started crying. A little.

WHATEVER GWAN HAD going, he was ahead of me, and that meant I needed a new plan. That meant I needed to talk to Dex. Because I didn't trust anybody, I doubled back on myself three different times to make sure I didn't have a tail. In theory, they could be tracking me by my military-issued comm device, but I'd spoofed my location to a different part of the base, so I wasn't too worried about that. They might also be watching Dex, but if anybody could protect himself in a situation like that, it was him.

I found him at his desk, walled off by stacks of equipment crates in the corner of the large sterile lab. A couple soldiers occupied other desks, but all of them had their heads buried in their machines or were staring at virtual projections. I found Dex himself watching the latest episode of a popular fantasy show on his work rig.

"Hey, Dex. How are you watching that on a government machine? Won't you get caught?"

He gave me a withering look. "Please."

"Have you looked at the info that you got from down on the planet?"

"Officially? No. That's my story and I'm sticking

to it. But if I had, I would tell you that right now, you should walk . . . no, you should *run* away. It's not too late. I could wipe everything and none of this ever happened. We go back to our regular lives."

"I could do that. But you know I won't, Dex."

He nodded. "Yeah. I know. I just want it on the record that I said it. Because you know how there are people who, when something goes horribly wrong, say things like, 'I don't want to say I told you so'?"

"Sure."

"That's not me. When I'm visiting you in prison—or at your funeral—I'm totally going to say it."

"Aw, Dex. You'd come to my funeral?"

"Let's hope not."

"So what you've got—"

"Is the type of stuff that people murder other people over."

"Can I see it without putting it on the net?"

"That's the *only* way you can see it." He unlocked a drawer with a biometric lock and took out a tablet. "This is a sandbox. It hasn't touched anything, it never will touch anything. Look into the red square."

I looked into the red square on the tablet.

"It's now coded to your retina. If anybody else tries to access it, it will wipe itself."

"Is this the only copy?"

He looked at me like I had a dick growing out of my head. "Of course it's not the only copy. But it's the only copy anyone is ever going to find. And as far as it matters to you, *yes*, it's the only copy."

"I don't want to get you in trouble," I said.

Dex laughed in his deep bass voice. "Sure. Because when have you ever done that?"

"I'm serious."

"I know you are. And you're not going to get me in trouble. Because when you walk out that door, we're done. We don't talk again, we don't even *know* each other."

"Seriously?" I asked.

"Seriously. This is too hot."

"But you still want your cut."

"If you somehow manage to live through this and get paid," he said, "then yes, absolutely I do. But I'm not going to hold my breath."

"So little faith," I said.

"It's nothing personal. Just playing the odds."

I had to respect that.

AFTER THAT SALES pitch from Dex, I couldn't *not* look. I could always reassess afterward and back out if it was too hot for me to handle. I think I even convinced myself of that—that I could walk away if I didn't see a clear path to victory. That would have been the smart play, and I consider myself to be a smart player. But then, most people probably overrate themselves, and I include myself in that. Either way, I disappeared into a maintenance shaft and opened up the files.

It took me five hours to get through it, there was so much stuff. I'll give this to Ma Ventnor—she kept detailed records. Payments received, payments made. Everything. Some of it was encoded and didn't have real names attached to it. But some of it did. And I was willing to bet that a professional forensic data analyst would be able to put together a lot more than I could. Not that I needed one.

What I put together was enough.

Two major defense corporations had made payments to Ma to keep the war on Gallia going. Big payments. Ma, in turn, had paid off government officials at the highest levels, both on planet and off. And some at lower levels. One in particular stood out. Colonel Dentonn. The record didn't detail the purpose of the payment. Perhaps it was just to protect the town of Kiergard. But it didn't matter. A colonel had taken money from a mobster, and that mobster was in bed with two defense contractors. Someone else could tie the pieces together and make a case. Not my job. My job was to take advantage of it, and if I couldn't do that, to blow the whole thing up.

Did I take it personally, though? You bet your ass I did. It made me mad as fuck to find out that the war was essentially a con. Which, I know, is a bit hypocritical, given what I do. I get that. But when I ran a con, I knew exactly who I was running it on, and those people were usually chasing something themselves. That's what made them good marks. They *deserved* what they got. In the case of Ma Ventnor and the defense companies and Dentonn, they were running a game on the entire galaxy and throwing away the lives of soldiers and even civilians, just so they could make a profit.

If that didn't make them marks worth going after, I'd retire from cons right now.

I don't want to overstate this and make it into some sort of ethical thing on my part. I'm nobody's hero.

I look out for myself. But sitting there in the dark maintenance shaft, I had at least a small shred of righteous anger tied up with my personal greed.

What I didn't have was a plan . . . or a team. And that presented a problem. Kendrick was still MIA, Putty was WIA, and Dex was done. Patel was on his way out, and regardless, I couldn't drag him into anything else. Rookie, Chang, and Erickson didn't fit for a situation like this, and Miller? I just didn't know. Martinez would be useful, but only if I needed someone to put a bullet in my head to give me a quick out. I didn't discount that possibility, but hopefully it wouldn't come to that.

My assets were my own wits and a tablet full of incriminating information, and I was facing off against the full weight of the military-industrial complex, to include the general and all the resources of the entire station.

Naturally, I went on the offensive.

CHAPTER 20

L IKE THE COMMANDER'S OFFICE, COLONEL GWAN'S personal quarters were smaller than I thought they'd be, utilitarian, with just a desk, a footlocker, a wardrobe, and a single bunk with a civilian quilt on it. A small rug covered the middle of the standard station flooring. He did have his own small latrine, with a toilet, sink, and shower. That was a nice perk. They could have spent a little more on security, though. Because you never knew what kind of miscreant might decide to break in. I guess with the senior officer quarters all being in one short hallway, they relied on technology and the common sense of the average soldier to keep them secure. But you can fool technology, and nobody ever accused me of having common sense.

I took a seat on the foot of the colonel's bunk and waited. His mattress was the same made-by-the-lowest-bidder model as mine, which surprised me. Why bother getting promoted if you can't get a better mattress?

Just another reason to get out of this organization.

It was probably two hours before he came in, but I wasn't leaving. Gwan wanted to separate himself from me. I hadn't figured out exactly what I intended yet, but regardless of where I ended up, I needed to reverse that, because no plan of mine involved Gwan winning the war and becoming a hero without fixing the bigger problem. Dentonn's name had been in Ma's files, and I believed that would bother Gwan. But to put that to the test, I had to talk to him, and it was a lot easier to do if he couldn't avoid me because I was sitting on his bed.

The door whooshed open, and I immediately recognized my miscalculation. It's easy to figure that out when you're staring at an angry colonel with a pulse pistol leveled at you.

Right. Officers carry sidearms, even on base.

Whoops.

"What the fuck are you doing in my quarters?"

I slowly stood and raised my hands. "I needed to talk to you, sir."

"What if someone saw you? There are cameras. And your locator."

"Nobody saw me, sir, and my locator . . . well, let's just say that it's not a problem."

He lowered his pistol toward the floor but didn't put it away as he considered my answer. "I could have you thrown in the brig just for altering your locator data."

"You'd have to arrest a third of the base if you did that, sir."

To his credit, he didn't push back on that. "I should have known you wouldn't have the sense to just go away."

"Nobody ever accused me of having sense, sir. After

all, I'm the guy who let a colonel manipulate him into stealing a drop ship and starting a war."

"And now you're here to blackmail me." He raised his pistol again. "Maybe it would be easier if I discovered an intruder in my room and shot him in my surprise."

"I'd prefer a different solution, if I'm being honest, sir. No blackmail. I just want to cut a deal. But I figure we have a problem. You already got what you wanted, so you have no motivation to help me. All I can do is threaten to fuck things up and hope that you'll work with me."

"I've got you on video discussing the entire event," he said.

"*Do you*, sir? You might want to check on that. Digital data is really finicky."

He considered it for a second, as if I might be bluffing, and then he laughed and holstered his pistol. "Well played. You really are a little shit." But there was no bite in the words.

"This is true, sir. A really sticky shit."

"So how about we cut to the chase and you tell me what you want."

"The first thing I want, sir, is to know what's happened to Kendrick."

"Corporal Kendrick is fine."

"That's not really an answer, sir."

"And that's not the tone you take with a colonel." He stared me down, but I stared right back. We were kind of beyond chain of command bullshit right now.

"Let's call him an insurance policy, then," he said.

"In case you decide that you're going to get out of line."

I considered that long enough for the silence to get awkward, but I couldn't see any way to pressure him. Gwan held most of the cards—or at least the cards that were currently on the table. I had my own, but I was keeping them in my pocket for now, saving them for the right time. "Okay, sir. If that's how you're going to play it—"

"I've got to protect myself. It's not personal."

"It *is* personal, though. I want you to take care of my team, sir."

"Your team other than Kendrick?"

"*Including* Kendrick. But that can wait until you've got your assurances, if that's the only way."

"Looking out for your people is at least honorable of you. We haven't prosecuted any of them. So there's that."

I didn't buy it. He was trying to show his beneficence, but he *couldn't* prosecute them without messing up his own story. "I'm looking for a little more."

"Of course you are."

"Hear me out, sir. I don't think you'll find it unreasonable. In fact, I think that some of what I want can benefit both of us."

"I doubt that."

I ignored him and started ticking items on my fingers. "First off, I want Patel's medical discharge expedited with the full medical pension that he's earned, and I want no charges against Erickson."

"She used nanite technology without authorization—"

"No, sir. That was all me. Sure, she injected them. But I paid for them. I can prove it."

He stared me down, trying to read me, but I wasn't giving anything up. It would be hard to call me a liar when I was admitting to a crime. "So you'll take the fall for that?"

"Yes, sir."

"Fine. Done."

"There's more, sir. Second, I want you to assess Erickson's credentials and, when you find what I know you're going to find, I want you to give her a job as a military doctor."

"You want me to make a medic into a doctor? I think you're overestimating the power of a colonel."

"What I want, sir, is for you to promise to look into it, and do everything in your power to make it happen. That's it."

"And you'll just trust me on that?"

"Yes, sir. If you say you'll do it, I trust that you'll do it." I knew he could lie, but he wouldn't in this case. He didn't have to, and Gwan was a guy who wouldn't waste a lie on something small.

He considered that. "Okay. I'll do it. What else?"

"The general told me I could be dishonorably discharged. In fact, she threatened me with it when I tried to go see you at your office. She said if I was a problem, that was what I had coming. I want you to *make* that happen. Dishonorable discharges for both me and Kendrick. I just want out."

"You want out of the service?" He sounded surprised, as if wanting that was a strange thing.

"Yes, sir. I don't fit here, and I definitely don't want to sit around with all of this hanging over my head. I'd rather move on and be done with it."

He looked down at the floor as he thought. "I can make that happen for you. Sure. We've got more than enough to make it stick. But Kendrick hasn't done anything to warrant a discharge."

"Sure he has, sir. He went AWOL. When he stayed down on the planet, that was intentional."

"That's ridiculous."

"Ask him, sir. Push him on it and see what he says."

"Okay. Sure." He didn't meet my eyes, and I marked that for a lie. At least I had found the line. And with that, I knew that he probably wasn't going to let Kendrick go, even when he got what he wanted. "What about the rest of the squad? Martinez, Putkin, and Stimpson?"

It impressed me that he could rip off their names off the top of his head. "As you mentioned, sir, no charges. I appreciate that. I don't need much for them—just owe them a favor."

"A favor?"

"Yes, sir. Down the road, each of them might ask you for a favor." He looked skeptical, so I hurried on. "Nothing ridiculous. Help with a future assignment, transfer to another unit. Little stuff that's hard for a soldier, but nothing for a colonel." It wasn't much, but it didn't have to be. I had them covered in other ways.

He grunted. "Sure. I guess I can do that. Anything else?"

"Just one thing, sir." I hesitated. To get him to bite on this, I had to give him part of the truth, which risked everything else. But I believed that Gwan was, at the heart of things, a man who wanted to do the right thing.

"Spit it out."

"It's about the war."

"We're going to win it. It's finally going to be over."

"Sure, sir. This one."

"Right. After twenty-two years."

"And I appreciate that. I really do. But there are eighty-seven other wars going on in the galaxy on planets just like Gallia, sir. Give or take one or two, depending on how you classify things."

"I'm aware."

"What if we could stop all of them?" I asked.

"We can't."

"What if there was evidence—"

He shook his head. "It doesn't matter if there's evidence if nobody wants to see it. You don't understand the forces at play here, and how high up it goes."

I did—maybe better than he did, given what I'd read in my secret files—but he wasn't ready to hear it. "We could try, sir."

"If I try, I run the risk of losing what we've gained *here*. Once we have success on this planet, I can use that to try to leverage change in other theaters."

I didn't agree, but I nodded, giving in. Gwan wasn't going to help, so I'd have to find another way. But he didn't need to know that. "That makes sense, sir."

"Tell me you're not going to do something stupid, Gastovsky."

"I'm not going to do anything stupid, sir. Just do what you can to protect my people and expedite that discharge. I don't want to be here any longer than I have to."

Gwan checked the hall for me before I left. It wouldn't do much good to defeat the cameras and the tracking system if I ran into the general in the hallway. When it was clear, he gave me the signal, and I got out of there.

It wasn't a perfect meeting. He wasn't going to do what I wanted, and I couldn't trust him with my information. But at least I knew where I stood and what I had to do.

I needed a new game, and that required help.

MILLER WOULDN'T HAVE been my first choice if I had other options. But as I've said, I play the hand I have, not the one I wished I had. My new plan called for a second person. I'd wanted it to be Gwan, as he was basically untouchable, but Miller was my next best bet. After all, she'd told me that she wanted to know everything. I had to test that, but first, I felt the need to address what had happened the last time I'd been with her.

We were walking through the hallways, specifically *not* holding hands. "So, are we going to talk about what happened?" I asked.

"What are you talking about?" She smirked. She knew exactly what I meant.

"When you kissed me," I said, loud enough so that people walking by looked at us and giggled.

"*I* kissed *you*?" She asked. "*You* kissed *me*."

She couldn't be serious. Could she? Had I kissed her? No, I hadn't. But the fact that she now had me questioning myself said something about my state of mind. "That's your story?"

"Story? That's what happened."

"*I* kissed *you*."

"That's how I see it."

We walked on quietly after that, until we reached our destination, because I needed a spot away from prying eyes and ears so that I could fill her in. And that's how I ended up alone with Kara Miller in a two-meter by three-meter supply closet that had no cameras and a lock on the inside of the door, all for the low price of fifteen credits paid to the enterprising staff sergeant who maintained it. That it also had a portable cot we could set up was a bonus. It gave us a place to sit.

"You know everyone is going to think we're having sex. Nothing we say after this is going to change that," said Miller.

That she understood this made me like her even more. "Sometimes you have to sacrifice for the cause."

"Easy for you to say. Your reputation is already shit."

"Very true. I'll do what I can for you. I'll tell people that I put my best moves on, but you wanted to take it slow. I mean, obviously I can't say you flat-out rejected me. Nobody would believe that."

She laughed. "I think *some* people would believe it."

"Yeah? Who?"

"Most of the women who know you."

I put my hand over my heart, wounded. "Ouch."

"Come on. We've only got thirty minutes. Which, now that I think about it, isn't a lot of time for what people think we're doing in here."

"What, like three minutes for the act, twenty-seven minutes to recover, right?" I gave a double fist pump.

"I want to revise my previous answer. *Every* woman who knows you."

As much as I enjoyed the banter and wanted to continue to see where it led—I had thought about that kiss a lot—she was right. We had limited time, so I went into business mode. "You said you wanted to know everything. Do you still mean that?"

"Absolutely."

"Why?" I asked. The answer mattered. I was about to involve her in something way beyond what she expected, and while I didn't want to scare her off of it, I also didn't want her to go in for the wrong reasons. I *thought* that I had a good read on her, but I wanted confirmation. Because we couldn't go halfway. Halfway got you all the trouble and none of the gain.

She thought about it for a bit, which I appreciated. She was taking it seriously, the joking and flirting over. "Because something big is happening, and we were part of it. And I get the feeling—it's just a feeling at this point—that there's more to it. And knowing that, I don't think I can live with turning my back on it. But more important, I can tell that means something to you, and I trust you."

"You *trust* me?"

"Well, not with everything. But in this case, yeah, I think that you're going to do the right thing."

Was I, though? I was definitely in it for myself, but I guess I could argue that I was doing the greater good on top of that. It's hard to say. What wasn't hard was the fact that I needed a second person, so my own personal bias was already pushing me toward telling her everything, to the point that I really didn't trust my own motives. So I did what I always do and went with my gut. "Okay."

"You're going to tell me?"

"Yes." I took a deep breath and dove in. "We've been at war forever, and neither side has taken a planet outright in over two decades."

"True, but that could speak to the nature of warfare, right?"

"What do you mean?" I asked.

"It's a two-sided affair. Holding a planet when the other side can drop in from space seems like a pretty impossible task."

"Exactly. So why do we even bother?"

"What do you mean?"

"If nobody can win on the ground because of what happens in space, why do we bother to fight on the ground? And why are we specifically prohibited from fighting each other in space?"

"We have treaties that prevent attacks against space assets. The casualties would be too high."

"And if you were trying to win a war, high casualties for the enemy are bad because . . ."

"Gah!" She threw her hands up. "You're questioning the entire nature of the last five decades of war."

I considered that. I hadn't thought of it that way. Turns out, I didn't have a problem with it. "Yep."

"I'm going to need more than that. You're got great instincts, but you're asking me to question the entire military establishment."

"Not just the military establishment. Essentially, I'm questioning humanity as a whole."

"You're pretty ambitious."

"Yes, I am. And here's why." I unlocked the tablet with my eye and handed it to her. "There's too much to read right now. Just look at the highlighted documents. It will show you how the Gallian mob is in business with two major defense companies, and how between them, they're making payoffs to government and military officials to ensure that the war continues indefinitely."

She read for ten minutes while I vibrated in my seat, my mind running through what I was going to do if she didn't buy it. Or, more important, what I'd do if she *did*.

"What's Dex think of this?" she asked finally.

"Dex is out," I said.

"He's out . . . so who's in?"

"On this? Me. And you, if you want. You can still walk away. Nobody knows I showed you, and we can both say I didn't. I'll take it to my grave." I found that I meant that.

"What is it that you want to do?"

"Release the data to the galaxy. People in the government, but more important, people outside. The press. Anyone who will investigate without worrying about the outcome."

"That might not be many people."

"It doesn't have to be. Just the right people. I think the media would do it. They'd at least get it out in the open. Whether anybody believed them or not, it's hard to say. But I think that in the hands of the right reporter, this is a story."

She considered it. "Sure. I can see that. Okay. I'm in."

"You sure? There's a lot of risk."

"I jumped on a drop ship with you down to the planet. I'm not afraid of risk."

She had a point, though they were different kinds of risk.

She continued, "Give me a couple of days to see what I can find out. Maybe I can come up with a way to get the information off the base."

"Yeah?"

"If this is true, people are dying for no reason. I think it's worth taking a chance. It's the right thing to do."

That's when I knew she was really in. Because that was Miller. She cared about the right thing. I appreciated that about her, even though I didn't always share that sentiment. But in this case, maybe I did. And that was a little too serious for me to contemplate, to the point where it made me uncomfortable. So I did what I always do when I get uncomfortable. I made a joke to break the tension. "Are you sure you're not just coming along for the ride due to your overwhelming attraction to me?"

She laughed. "Not everything's about you."

I laughed too. "I noticed that you avoided my question."

"Did I?" she asked. Still a horrible liar, which I also now found pretty irresistible.

"So . . . we've got like five minutes left. You should probably take off your top."

Miller laughed again. "Yeah? I don't see that happening, but I'm intrigued. Why? Shoot your shot, Gastovsky. Convince me."

"Well, we need to do it to maintain our cover. You see, there's a secret network of men that talk, and since people will know we were in here together, I'm going to be under obligation to describe your breasts to the group in explicit detail."

"What? Ew! Really?"

"No, not really. You have my word; I'll keep your breasts completely to myself."

She shook her head, smiling, unsure what to do with me.

"So . . . is that a no?"

"You're such a dumbass," she said, but she was still smiling.

"Yeah, but you *liiiike* me."

CHAPTER 21

S HE DIDN'T SHOW ME HER BREASTS, IN CASE THAT'S
important to know.

Instead, she went to look for a way to smuggle the
info out, and I went back to my normal routine. We had
time on our side. The general had told me to back off,
and until I made a move, it should appear that I was
doing exactly that. I'd confronted Gwan, but I didn't expect him to go running off to tell anybody. He'd gotten
what he wanted after all. Sure, he'd be keeping tabs on
me, and so would the general, but I could act natural for
a while and bore them into not paying attention.

It did mean cutting out some of my extracurricular
activities. I'd hate for the leadership to be watching me
for one reason, only to stumble over an unrelated smuggling operation. But if what I had planned worked, I
wouldn't need that setup anymore anyway.

The good thing about keeping quiet is that you can
hear trouble a lot more clearly when it comes.

The first indicator of something wrong came when
the personnel sergeant messaged to tell me that we had a
new soldier arriving at the squad. Sure, Putty was done

in the infantry, so technically I needed someone. But I hadn't put in a requisition, and I'd never known the personnel department to be that proactive. I wanted to call up and question it—hell, I wanted to call up and tell them to fuck off—but I couldn't. That would tip off that I suspected something, which would lead to questions about *why* I suspected something. I didn't need those kinds of things floating around. So I did what every good sergeant does when the bureaucracy does something he doesn't like.

I swore and kicked things.

"Everything all right?" Patel lay on his bunk, his tone mocking me. He'd be leaving the squad too, once his discharge came through and he processed out, but the military didn't do anything fast. Which was another reason that the new soldier showing up so quickly made me suspicious.

"A new soldier is coming in to replace Putty," I said. "Martinez, do me a favor and go retrieve him from admin."

"Roger." Martinez got out of his bunk and headed out.

"Since we're getting a new soldier, this means you can't call me Rookie anymore." Rookie sat on his bunk, looking very serious about the topic, which distracted me from my personnel problem.

"Pipe down, Rookie," said Patel. "You don't get to make that call."

"But I'm a veteran. I've been through more than a lot of soldiers up here on base."

"Rookie is more of a state of mind." Patel rolled over on his bunk, pretending that was the end of it.

"That's just it. I don't *feel* like a rookie anymore."

"Yeah. It's more a state of *my* mind than yours. I don't make the rules."

"But you're absolutely making the—"

"Let it go, Rookie," I said. "He's fucking with you. What do you want us to call you?"

"You could use my name, like you do with Patel and Martinez," he offered. When neither Patel nor I responded, he added, "Stimpson. Carl Stimpson." He paused again. "That's my name."

I'd used his name before, but it was funny to make him think that I'd forgotten it. Funny in an asshole kind of way, which . . . welcome to the augmented infantry. "What do you think, Patel?"

"Stimp?" asked Patel.

I thought about it. "There's a guy over in Bravo who goes by Stimp. We don't want people getting confused."

"Oh, right. I know Stimp. That won't work."

Stimpson looked back and forth between us, rapt, as if we seriously held his future in our hands. Which we kind of did. Whatever we called him would probably stick.

"We could go with Stumpy," offered Patel. "It sounds like Stimp."

"I really wish you wouldn't," said Rookie, who clearly didn't get how this game worked.

"Stumpy works. Or, you know, the other Stimp is a shorter guy. We could go with Big Stimp. Or Tiny," I suggested. "Classic reverse nickname."

"Oh, good one," said Patel. "And the ladies will wonder why he's called Tiny."

"I fucking hate you guys." Rookie stomped out of the room, almost running over Martinez and the new rookie, who we definitely couldn't call Rookie, one, because it would be confusing, but more important, because it would piss off Stimpson that we didn't.

"Call him Stimp?" I asked Patel.

"Yeah. Fuck Bravo Stimp. That guy's a dick."

"Who we got?" I asked, turning my attention to Martinez and the new soldier.

"Corporal James Galandro," said the short, wiry man.

"Corporal?" Not a rookie. That didn't make any sense to me, which kind of fit. On any other day, I wouldn't have thought twice about it, but today? I smelled a rat. I didn't need a corporal. I needed another heavy, and I didn't know much about Galandro, but he was no heavy. He was an obvious plant, though who specifically planted him I couldn't be sure.

"That's right," said Galandro. "Transfer from Foxtrot. They broke our company up for parts after we got creamed yesterday."

"I need a heavy."

"Don't know what to tell you, sergeant. Orders, right?" Galandro's tone gave an air of, *What can you do?* And he wasn't wrong. It's exactly how any soldier would act. It would suck to be a corporal and get reassigned to a unit where you didn't know anybody. And to have someone question it? That would piss anyone off.

"Foxtrot. You guys were down in the big attack, right?" I asked.

"Yeah, that's right," he said. "We were the only company that hit heavy resistance. Just lucky like that, I guess. Got caught in a kill zone of a dug-in infantry unit complete with bot tank support."

"They pulled the whole company out?"

"What was left of us," said Galandro. "It was a shit show from the start. We had tons of support. All we had to do was wait for it, but the captain kept pushing us forward. Felt like he wanted to win the war on his own. You know?"

That sucked. It's easy to forget that wars aren't homogeneous. You can be winning overall, but still losing in some places. "Sorry to hear that, man."

"Never liked him. The captain. Always looking up, never down. That kind."

I really did feel bad for him, mole or not. He'd probably lost a lot of friends. "That's your bunk. We'll get Putty's stuff stowed here in a minute."

"You guys are the squad that led the attack, right? Behind the lines?"

"Yeah, that was us," I said.

"Well, if I had to be reassigned, I guess this is a pretty badass place to get."

"Yeah," I said. On the surface, Galandro was a good fit. He'd been there, done that, and wouldn't be in awe of us like someone getting ready for their first mission. But I didn't trust him. The timing was too convenient.

Paranoia is a bitch.

PUTTY SNUCK UP on us. Rather, he showed up in the door, and there he was. I froze, but thankfully nobody noticed me tearing up due to the shenanigans of others.

"Who is that in my bunk?"

"What are you talking about?" asked Stimp. "That's not your bunk. It's Galandro's."

"But it *was* mine. You know that, Rookie."

"What?" asked Stimp. "Who's Rookie?"

"Very funny, Rookie."

"What are you talking about?" asked Patel, catching on. "That's Stimp. He's been with us a while. He's a badass in a fight. Saved my life."

"Stimp is over in Bravo," said Putty.

"Fuck Bravo Stimp," said Patel.

"Guys. I'm back," said Putty.

"What, you want a fuckin' hug or something?" asked Martinez, from flat on his back in his bunk.

There was silence for like three seconds, and then everybody started laughing at once, no longer able to contain it. Even Galandro, who didn't have the back-story, got in on it. He understood. It might seem kind of callous, a guy wounded the way Putty was, coming back and us giving him shit. But it wasn't. In fact, it would have been messed up if we *didn't* bust his balls. If we didn't give him a hard time, we'd be saying he couldn't take it. That he wasn't one of us anymore. You only messed with someone if they belonged.

"Good to see you, man." I walked over to hug him. He smelled like hospital, all clean linen and medicine.

"Good to be back. They've assigned me to temp billets."

"Fuck that," I said. "You'll stay with us until you get your new assignment. Take Kendrick's bunk. If he comes back, we'll figure something out then. You find out your new assignment yet?"

"Nah. They want me to go for aptitude testing after I finish physical therapy."

"If they want to find out what you're good at, that's going to be a pretty quick test," I said.

"I tried to tell them," said Putty.

Looking at his arm in his uniform, I couldn't spot anything different, except for the hand, which looked a little too perfect to be real. I gestured to it. "How's it feel?"

"A little weird. Like, you think it's supposed to work like power armor, where you're extra strong, but you're not. It's like . . . a regular arm. I don't know . . . I'll get used to it pretty quick."

"I got you."

"You think there's any way to game the aptitude test? Like, what's the easiest job in the military?"

I laughed. "Trying to slack off before you even know your next job."

"Well, yeah. I'm a hero. Time to rest on my past accomplishments. It's the way."

"With a slogan like that, you're a perfect fit for recruiting. Let's take a walk." I put my arm around him and guided him out the door.

"So . . . you and Miller, huh?" Putty raised his eyebrows in a ridiculous way.

I shoved him in his good arm, pushing him away. "You heard about that?"

"Come on, Gas. *Everyone* has heard about that." He looked back toward the door. "Guarantee the squad knows, even if they're not saying anything."

"Yeah, they know."

"So?"

"So . . . what?" I knew exactly what he meant, but I wasn't going to make it easy on him.

"Come on! I've been in the med bay, nearly dead, and this is how you treat me?"

"You could go ask Miller about it." I gestured to her door.

"No, thanks. I lost an arm. I think I'll keep my balls."

"Wise man."

"So? Really. How'd it happen?"

"Nothing happened," I said. Which was the truth, even though neither Putty nor anybody else was going to believe me. But I'd stick to the truth on this one. Screw them.

"Nothing. Right. Just like when I say nothing is going to happen between me and your sister. Spoiler alert: I really don't mean that. Speaking of your sister, remember when you told me if we got out of there alive, you'd introduce me?"

"Turns out I was lying," I said.

"Gas Gas Gas Gas Gas. Is that any way to treat a war hero? I mean . . . you're not implying that your sister is too good for me, are you?" He moved to the right side of the hall to let three soldiers pass by from the opposite direction.

"Absolutely not. I'm not implying that at all. I'm straight-up saying it."

Putty put both hands to his heart. "That hurts, man."

I laughed, but the interaction had an effect on me. I decided not to bring Putty in on the next job. Miller was taking a risk, but she could survive it, because she was clean. Putty? Not so much. If they started digging on him, they'd find stuff, and he didn't need that. "You're a war hero. You'll get over it."

"Truly I will. Do you think Miller has a hot friend?"

"I'm glad to see that despite your new appendage, you're still the same old idiot."

"Yeah, I'm kind of great."

CHAPTER 22

WAITING HAD BEEN KILLING ME, SO I WAS PRIMED to go when Miller appeared at our door. She inclined her head for me to follow her out, which maybe she thought was subtle, but wasn't lost on anybody else in the room. Mercifully, Patel, Stimp, and Martinez pretended they didn't notice. Regardless, my face still warmed as I walked out the door.

"We've got to stop meeting like this," I said.

"Yeah yeah. Find us somewhere private." She had an envelope under her arm, but I didn't ask about it. Not there.

Instead I waggled my eyebrows at her. "You don't waste any time. Can't you even buy a guy a drink?"

"I am going to punch you in the nuts."

I cringed but recovered quickly. "I'm not really into that . . ."

She threw her hands up and stomped off as I hurried to catch up. Sometimes I have that effect on people. What can I say?

"People aren't going to believe me when I tell them

we're not doing it," I said. "Hell, they didn't even believe me after the first time."

"You *talked* about it?"

"I had to. Putty brought it up."

"*Putty* heard about it? In the med bay?"

"I'm afraid so."

She considered it for a moment. "So . . . what'd you tell him?"

"I told him the truth."

We turned the corner into the main corridor. "*Everything?* You think you can trust Putty to keep a secret?"

"No! Not everything. Just the truth about you and me. I trust Putty with my life. But with a secret? No chance."

"Okay, we're on the same page then." She smiled. "Did he believe you? About you and me?"

"Absolutely not."

Miller laughed. "Hard to blame him."

"That's true. Nobody is going to believe that you could resist me." I checked to make sure she was smiling. "So you're okay with it? With people thinking we . . . you know."

"What choice do I have?" She looked at me for a few seconds, her brow furrowed as if she were considering something. "Besides, it works better for me than it does for you."

"How do you figure that?" I asked.

"I'm the woman sleeping with that handsome stud, Gas." She blinked her eyes and put her hands under her chin. "He's so dreamy."

I laughed. "Whatever."

"On the other hand, you're now off the market. No woman wants to mess with Killer Miller. Nobody is going to sleep with you."

I thought about it for a minute, considering my words. It felt like there might be more behind her statement than the joke, and you know . . . I found I didn't mind. "I think I'm okay with that."

"Yeah?"

"Yeah." We walked in silence a bit longer. I didn't have an appointment for the supply closet of love, so I led us to the maintenance bays and searched around until I found one with only bots working, which wasn't hard to do. We accidentally interrupted a couple behind a large processing unit but got away without it being too awkward and found our own dark corner.

"You know all the hookup spots, don't you?" asked Miller. "I'm not sure what a lady is supposed to think about that."

"What can I say? I'm resourceful. It's why people like me."

"People like you?" She shoved me in the shoulder. "We can talk here?"

"Definitely. There are cameras in the bay and they'll know we're here, but they don't cover this spot. Which is why people come here."

She leaned back against the wall. "So you're saying the command knows that couples come here and avoid the cameras, but they don't do anything about it?"

"I'm sure they know what's going on. They're not stupid. But by making us sneak around for it, it gives them deniability. They don't have to deal with it, because it's not supposed to be happening. Besides, someone would move the cameras anyway."

"That seems like a pretty dangerous situation from a base security perspective."

I leaned against the wall beside her, our shoulders almost touching. I wasn't worried about anyone over-hearing us—the hum of machinery would drown us out. I just wanted to be closer to her. "Yeah. I'm not saying they've really thought it through. More like *not our problem*."

"That's . . . well, anyway, we've got more important stuff to deal with."

"Right. What did you figure out?"

"We can spread the word. You've seen how fast rumors fly here. We tell a few soldiers and it's all over the base in no time." She looked at me with big eyes, and again it was hard to concentrate.

"What? No! We can't do that," I said.

She looked confused. "Why not? People need to know."

"Yes—the *right* people. I thought we discussed this." I, in fact, knew that we had discussed this, as she'd made a point of repeating those exact words to me.

"Why wouldn't soldiers—the people on the actual front lines—be the right people?" she asked, fixing me with a glare.

"Because everybody we tell, we put in danger. What do you think they're going to do to soldiers they catch spreading that story?" I almost said, *What do you think they're going do to us?*

"This is bullshit. Soldiers aren't going to stand for it."

I understood her position. I really did. She was all
about doing the right thing, but in this case, the right
thing ended very poorly for her and me. "You think
they're going to care?"

"Of course they will," said Miller.

"Nope. I mean, some will. Maybe ten, or even twenty
percent. But most are just here to do a job. Some even
like it."

"Twenty percent is enough." Now she just wasn't
thinking.

"To do what? Mutiny? Because I have some bad news
for you about how those end."

"Gah! You're impossible!" She was mad, and part of
me knew that it wasn't at me, but it still sucked, having
that anger focused in my direction. But she was going
to get people hurt or killed, and as much as I wanted to
stop that angry look she was giving me, I couldn't do it.
Not at that cost.

Still, I tried to explain. "The world is wrong. That's
not new information. But we can't involve other soldiers.
We've got to get the information off base. As long as it's
here, they can contain it. They control everything."

"Okay," she said, calming herself. "I was afraid you
were going to say that, so I did some checking, and
there's one other way."

"Lay it on me."

"Everything digital that leaves base goes through one
place. Nothing gets out of there unchecked," she said.
"When we as individuals hit send, our data doesn't go
out in real time, but gets aggregated via the long-range
comm unit that transports it to nodes throughout the

galaxy, where it gets further broken down to its destination. Though all of that is automatic, and almost instantaneous."

"Right. I send a note and my mom gets it a couple of hours later, even though we're nine hundred light-years apart." I hadn't thought about how that applied to our current situation, but it made sense.

"So to get our data out, we have to get into central comms and bypass all the station filters."

"Okay. What's our play?" I asked.

"Sex vid."

"Well, the lighting isn't great here, but I guess—"

"Just stop with the nonsense this *one* time?" she asked, cutting me off.

I stopped talking.

"There's a black-market industry where soldiers send large packets of data off base . . . you know . . . to lovers far away."

I was definitely aware of this enterprise, even if I didn't have my fingers in it. "Sex vids."

"Exactly."

"That's great. We can use that. Unfortunately, normal soldiers don't have the entire command structure watching them as they try to send off their happytime vids."

"Right. But we can get a mule," she said. "Anybody can send the stuff."

I considered it for a bit, but I couldn't do it. Part of it was that I had to see this done myself, but the other part was that I couldn't implicate anyone else. They'd pay too high a price if they got caught.

"I've got to send it myself."

"I understand," she said, and her face said she meant it. "But you'll have to figure out how to get to central comms."

I nodded. "Right."

"So," she said.

"So."

"We going to do this thing?"

I almost made a smart remark, but thought better of it, even though I had a feeling that she was setting me up with a double meaning on purpose. But I played it straight. "Yep. Let's do it."

"We're not going to end war, you know."

"No. Of course not. But we might change the way people think about it for a while."

"You know, you're kind of sexy when you're self-righteous," said Miller.

"Yeah?"

She smiled and put her hand on my forearm. "Yeah. And once we do this, it could go really wrong. We might not get another chance."

"We've got a lot to do," I said, but there wasn't a trace of protest in it. I was just giving her one more chance to change her mind.

"The data will still be there tomorrow."

CHAPTER 23

THE NEXT MORNING . . .
    Say what you want about me, but I don't kiss and tell. Not too much anyway. And not about this. If anybody wanted the scoop, I intended to direct them to Miller for answers. I figured that would put an end to their curiosity in a hurry.

Putty pulled me aside in the squad room, gesturing for me to follow him out the door.

We barely got outside before he started speaking. "Killer has turned on you."

Confused, I couldn't respond immediately beyond, "Huh?"

He gestured with his head for me to follow him farther down the hall, away from our rooms. "Miller. She's fucking you."

"I told you we weren't—"

Putty grabbed me by one shoulder and spun me to face him. "Stop it, Gas. This isn't a joke."

That's when I started to panic. For Putty to be serious about something . . . I hadn't seen that before. "Go ahead. Tell me what it is."

"She's met with several people—at least two that I know for sure—and she's feeding them some conspiracy bullshit about us not trying to win the war."

"That's—"

Putty cut me off before I could interrupt. "Gas, she's telling people that you're going to expose it."

I sighed. That was unfortunate, if not unexpected. To my credit, I didn't overreact, because I didn't believe that Miller was trying to sabotage me. What her action told me was that she didn't trust me, so she had gone rogue and started implementing her own agenda. She had agreed to follow my lead, and I had hoped—even expected—that she would. Turns out, I was incorrect. That's the problem when you work with somebody who truly believes in right and wrong. Looking back, I should have seen it coming.

Shit. I needed to figure out what it meant, where it put me.

I definitely needed to move up my timeline. But first, I needed to square up with Putty, who was still standing there, hand on my shoulder, waiting for a response. "Yeah. About that. She's not wrong."

Putty looked like he wanted to speak, but for once held his tongue and thought first. "Okay," he said finally. "I trust you. But I don't trust Killer. What do we do?" And just like that, he was in. I'd almost gotten him killed, but he still trusted me. That put some things in perspective in a hurry. Namely, it wasn't just myself that I was risking.

"Here's what we're going to do . . ."

IT TOOK ME until the next day to prepare to go to central comms and broadcast my information, because I couldn't go directly. I also had to avoid whoever was watching me, in person, via tracker, and by camera.

I had to disappear, which I had done for short stints previously, but is harder than you might think on a station with forty thousand residents. We had access to the cameras—I wouldn't stand a chance if we didn't—but simply cutting the feeds off as I went would paint a target on me as sure as the cameras themselves. I had to actually disappear.

To do that, I needed help, so I recruited what I called my B team, a group of people who wouldn't know anything beyond their specific role, thus keeping them from the majority of any potential repercussions. I concocted a cover story that the command had ordered Miller and me to stay apart, and I needed to get off surveillance so we could hook up. Since the rumor had gotten around the base that we were together, everyone believed it. It seems like an overly simple story, but simple stories are the best kind. Every soldier sees it as their solemn duty to help their fellow soldiers get laid. It's one of those rules they don't teach you in basic.

To kick things off, four of us stood talking inside of one of the big 3D printer bays. We had no reason to be there, but there was no reason for us *not* to be there, either. What nobody would notice at first glance was that we all wore identical uniforms, were all male, and all had about the same build. Why would anyone pay any attention to that? Things like that happened all the time on a military station. The cameras also wouldn't see the fifth member of the team, dressed the same, since he was standing in a dead spot.

After about twenty minutes hanging out and chatting, lulling anyone watching into complacency, another member of our team—one of Dex's tech wizards (Dex was back in. I'd had to beg)—cut off the camera that covered us for forty seconds. It had to be that long. There were eight doors I could reach in forty seconds. Even if somebody was watching in real time, by the time the camera in the printer bay came back on, they'd have to look for me in a bunch of different locations. Instead, they'd find four identically dressed soldiers with their heads down, faces avoiding cameras, none of whom were me.

And that's how I came to be sitting alone in the dark inside an empty recycle bin, having never left the room. Several hours before our staged conversation, two other soldiers—who knew nothing other than that they were part of a clandestine operation, and getting paid well for it—had made sure that the wheeled cart that handled misprinted materials for recycling had enough room to comfortably fit one average-sized soldier. The cart was rarely used, since the printers ran automatically, but for whatever reason, probably years ago, some facility manager decided the room needed a recycling cart.

I sat there for three and a half hours. At that point, if somebody *was* following me, they would be panicking. But by that time, they'd have to search the entire base to find me again. There was some chance that they'd physically dispatch people to look for me. They probably wouldn't, but on the off chance that someone thought, hey, why not check the recycle bin, I had a story ready. Because technically, I hadn't broken any rules. Sure, it was weird to hide. But it wasn't against the law.

You know, except for carrying all kinds of classified information on a small disc in a secret inside pocket of my uniform shirt.

The downside was that I couldn't know how hard they were looking. We'd considered using a comm device, but anything electronic created a chance to find me, and while I hated being cut off, we couldn't risk that. Instead we had a manual abort. Three soldiers were going to walk by as I snuck into central comms: two women and a man. If the man was in the middle, the mission was a go. If he was anywhere else in the group, I'd keep walking.

First I had to get there, but it was an easy enough trip. Two soldiers came and wheeled the recycling cart out of the room and down the corridor to the appropriate chute. Once there, they waited ten seconds for someone else to switch the camera off, then flipped the lid open. I hopped out and moved quickly out of the camera's view while the soldiers pulled the few items of recycling from the bin and disposed of them.

Only one more camera covered the space between me and my destination, and I assumed that one was off too, though I had no way to tell. Two consecutive cameras going out would be a sign to anyone paying close attention, but we didn't have any better options. It would take a really astute observer to piece it together, and by the time they did and could react, I should have the data well on its way. Once I launched it, they could grab me, but they couldn't erase what I did. They would catch me after the fact, regardless. Once the data got out, authorities would track it back to its source. Me. There was a good chance that I'd be celebrating from prison. Revealing the truth and exposing a conspiracy didn't mean I wasn't breaking the law. So I'd focus on getting the data out and worry about avoiding the consequences later.

I walked at a steady pace, trying to look like I belonged. Just another soldier. Move along. Nothing to see here. I watched for my signal—the three soldiers—but they didn't appear. I only had another thirty meters to the door, so I slowed a bit to give them more time. *Where are they?* My mind raced through possibilities, and of course I jumped to the worst. We'd been compromised. More likely our timing was just off—after all, there were a lot of moving parts, and syncing them down to the second through people who didn't know the entire operation was bound to have glitches. It could have been as simple as a higher-ranking person interrupting the trio to speak to them. They'd have no choice but to stop.

And then I was at the door, and I had to make a choice. I glanced to my right, hoping that three soldiers would walk around the next corner, but I couldn't wait long. The camera hack would end in a few seconds, and I needed to be either gone or inside by then.

I held my breath and opened the door. Inside, it took a few seconds for my eyes to adjust, the room lit only by a single overhead augmented by video screens and thousands of tiny LEDs from all the equipment. The square room measured maybe eight meters on a side, though it felt cramped with all of the terminals, servers, and other high-tech stuff I couldn't identify. Two soldiers sat against the far wall, backs to me, and they didn't turn. The third person in the room, a short master sergeant, nodded her head to an empty seat facing the wall to my left. My research told me that the facility had an on-duty staff of four, leaving one soldier unaccounted for. Perhaps that was part of how this worked. I didn't know. I didn't need to. Just like the master sergeant didn't need to know what I was sending out. She'd been paid, in whatever currency she took, by someone else on my team, and now I had my access.

I sat in the chair and examined the interface. The screen on the terminal already had the page I needed open. All I had to do was address the message, load the data, and send. I pulled the data drive from my inside pocket and inserted it.

Behind me, both doors whooshed open. A female voice shouted, "Everyone step away from the terminals."

I sat frozen. Then, after a second, I turned to see what had happened. Three SPs had come in through the far door. The techs at the other two terminals hadn't moved, either, so I stayed put.

"Now!" shouted the lead SP.

The next few seconds passed in a blur as everyone moved at once, bumping into each other in the now crowded room, three or four additional SPs having entered from the same door I had. For a second, I lost track of everyone except the two SPs who forced me to my knees, wrenched both my arms behind my back, and flex-cuffed my hands together.

I was facing my terminal, so I had a front row seat as another SP went to the workstation and ejected the data drive. "I've got it, Sergeant!"

"Good," responded the SP sergeant, her voice calmer now. "You and Smithwick take it to exploitation. Gervais, Mattingly, take the master sergeant to D Cell. Eicholtz, you stay here with the other two. Once we're gone, they go back to work until their relief arrives. Command has called in the next shift. If they haven't arrived in ten minutes, contact me via comm."

"Roger, Sergeant," came a chorus of voices. I didn't know this SP, but her squad had its stuff together. Everyone but the two SPs with me started moving.

"Get him on his feet," said the sergeant. "Let's go."

The two soldiers lifted me to my feet—I didn't resist— and they shoved me toward the door. They weren't gentle, but they weren't trying to punish me, either. Just doing their job. One walked on either side of me, and the sergeant walked in front. I didn't recognize any of them.

"Where are we going?" I asked.

"Shut up. Don't talk," said the sergeant, without turning around.

No problem. I had a pretty good idea anyway. I knew the way to D Cell, and we were headed that direction, right up until we passed the corridor where we should have turned. Okay. So, not D Cell. I kept my eyes focused on the dark skin of the SP sergeant's neck, not making eye contact with anybody. I don't care who you are or what you did, getting perp-walked was embarrassing.

They had me dead to rights trying to broadcast sensitive information, so this ended only one way for me. Well, two ways, I guess. Prison or death. Three if you count *accidental* death as well as court-ordered. It seemed a pointless distinction to me: dead is dead after all. I sound flippant about this, and that might be hard to believe, but I remained pretty detached about the whole thing. I kept trying to remember my mantra: wherever I am, that's where I want to be. That included being in cuffs and marched to an undisclosed location. All I had to do was find a way to turn it to my advantage, and I couldn't do that if I panicked.

We took two or three turns and stopped in front of a door in a part of the station I'd never visited and waited. It didn't have an entry pad, which was weird. After a few seconds it opened, and we went through into a narrower corridor. The door closed behind us, and something about the atmosphere changed. It felt as if the pressure had risen slightly, plus there was the sound. Not really sound so much as *lack* of sound. Everything was muted. Duller. They had probably built some dampening element into the walls, ceiling, and floor. Which meant we were in some sort of facility that handled classified information.

We passed only one other person, a light-skinned man in uniform sitting behind a square window about four meters past the door. Probably the guy who let us in. At the far end of the hall, we stopped in front of another door, which also opened without us doing anything, and they pushed me through into yet another corridor, this one with three doors on each side. The sergeant stepped aside, and the two soldiers guided me to the second door on the right, where they stopped me, and one of them removed my flex-cuffs with his cutter.

"In you go," said the sergeant, and I complied. What else was I going to do? I appreciated the gentle treatment thus far, and I didn't want to give them any reason to change that now.

The door—several times thicker than the standard station doors—zipped closed behind me, and I was alone. I couldn't even hear the SPs outside of it.

My cell measured maybe three meters wide by two deep and had a narrow cot with a thin mattress bolted to the back wall. A chemical toilet that seemed to grow straight out of the floor in the corner comprised the only other furniture in the room. The door had a head-sized window in it, but from my side, it was opaque. They could look in to check on me, but I couldn't look out. Not that they needed to look in. Two cameras stared at me from recesses in opposite corners of the ceiling, which was higher than I could reach even if I jumped.

I didn't bother to check the door. You don't build a secret detention cell without making sure it works. Instead, I sat down on the bunk and assessed my situation. Which . . . well . . . I was fucked. That part of the assessment was easy. But why was I there instead of in the regular D Cell? That was a problem. Inside D Cell, I knew people. I had considered the possibility, and if they'd taken me there, I had help. Here? Maybe not. The fact that they even *had* a super-secret detention area that average soldiers didn't know about seemed an ominous portent. And the soundproofing didn't make me feel better about it. Kind of a *nobody can hear you scream* vibe.

Nope. Didn't need to think about that. Of course, I *did* think about it. I couldn't *not* think about it once I got it in my head. But I tried to focus on other things and prepare mentally for whatever came next. I wondered how many more of the team they'd rounded up. Maybe none. The guys who had helped me hide in the bin—they didn't know they were doing anything more than helping me out. That didn't mean the command wouldn't detain them anyway, at least until they could debrief them and find out what they knew. They might even hold them for a couple of days to scare them. But in the end, they'd probably walk, maybe with some additional duty or other administrative punishment.

And I wondered who'd caught me. Was it Gwan, deciding that he needed to wrap up a loose end? Or was it Dentonn? If it was Dentonn, that opened the possibility that Miller fed him information, but I didn't believe that. At least, I was trying not to believe it. Putty had said she'd turned on me, but I didn't think so. Sure, she hadn't followed my plan. But once I knew that, I'd accounted for it and adjusted my own actions accordingly.

Weirdly, what really kept running through my head was that I was hungry. I hadn't had dinner, since I'd been hiding out, and it was probably close to 2100 hours by now. I had no way of knowing since I'd left my device in the barracks so they couldn't track me. I sat there

for maybe thirty minutes, maybe longer—hard to say—
before I decided that nobody was coming, and lay down.
Whatever they had in store for me, I'd be better off if I
faced it well-rested. I closed my eyes and tried to sleep.
It evaded me for a long time, but eventually I drifted off.

than any other mess hall breakfast was the plastic flat-
ware in place of metal. He even brought me sugar packets and cream for my coffee.

"Thanks," I said. Cultivating a decent relationship
with the guard seemed like as good an idea as any right
then. I didn't hold it against him. *He* didn't put me in
prison.

After breakfast and taking care of my business, I
took stock of my situation and thought through my next
move. I considered asking for a lawyer, but somehow I
didn't feel like the law really applied to me at the moment. Not the parts where I had rights anyway. Escaping
the cell seemed impossible, but I had to at least think
about it. I didn't have a shower, so at some point they'd
have to take me out for that . . . maybe. That could present an opportunity. The guard was complacent, and I
thought I could take him, especially with surprise on
my side, unless he had a partner. That gave me another
option, though escaping my room without a way to
escape the facility overall might create more problems
than it solved. And even if I made it out of the detention facility, I was still stuck on a space station where
I didn't clearly understand my enemies. Without help,
they'd simply recapture me and bring me back or put
me somewhere worse. In the end, that's what I needed.
Help. I decided that I'd focus my escape efforts on that,
though at the moment I didn't know how.

I didn't let any of this show on my face. Without a
doubt they were watching my cell via camera, and
I wanted to project calm, that I was exactly where I
wanted to be. I didn't expect them to buy it, but I also

didn't want to give them the satisfaction of seeing me worry. And either way, they hadn't beaten me yet. I still had Miller and Putty. Even though it was against our agreement, Miller had told other people and worked toward her own means of getting the news off base.

Probably.

And then I sat there. All day. Other than someone bringing lunch and dinner, I didn't see or hear a soul. That might sound relaxing, but after a while it started to get to me. It's hard to maintain the illusion that you're where you want to be when you only have yourself to convince. It was a deliberate tactic on their part—to leave me alone so I'd get in my own head—but even knowing that, I struggled. They were showing their power. They didn't have to do anything to me. They could just leave me here in secret prison forever. Someone would ask questions about my disappearance, but much like they had done with Kendrick, nobody had to answer them. I would have killed for a vid player or even a book.

They were kind enough to dim the lights for what I assumed was night, though they didn't turn them off all the way. I slept fitfully, second-guessing myself even in my dreams. I hit my low point right before what I estimated as morning, almost ready to give up, but I caught my first break in the form of breakfast. Specifically, the person who delivered it: SP Sergeant Ken Burrows. They didn't speak to me, but their presence alone meant I might have help on the inside, and I had to fight to suppress a smile that someone might see via camera. They didn't work here—not on a regular basis—so someone had made this happen. I didn't acknowledge that I knew them in any way, but when they handed me my tray, the eggs and bacon made a smiley face on the plate, hidden from the cameras by Ken's strategically placed body. When I took it from them, I messed it up so nobody would see it. Message received. I still didn't smile when they left. I kept that on the inside. But I was back.

Back where I wanted to be, even though I hadn't moved.

My interrogation came a couple hours after lunch. I had a processed turkey sandwich, if that's important. Two guards came and got me, flex-cuffed me, and marched me out of the cell block and through another door with no switch or handle. We hadn't gone far, hadn't left the soundproofed facility, when they stopped in front of yet another door and waited. This one opened into a room with a table and three chairs, all bolted to the floor. Inside waited a tall female soldier wearing a uniform with no rank on it.

"Uncuff him," she said.

"You sure?" asked one of the guards, as if they hadn't rehearsed this little number ahead of time.

"He's not a threat." She looked at me. "You're not going to cause problems, are you?"

"No, ma'am." I didn't make her for an officer—she didn't have the look. But I gave her the title anyway, so maybe she'd underestimate me. I didn't expect to be talking to her for long, but she was there and that made her the enemy. Anything I could do to deceive her, I would, just on principle.

"See? Uncuff him."

The guard followed her instruction and guided me into the room via a hand on my back. Once inside, the door zipped shut behind me. In theory, we were alone. In reality, we had company in the form of cameras in three corners of the room and a two-way mirror on the back wall. If I tried anything, the guards would return in an instant. No doubt about it. They were showing me the illusion of trust but nothing more. Still, I could play the game. "Thanks for that."

"No problem, Gas. Do you mind if I call you Gas?"

"Everybody else does."

"Have a seat." She gestured for me to take one of the chairs with its back to the two-way mirror, and I complied. "You're in a lot of trouble, Gas."

No shit. "I kind of got that impression. The secret prison sort of gave it away."

"It's worse than that."

"Yeah?" Anything she said would give me information, so I was in no hurry for her to stop talking.

"Everyone is turning on you."

"Are they?" It was a soft gambit. They'd caught me trying to smuggle data off the ship. Nobody needed to turn on me. They already had the evidence. "Who?" I asked.

"Everyone."

"I need names," I said.

"I can't give you names. It's against policy. For their protection. You understand." She spoke in calm, measured beats. Almost soothing, the way someone might sound on an easy listening music channel.

Sure. Because I was a threat to them from inside a

secret cell. Nope. Didn't buy it. And since she wasn't giving me anything I might as well get rid of her. "Then I guess we're done here."

She smiled, flat and thin, no teeth showing. "We're done when I say we're done."

"Sure." I smiled back, hoping mine was a little more natural-looking than hers.

"When did you decide to turn traitor?"

So that was her game. They *didn't* have video of me confessing, and they wanted it. Good luck with that. I sat silent.

"Did anyone influence you?"

And now she wanted me to take the bait and try to shunt my own culpability off on someone else. Except there wasn't anyone, unless I wanted to try pinning it on Gwan. But if they wanted that, it told me something. It told me that Gwan wasn't the one running the interrogation. That left Dentonn. I sat there in silence. I didn't sneer or anything. In fact, I tried to keep my face as emotionless as possible.

"You're not helping your cause here."

Silence.

"I can't help you if you don't give me something to work with."

But that was the thing. She couldn't help me anyway. I knew this because I talk to people, and people talk to me. I ask them about their jobs, and even the people who do secret stuff like to talk about themselves over a beer. After all, people like me, and what could it hurt to share? So they did. I had learned about interrogators by listening to them talk about themselves during card games or sitting in bars. I wouldn't give her anything, because why negotiate with someone who didn't have power? Interrogators were basic cogs, like me.

She could hint that she could do stuff for me, even promise it, but in the end, the decisions came from higher.

"You really want to play it this way?"

"What I want is to stop wasting time," I said. "So why don't you get whoever is watching behind the camera to come in here and negotiate like adults."

"There's nobody watching, and there's nothing to negotiate," she said.

"Sure there is. Colonel Dentonn is watching, aren't you, sir? He's a cowardly fuck who sends other people in to do his dirty work."

"Disrespect toward a senior officer is a crime. We could lock you up just for that."

"Two problems with that threat," I said. "One, I'm already locked up, and you can't lock me up twice at the same time. Wait . . . can you? Do you have some magic lockup device I don't know about? Hmm. No, you couldn't. Right?"

"And the second thing?" The frustration was beginning to show in the lines around her eyes, the set of her mouth. I tend to have that effect on people. It's a gift.

"Second thing? Oh, right. For that to be disrespect toward Colonel Dentonn, you'd have to prove that he's *not* a cowardly shit who hides behind walls and watches other people do his dirty work. Good luck with that."

Her lips quirked up for a split second before she regained control. She knew. She wasn't on my side, but she knew Dentonn was a shit. I could use that. "There's a lot of evidence against you."

"Evidence of what crime?"

"You stole a *drop ship*."

"Did I?"

"Do you deny it?"

I looked away from her and stared straight at the camera in the corner. Right at Dentonn. "I was *on* a drop ship. But go ahead—run the video of us getting on it and see who got on first. I'll give you a hint: it was Sergeant Miller. You want me to tell you whose orders she was following?"

My interrogator sat there, unsure what to ask next, meaning that we had ventured off her script, and I had the person putting questions in her ear scrambling. Unless I missed my guess, someone was pulling that footage and looking to see if I was bluffing, which I wasn't. If they dragged Miller in, maybe they could discredit my story, depending on what she said. But she wouldn't lie, and Dentonn *had* told her to follow me, so that much would come out. The thing is, on camera, she *didn't* follow me. She *led* me. She got on the drop ship first. So my lie had video evidence, and Miller's truth didn't.

None of that mattered except in how it affected Dentonn. I wanted to piss him off. On the surface, pissing off a guy who had you under control in a secret prison probably sounds like a bad idea. But that's the thing—this is the only place my plan could work. Dentonn had to believe he had me under his control, or he wouldn't talk to me. I needed to anger him enough to cause a mistake.

When the door to the interrogation room zipped open and he flew in, face red, I had my first sign of success.

"Hey! Colonel Dentonn! Good to see you, sir!" I said, waving.

He plowed into me, knocking me off my chair. I hit hard on my shoulder and back, and my head smacked into the floor. Bright spots flashed in my eyes.

"Ow."

The interrogator sprang up and attempted to get between us. "Sir, you can't—"

"Get out!" he spat, cutting her off.

She stared at me on the floor, and then back at him, standing over me, fists clenched. "No, sir. I'm not letting you beat a prisoner. I don't care who you are."

Good for her. She was a stooge, but she had a moral code.

Dentonn unclenched his hands and relaxed his shoulders. He gestured to me on the floor. "That was an accident. Please help the sergeant up, and then leave us." As if to show that he was no threat, he walked around the table and took a seat where she'd been a moment before and tried to look nonchalant.

I almost laughed at the ridiculous sight, but I covered it as I let the interrogator pull me to my feet and get me situated back in my chair. She lingered several seconds looking at us before she finally left. "You've got a problem, sir," I said.

"Yeah? Not as big as yours."

"Maybe not."

"Enlighten me. What's my problem?"

"You have a loyalty problem. You've got people here

who will do what you say, but they're not bought and paid for. If they see a crime, they're going to tell the truth. At least some of them. To protect themselves if nothing else." I wasn't really trying to inform him. I was playing to the audience outside the room, reminding them of their duty. I had no doubt that Dentonn killed the cameras before he came in. But I also trusted soldiers. In this case, I trusted their curiosity. The chance that someone was at least listening in was about a hundred percent. I wondered if Dentonn knew that, or if, in his senior officer arrogance, he actually believed they'd follow his order not to eavesdrop.

Not that any of that mattered much. Dentonn was already screwed. But I couldn't tell him that, because if he knew, then I became expendable, which seriously degraded my long-term health prospects. Not that he would have believed me anyway. But even as we sat there, Miller was smuggling the damning evidence against him off-base by giving a data drive to every soldier leaving the system for any reason, with the instructions to send them to various news outlets as soon as they reached a distant station. He had me detained, but he didn't understand I *needed* that to happen. I let myself get caught so Dentonn focused on me. It kept him looking at what he expected to see, and that blinded him to the real operation. The one that I never touched.

The thing is, I didn't want to *stay* in custody, so I had more work to do.

As if understanding my play with his people, Dentonn fired back. "You're a criminal. No decent soldier is going to believe a word you say."

"Maybe not. But *you* do."

"I don't believe you at all."

"Yes you do. Because you're a criminal, and you know how it works."

"I'm not—"

"You took money from a criminal organization to influence how you ran the war."

And then he did something I didn't expect. He smiled. "You think you're clever, trying to tell your story to anybody watching. But nobody can hear you. I didn't just turn the speakers off. I disabled them. They can see you, but there's no sound."

I nodded absently, almost in appreciation. It was a nice move, cutting me off like that, if it was true. I respected an adversary who at least looked a few moves ahead. "So why are we here, sir? Are we negotiating?"

"Negotiating? No, I think not. I just wanted to look you in your smug face and tell you that you're never leaving here alive."

"And here I thought you wanted a confession." I tried to look scared, or, if not that, at least cowed. I needed his attention focused on me a little longer, until the evidence was out in the world. *That's right. Keep looking at the shiny object in front of you.*

"I would love to have a confession. But somehow I don't think you're going to volunteer."

"You let me walk out of here, and I'll go on camera from a safe location." He wasn't going to take that offer, but he expected me to make it, so I did.

"I'm not giving you shit."

"That does seem to put us at an impasse."

"It doesn't put me anywhere. But it puts you out an airlock. Goodbye, asshole. We won't see each other again."

Hopefully he was right. About the last part—not the whole being murdered thing—but I resisted the impulse to say so. He needed to believe it was his choice.

I needed him to believe he was actually in control.

CHAPTER 25

I T'S WEIRD SITTING ALONE, WONDERING HOW SOME-one is going to try to kill you. He said airlock, but I doubted that. That seemed a little melodramatic. Not that I wanted to find out—it seemed a pretty shitty way to die.

I know that I have to trust the team, but that's a *lot* of trust when you're counting on them to figure out the plan for your death and thwart it. Granted, I'd put some of the pieces in place myself, but Dentonn had changed enough things that everyone involved would have to improvise.

News came with dinner this time.

"We've got sixty seconds where the cameras are on loop," said Ken, as they handed me my plate.

"How's it going to happen?"

"Drugs in your food. You'll eat it, get tired, go to sleep, and never wake up. They'll make it look like an overdose—that you had the drugs smuggled in some-how."

That had flaws, but I didn't have time to go into it. "So . . . ?"

"There are no drugs in the food, but nobody knows that. Eat it, wobble a little, and go to bed. They'll never know."

"They might figure it out when I'm still alive in the morning."

"You won't be here." Ken glanced down at a mechanical timer they had—they weren't carrying their device. "I've got to go. Be ready."

I DIDN'T SLEEP, of course. I just lay there, back to the cameras for I don't know how long, trying not to move. I estimated that it was past midnight when my door zipped open. There was no warning, and nobody there. It just opened. The thought crossed my mind that it was a trap, that I'd walk out the door into the waiting arms of a squad of guards, and I hesitated for a moment. But to what end? They already had me, and it's not like an attempted escape charge would significantly change my sentence. There were still the cameras. But if someone could pop the door open, I had to trust they had handled video surveillance as well. I stared directly into one and smiled. Then I walked out the door into the sound-proofed hallway.

I stood there for a moment, unsure what to do, assessing the situation. I was alone. If nothing else, it seemed like a good chance to look around. I peered through the window of the cell next to me, but it was dark inside and I couldn't see anything. So I walked toward the exit door.

It opened as I approached.

Okay then. I hurried through, and then hustled down

the corridor to the last door, expecting that to open too. I stopped in front of it when it didn't. What the actual fuck was going on? As if in answer, the door opened to someone standing slightly backlit in the relatively brighter outer corridor.

Miller, standing there giving me that cute half smile she had. "Hi."

"Hey." It took me a second to notice the two guys with her, standing back and off to either side.

"Let's go," said one of the men.

Miller turned with them, and I followed. I didn't know them, but I knew who they were. I could tell by how they moved, how they communicated with each other without speaking. Special forces. As regular infantry soldiers, we didn't see them much, but when we did, they stood out even as they didn't stand out. That makes no sense, I know. It's hard to explain. They didn't do anything to stand out, which made them . . . something. And as much as we in the augmented infantry liked to think of ourselves as badasses, every one of us knew the truth. These guys were badder. So much so that despite my burning questions, such as, *How and why did you get involved with this?* I didn't speak to them. Instead, I focused on Miller. I certainly hadn't expected her to be part of my escape. But she was here now, with this rather impressive duo, and I was glad to see her. Even if I hadn't been, it wasn't like I was turning back to my cell and my almost certain death.

Without ever saying a word, our two new teammates dragged us along to the outer ring of the station to bay foxtrot 4 and a waiting ship. They didn't run, but I had to hurry to keep up just the same, their gaits effortless and efficient. Martinez stood outside the ship's entrance with his rifle, pulling security. I must have hesitated, because Miller tugged me by the forearm, dragging me through the port onto the vessel, as our two escorts disappeared silently down the wide corridor. Inside the ship, Dex was tapping furiously on a keyboard that he had plugged into a console on the ship. A woman I didn't know, dressed in civilian clothes, was busy running through preflight checks. Miller hugged me.

"I didn't expect to see you," I said to Dex.

"Miller can be very persuasive," he replied.

"Where's Kendrick?" I asked.

Miller looked down at her feet, then back at me. She shook her head.

"We can't leave him behind."

"I tried," she said. "Dex found his location, just like you planned, but it blew up. We couldn't get to him. The operation got compromised and people backed out."

I considered it for a second, but *only* a second. Kendrick had been with me on the job since the start, and if I left him behind, he was at best going to spend his life in prison. At worst, he was a dead man. I couldn't do that, even to save my own skin. "We don't leave people behind."

"I know, but there's no time," said Miller. "Every second we delay increases the chance that we get caught. At some point, someone we haven't coopted is going to figure out what we've done to the cameras. Besides, there's no way to get in to where they're keeping Kendrick without tipping off—"

"Buy me ten minutes. I'll wing it," I said.

"We can't—"

"Ten minutes. Please," I said. "I have to."

She stared me down for several seconds, and then nodded.

"Dex, show me a map of where he's at."

Dex keyed some things into his setup, and then stood and brought me a handheld device. "Here."

"Martinez, with me," I said as I exited the ship.

"Roger."

"Kill the cameras if you can, Dex, and be ready to pop the doors when I get there," I called over my shoulder. I didn't look back. I couldn't bear to see whatever look Miller was giving me. She'd risked herself to free me, no doubt calculating every chance. And here I was rolling the dice and improvising.

But we don't leave anybody behind. Not unless we were doing it on purpose. This was my mess, and I was going to clean it up.

Martinez and I double-timed it through half a klick of corridors. The few night shift people we passed paid us no attention. Soldiers running weren't a common sight, but weren't so rare to be worth notice. We reached a door that clicked as we approached. I tried the hand pad, and it whooshed open.

I glanced at the device that Dex had given me. "Third door on the right."

Kendrick's door wasn't locked, so I entered without knocking. There were seven other rooms in the block, and I didn't want to make any more noise than necessary.

Kendrick woke when I entered, disoriented. "What? Who's there?"

"It's Gas." I found the light switch and touched it to bring on the overhead, then squinted against the bright light.

"What's going on?"

"Boots and pants and let's go. We're getting off the ship."

He was up and moving instantly, sliding into his pants and then pulling his boots from under his bunk and jamming his feet into them. "What's cooking?"

"We've got a ship. You and I are getting the fuck out of here. The heat is high."

"Let's roll then." I loved that he didn't waste time with more questions. I trusted him, and he trusted me.

We almost made it back without a hitch.

"Halt!" A hundred meters and one turn away from our escape ship, a male voice called from behind us.

Martinez and Kendrick looked to me. I considered running for the ship, but the distinctive sound of weapons slapping against shoulders made me think better of it, and I skidded to a stop, the others following suit. I turned, already having digested and identified the voice. "Colonel Dentonn. Sir."

"Hello, Sergeant Gastovsky. Going somewhere?"

"You know how it is, sir. Always busy."

Dentonn smiled. He could afford to. He hadn't drawn his sidearm, but he had three SPs with him, all of whom had their weapons poised and ready to fire. What was worse, I didn't recognize any of them. They weren't mine. "I'm afraid we'll have to put your little trip on hold."

To my left, Martinez had his rifle at the low ready. He was the best I had, but at this range, he'd be dead before he ever got it to his shoulder. "Can we talk about it, sir?" I asked, stalling. What can I say? I was winging it, and that's the best I could come up with.

"There's nothing to talk about," he said, not taking the bait.

Heavy steps sounded behind me, but I didn't turn. I didn't need to. We were pinned in. I calculated the value of calling him out for trying to kill me to try to sway his soldiers to my side, but he'd just deny it.

"What happens now?" I asked.

"Drop the weapon and go to your knees," said Dentonn.

"I don't think so," responded a mechanical voice behind me.

It couldn't be. I turned to look.

Putty. And he was in heavy armor. That was supposed to be impossible—his armor shouldn't work with his prosthetic arm—but I'd figure that out later. Because there were still three soldiers with weapons pointed at me. On the other hand, they didn't have power armor, so we had them outgunned by about a hundred to one or so. I turned back to Colonel Dentonn.

"So, what's your move, Gastovsky?" I had to give it to him. He looked as calm as if he'd planned all this himself. He clearly didn't recognize the scope of his problems. Or maybe he was in denial.

"We're leaving," I said.

"Are you? Right now there are alarms blaring and security scrambling from all over the station."

"I doubt it. My people own the cameras and the alarms. This is just you and me." *I hope.*

"So then we're at a standoff," he offered.

"An impasse, perhaps," I said, reminding him of our conversation from earlier.

He shook his head. "You're not going to shoot us. If you do that, you're murderers. Even if you do escape, you'll be hunted wherever you go, and when you're caught—and you will be caught—you'll spend your life in prison. If you're lucky."

"My other option is to surrender here and spend life in prison." I paused for effect and met his eyes. "If I'm lucky."

His eyes widened slightly at that, as he realized that I knew he'd tried to have me killed. I guess they didn't teach him in officer school that you can't threaten someone who has nothing left to lose. His three SPs had lowered their weapons, probably from a self-preservation instinct, but now they were glancing at each other.

"Flex-cuff the colonel and walk away," I said. "We'll release the camera footage. Nobody can blame you for it when you're facing a guy in heavy power armor."

Two of the SPs openly looked at the third now. She considered it for a moment, and then said, "On your knees, please, sir."

To Colonel Dentonn's credit, he didn't question it. He didn't yell or threaten. He recognized the losing situation for what it was, and he knelt, and would survive to fight on another day.

"Ankles too," I said. I couldn't have him following

us or running to get more help before we could take off. We'd need a head start if we wanted to disappear.

"You're not a hero, you know," said Dentonn.

"I know I'm not, sir. I never claimed to be one. Some of these folks are heroes, though," I said, thinking of Putty and Martinez and all the rest who risked themselves on this mission. "But not me. I'm a misfit." I turned to the others. "Let's go."

"You know they'll hack your ship and shut it down before you can get away," said Putty, as we made our way quickly to the waiting ship.

"They can fucking try," I said.

MILLER WAS WAITING at the ship, and from the way she was pacing outside the hatch, she wasn't happy about it. She smiled when she saw me with Kendrick, but her eyes went wide at the sight of Putty in his massive armor. "I thought they couldn't make armor work with a prosthetic," she said.

"I know a guy," said Putty.

"We need to get out of here." She turned to me. "And you need to get on that ship. I know you can't tell me where you're going."

"I can't. And things are going to get hot around here for a bit. They might come after some of you, but it should blow over. There were so many different people involved in making this happen that they'll be chasing it for a year before they unravel it all."

"I'll be fine," she said. "And I'll take care of the team. Don't worry about it."

"And take care of yourself."

"You too."

I wanted to go to her and kiss her. I should have, but I was a coward. Too many people watching. But not knowing if I'd see her again? I should have done it. I'm chickenshit. I stood there, silent.

"Are we going to do this, or what?" she asked, finally, turning away.

Maybe she was chickenshit too, but that didn't cross my mind at the moment. Only that I shouldn't have let her go.

KENDRICK WAS ALREADY strapped in when I went aboard. "I can't believe this whole thing worked. It *is* going to work, isn't it?"

"We'll know in about thirty seconds," I said.

The ship shuddered with a metallic *thunk* of clamps releasing. Then we drifted away for a moment before accelerating. The force of it pushed me back into my cushioned chair.

"Are they going to chase us?" he asked.

"Maybe, but I don't think so. There are supposed to be discharges for both of us in the system, and there's at least one senior officer with a reason to make sure they're honored. Technically we're not soldiers anymore."

"Sure, but we still did some shit. They won't be happy about it."

"Some of them won't, that's for sure. But others? They won their war, and they get to tell the story their way. If they drag us back, we're going to tell our own version, and they don't want that."

"So they'll hunt us down and kill us quietly," he said.

"If they can find us, they might. But it's a big galaxy, and we're about to be very, very rich."

"Yeah?"

"I figure we've got a day, maybe two, before the news breaks about the war and the mob and the defense contractors and Dentonn. You know all that money we've made doing less than legal things the last couple of years? I used it to short those two defense contractors with leveraged positions. We're already showing a nice profit with news of the war ending. But when the other shoe drops?"

"Nice," said Kendrick. "How much?"

"I can't say what the haul will be when all is said and done. But a lot. A fucking *lot*."

EPILOGUE 1

2 Days after Gas's Departure

SERGEANT KEN BURROWS LED THREE OTHER SPS down the wide corridor to the main door of the combat information center. Their heart was beating a bit quicker than normal, because while it was a routine mission to arrest someone, it wasn't just *anyone*. They put their palm against the biometric reader, and their SP override caused the door to open. They led their team inside and paused, looking up at the tiered rows of operators, their faces glowing from the radiated light of their digital readouts. They took their time, scanning the room until they located their target: the command terminal. They headed up the stairs bisecting the giant beast that commanded all aspects of the war and stopped at the fourth level. They didn't look back, trusting their team to follow behind and do their jobs. "Colonel Dentonn?" they asked.

An older man with a weathered face peered up from his screen. "What do you want—" His voice trailed off when he recognized Ken's SP brassard. That happened a lot. "You don't have authorization to—"

"Sir, you're under arrest," said Ken, cutting him off. They said it louder than necessary, to make sure that the soldiers in the area overheard it, despite their headsets.

"What are you talking about?" asked the colonel, but his darting eyes told Ken he already knew. Maybe he didn't expect it to happen like this, in public, but he knew.

"Sir, step away from the monitor and put your hands on your head."

"I'm not going anywhere."

"Sir, this is your last warning. If you don't comply, we will detain you by force."

Dentonn wavered for a few seconds, as if deciding, and then got to his feet. He wouldn't meet Ken's eyes.

"Sir, put your hands on your head."

Again the colonel delayed, but ultimately complied, slapping his hands on his head like a surly teenager.

"Thank you, sir." Ken looked over their shoulder to another member of the team. "Cuff him."

"You don't need to handcuff—" the colonel started to say, but the woman Ken had tapped for the job wrenched one of his arms down behind his back, and within three seconds had his hands secured. If she did it a little harder than she needed to, Ken didn't notice. Not officially anyway.

"What are the charges?" the colonel asked as they marched him back down the stairs, a true walk of shame in front of his entire department.

"Attempted murder, to start, sir," said Ken. "I'm sure there will be more. But for now, that's enough."

"I didn't—"

"Sir, I recommend that you remain silent," Ken of-fered. As they reached the door, Ken swore that they heard a couple people clap, but maybe that was their imagination.

47 Days after Gas's Departure

DR. FARRAH ERICKSON studied the screen in front of her, using the display to guide the remote array inside her patient's abdomen. The woman was sedated, so she wouldn't feel any discomfort, and if Erickson did her job right, she'd be back up and ready for duty in twenty-four hours. Not that duty was so important on the station recently. The war was over, and all that remained was to clean up the mess and manage the peace. Soldiers had begun to receive orders for new assignments, which had worked in her favor, as doctors were in demand in the military—they could never keep civilian practice from poaching them—and several had already departed, making way for her to take on added responsibilities.

She wouldn't be leaving the service. Not until she figured out if her credentials would hold outside, or if she could only practice military medicine. She had things to work out with that, adjustments to make, but she didn't mind. She was in her element again, and that was all that mattered.

"Got you," she said to the blockage obstructing the patient's small intestine. She triggered a micro-laser to begin reducing it, feeling a sense of satisfaction as it began to dissolve.

53 Days after Gas's Departure

"CHANG, YOU'VE GOT a package. It's big," Jenkins, a tall, thin private first class with a wispy mustache that he should probably have reconsidered, called to her from across the maintenance bay.

That was weird. She hadn't ordered anything, and nobody ever sent her physical mail. "What is it?"

"I'm a mail clerk, not a psychic. It's fucking heavy, that's what it is. You want it or not?"

"Sure. Set it down." She headed over to where Jenkins waited and pulled a cutter from her tool belt to open the package. It was long—almost as long as she was tall, which wasn't very. There was no return address on the package, no indication of where it came from other than the vendor name, a store she hadn't heard of from another system. Her name and unit were on the label in nondescript print.

"You think it's a bomb?" she asked.

"Why would you fucking ask—"

What the hell, she figured, and cut into the packaging.

"Holy shit," said Jenkins. He saw the logo on the inside packaging just before Chang did.

"Holy shit," repeated Chang. It was a hoverboard. But not just *any* hoverboard. It was a competition-grade Zoomie hoverboard. One that cost more than Chang made in a year as a soldier.

"I thought you didn't have a boyfriend," said Jenkins.

"I don't."

"Well, somebody sure as shit loves you, to send you something like this."

She nodded. "Yeah. I guess you're right."

66 Days after Gas's Departure

"STIMP, YOU'RE TOO soft." Putty glared at the tall, lanky soldier, but it didn't seem to have any effect. He really needed to work on his glare.

"That's not what your sister says," Stimp said.

"I don't have a sister, asshole."

"Not that you know of," said Stimp.

"What does that even mean?" asked Putty. "You know what? Never mind. But I'm serious. You can't give away product on an IOU. It's a cash business."

"Jameson is good for it, and she really needed her Viper. If she doesn't pay up, you can take it out of my share."

Putty shook his head. "What were you even thinking?"

"I was thinking that Jameson is hot," said Stimp.

"You can't give out freebies to a woman because you think she's hot. I swear, I work with idiots."

"That makes you the king of the idiots," offered Stimp.

"I'm going to bitch slap you with my cybernetic arm."

"Don't treat your girlfriend that way," said Stimp.

"Are you saying you're my girlfriend, or my arm is? Because your modifier is dangling."

"That's what your sister said."

"I liked you better when you were still a rookie and were scared of space whales," said Putty. He wasn't really mad. With more soldiers flooding back up to the base as they transitioned away from the dwindling war zone, demand for his services was up. Not that he needed the money. He had twenty months left on his contract, and then he was set for life. But running Gas's old empire helped pass the time, even if he had to deal with Stimp.

81 Days after Gas's Departure

MARTINEZ BELTED OUT the last note of "Timeless," a rock ballad by the legendary Canyon Stirling, holding it for a full eight seconds. When he finished, he stood on the small stage of his favorite bar on the station as applause erupted from every table in the place except one. He gave a slight nod in place of a bow, and walked over to the one silent table, where Putty and Stimp sat with their mouths open.

"How . . . what . . . do you—" Stimp stammered.

"What my less intelligent friend is trying to say," said Putty, "is that we didn't know you could do that."

"Do what?" asked Martinez.

"Sing."

Martinez shrugged. "Okay."

"Like, that was really good," said Putty.

"Sure," said Martinez. "Thanks."

"But you never talk," said Putty.

Martinez looked at him. What did he want him to say? He shrugged again.

"You know," said Stimp, "with the Gas-funded retirement plan, you should get out and pursue this as a career. You're *really* good."

"Eh. I like it here." Martinez thought about explaining himself, his reasons for staying in the military despite riches waiting for him on the outside, but then he decided against it. It wasn't anybody's business.

141 Days after Gas's Departure

CARL "DEX" DEXILL stepped off the military transport onto the platform of the terminal in the orbital station above the resort planet Mandel 3, and he never looked back. As far as he was concerned, if he never saw anything military-related again, that would be just fine. With his height, he could easily see over the crowd and spotted the public terminals he was looking for. Within a couple of minutes, he'd paid four credits—a ridiculous price, but that's what happened in an orbiting terminal—and had seated himself in front of one of the screens. A minute later, he had overridden the station protocols and had his own untraceable dark network connection.

He overrode the biometric locks—he didn't want to leave that data anywhere—and accessed his account on Sandaria, a planet known for its banking and its discretion. As promised, Gas's information led him to a welcome screen, and one more click took him to his account. The balance read 7,314,811.

Dex smiled.

A few seconds later, his fingers were flying again, and he transferred fifty thousand to a personal account under a fake identity that he could access from his current location. Fifty K wasn't much, but it would get him started. He was going to ride down the space elevator in style. First class, all the way.

Dex didn't really have a plan beyond that. He wasn't much for plans. All he knew was that he had money, and he was going to enjoy it.

297 Days after Gas's Departure

VIHAAN PATEL OPENED the door to Toys and Tech, a chime announcing his presence. He hadn't gone ten paces before the manager came through a hidden door from the back room and onto the floor to intercept him.

"Vihaan, what are you doing here?" His sister Aadya wore a black blazer over a white blouse and black slacks, and despite the innocent query, the tightness of her face said that her question held more than it seemed.

"What? I'm just checking on my store."

"You mean *my* store. You made *me* the manager."

"Yes. You're the manager of *this* store. But I manage the chain." Vihaan had four stores open already, with two more scheduled to open in the next three months and another three by the end of the year.

"I'm twenty-two. I don't need you checking on me every day."

"I don't come in here every day," he protested.

"You were in here four times last week, and this is your third visit this week." She glared at him, and he felt his face heat. Thankfully the store had just opened, and there were no customers yet to witness his embarrassment.

"Maybe I just want to see my sister," he offered.

"You have five sisters."

"Yes, but you're my favorite."

She glared at him for three or four seconds, and then she couldn't hold it in and laughed. "You are so full of garbage."

"Yes, but you love me."

"I guess." She walked over to him and gave him a hug.

"Now, let's talk about that sale display there on the endcap of aisle three," he said.

"Gah!" Aadya pushed him, turned on her heel, and strode to the back room, ignoring him.

347 Days after Gas's Departure

I CAUGHT MILLER'S FACE IN THE MIRROR BEHIND THE bar at which she was seated almost as soon as I entered. The room reeked of elegance, all dark wood and hushed sounds, and the racks behind the bar held some of the best whiskeys in the galaxy. That was precisely why I'd picked it. It was only a few kilometers off the military base on Lagrum 3, but the cost of drinks ensured that it didn't attract a lot of soldiers as clientele. I was sure that Miller saw me approaching via the mirror—she wasn't one to be caught unawares—but she didn't turn around. She wore a black dress with thin straps that showed her shoulders. I'd never seen her in a dress before. I'd barely ever seen her in civilian clothes. Not going to lie—I liked it. Even from behind and sitting down, she looked good. She still had her short military haircut, which showed off her neck, and I have to admit I took a few extra seconds reaching her, just taking it in.

"You always drink alone?" I asked.

"I'm not supposed to be alone," she said. "Some ass-hole told me to meet him here and then showed up late."

"He's only four minutes late, and he's probably worth it," I offered.

"Pfft. I doubt it."

I took the seat next to her. "What are you drinking?"

She showed me her glass. "A ridiculously expensive whiskey. You're paying."

"Happily." I signaled to the bartender to bring me one of the same. "How's the new duty assignment?"

She shrugged. "Not bad. They promoted me, and I'm training recruits. It's a lot of work, but it's only a two-year stint, and then I can go back to the field. How about you? How did you get out of the military without them coming for you?"

"Dishonorable discharge," I said. I hadn't been sure that Gwan would come through on those for Kendrick and me, but he had. I mean, it hadn't really cost him anything, but you never knew with officer types.

"Huh," she said. "Doesn't seem to be hurting you much. You look good."

"Thanks. You know . . ." I hesitated. I'd been running through what I intended to say to her every day for almost a year, and now I found myself seated beside her, and I couldn't get it out. "I'm just going to lay it out there."

"What?"

"Our last set of activities netted a significant windfall."

"You mean you weren't just doing it for the altruistic

value? This is my shocked face." She stared at me, her lips in a flat line, her face expressionless.

I laughed. "There's an account for every member of the team that they can access as soon as they separate from the service. It's too risky while they're still in."

"That's big of you."

"You were part of the team. There's one for you too."

This time she didn't immediately respond. I think I'd actually surprised her. It surprised *me* a little bit that she hadn't heard from one of the others. "How much?"

"Quite a bit."

"Give me a number."

"Seven-point-three million. Give or take."

Her eyes got big. "Each?"

"That's your cut, yes."

"That's quite a bit."

"Right. Like I said."

"It still doesn't make up for you not contacting me for almost a year," she said, but her voice lacked venom.

"I didn't have a choice."

"The words you're looking for are, 'I'm sorry.'"

"I'm sorry." And I was. I'd missed her a great deal more than I'd expected, and just sitting there with Miller was making me happier than I could remember being.

"Better."

"But there were people looking for me, and they were watching you. It took me a while to lose myself and for them to get bored of you."

This time she didn't look surprised at all. She knew. Still, she said, "You could have stopped at the apology."

"I wanted to explain myself. I wanted to contact you, but it wasn't safe. I guess I need to know you believe me."

"But we're safe now?"

"Today, here, yes."

"I believe you."

I don't think hearts actually melt, but the way her eyes bore into mine, something was definitely happening inside my chest. I swallowed.

"I've still got to be careful. You will too, after you get out, though not to the same extent. You'll get instructions when you receive your account info. The money makes it easier."

"I imagine it does. Let me ask you a question. Did you know all along that I was going to go rogue and send that data off base without you? Was that part of your plan and you didn't tell me?"

"Would I do that?"

"Do what? Use me?" She was trying to keep it light, but the hurt sat there in her tone, just below the surface. Like me, she'd probably thought everything through for most of the past year.

"I was going to say *show them what they want to see so they don't recognize what you're actually doing.* But yeah, I guess your point is true too."

She considered it for a minute, as if now that I'd answered her, she didn't know what to do with it. Finally she spoke. "It sounds better the way you put it."

I smiled, relieved. "I'm really glad you see it that way."

We sat there in silence for a minute, until it started to get awkward.

Or, more awkward than it already had been for me.

"So," she said.

"So," I said. "Are we going to do this thing, or what?"

She smiled.

ACKNOWLEDGMENTS

This book took a few drafts to come together, and I can say with a lot of confidence that it wouldn't have happened at all if I hadn't had a good deal of help.

Some of that help came in the form of great notes from early readers Patrick Mammay and Ernie Chiara that helped me build out the story and the character arcs. Rebecca Enzor read a few key scenes and gave me notes on those to help me build out the romance aspect of the story.

Jason Nelson gave me a ton of notes on the technology. He has done that with all my books to one degree or another, but it was even more significant with this one. His advice completely changed how I wrote some scenes, and even a whole section of the book. I'm not exaggerating when I say that this book wouldn't exist without him.

Dan Koboldt reads everything I do and always gives me great feedback that improves my books. More than that, he's my sounding board regarding the business of writing. He has a great way of looking at the industry and often helps me see things in ways that I might not have considered.

I couldn't do any of this without my agent, Lisa Rodgers, who has an exceptional editorial eye and a seemingly inexhaustible patience to deal with my random questions and insecurities. She listens to what I want, and she figures out how to make it happen.

I would like to thank the entire team at Harper Voyager for their support. Every time I interact with someone there, they make me feel like this is the most important thing that they're doing, even though it most certainly isn't. Thanks also to the people I don't ever see, working behind the scenes to get my book out in the world and where readers can find it.

I especially want to thank my editor, David Pomerico. When he read what I thought was the final draft of the novel, he asked me one question: "Is this the book you meant to write?" He went on to say that if it was, he'd help me work on it and get it where it needed to be. But also that he didn't think it was. That I meant to write something else.

It takes a lot to ask that question. It takes skill and experience to see beyond what is on the page and into what the author intends. More than that, it takes guts to say it. It takes a lot of confidence to take that big of a swing at something. And here's the thing: he was right. It wasn't the book I wanted to write. So I asked him for five weeks and I rewrote most of the book, including the entire third act. I wrote the book I meant to write from the start, the book that David knew I wanted to write. It's a much better book than the one I wrote initially.

I'd like to thank everybody who read my previous books, and especially those who were excited to get the third one when it came out. That was the first time that I think I realized I had fans. People were excited to read it, and that made the release of that book a lot of fun. It also made me want to write more.

Lastly, I would like to thank my wife. I am blessed to have her in my life in so many ways. She is absolutely the most supportive partner a person could ask for. Making a book takes a lot of people, but the act of writing itself is somewhat of a solo endeavor, and that means time alone. She is so gracious about that and takes care of so many things to help protect that time for me. You're the best, honey.